The *Unintended* Hero

by

Rita M. Reali

Little Elm Press

This is a work of fiction. Any fictional characters' similarity to actual persons, living or dead, is wildly coincidental. Real sites used in this book may include features that have been deliberately fictionalized.

Copyright 2020, Rita M. Reali.
Cover by Al Esper Graphic Design.
Author photo by J. Addeo, November 1991.

No part of this publication may be reproduced, stored in any retrieval system or transmitted in any form or by any means – electronic, mechanical, photocopying, recording or otherwise, whether currently in existence or which may exist in the future – without the expressed written permission of the publisher.

For information regarding permission, contact Little Elm Press: permissions@LittleElmPress.com.

Contact the author via email: **Rita@LittleElmPress.com**. Like **Rita M. Reali, Author** on Facebook for news about upcoming events and book releases. And be sure to join our Facebook fan group, **The Sheldon Family Saga**, to connect with other readers (and the author), ask questions or vent about your least-favorite characters.

Reali, Rita M.
The Unintended Hero

ISBN: 978-0-9966800-4-2

Printed in the U.S.A.
First American edition, September 2020

Acknowledgments

Many thanks to my physician and friend, Dr. Kimberly S. Peaslee, for her generous assistance in adding medical credibility to my fiction – beginning with her lending me her favorite college medical reference book to research tissue damage, through letting me pick her brain about gunshots and blood loss, which made for creepy dinner conversation... but still ;-). Even during the midst of her response to the Covid-19 crisis, she took time to respond via Facebook Messenger to my questions about gunshot wounds. Without Kim's valued input, *The Unintended Hero* would have fallen flat, medically.

An equal measure of thanks to my longtime friend, mentor and favorite editor, Elisa Krochmalnyckyj, who spiffed up the news copy contained in this book and then edited the completed manuscript. With her practiced journalistic eye, Elisa quickly discerned what I had initially intended to be a news article in a local newspaper was actually a page-one editorial that simply required a bit of polish.

Copious thanks to:
– My husband, Frank, for putting up with my obsessions, my mumbling to myself (including in my sleep – don't you love the term "somniloquy"?) and my frequent jabbering about everything from architecture and Lisbon to fictional airlines and Yale.
– My sister by choice, Monica Hackett, for the nagging.
– My friend and fellow award-winning author Dee Lynk, for her continual enthusiasm for the stories I weave.
– Karoline Barrett, Joseph Clarizio, Anne Looney Cook, Kimberly Dwelley, Tracy Osborne, Virginie Reali, Cacilda Rego, Cindy Sarty and Kathryn Uziel.
– Members of the Write Away! writing group, for their support and encouragement along the way.

And endless thanks to you, my dear reader, for being the reason I wrote this in the first place.

Dedication

For my dear friend, life coach and persistently joyful sister in Christ (fellow Daughter of the King), Christina M. Eder (of GuestStarCoaching.com), whose gracious support and endless encouragement helped me stay on track during the final months of writing this novel, rediscover my writing mojo and understand the importance of being able to both offer and accept comfort.

∞

For my sweet friend and choir director, Marian Sullivan, whose encouragement and enthusiasm for my storytelling (especially at the height of the Covid-19 mayhem) helped me maintain my momentum. Her gentle support and her valued feedback made a real difference in the final version of this book.

∞

And for my sister-in-law Donna Reali, who has long been a staunch proponent of and advocate for my writing. You are one of the strongest women I know, and I want to be like you when (okay, *if*) I grow up.

Prologue

(9:49 a.m. Saturday, September 11, 1993)
Marie fidgeted with her bouquet. "Is it time yet?"

"Almost," Michaela replied, adjusting her sister-in-law's veil. "I meant to ask you: Since you opted against my sapphire earrings, what did you choose for your 'something blue'?"

"I'm surprised you didn't notice." An enigmatic smile played about Marie's lips. She hitched up the hem of her wedding gown a couple inches to reveal peacock-blue leather pumps.

"Ooh! I hadn't noticed! Although, now that I think about it, you do look a little taller than I remember." She bent down to take a closer look at Marie's footwear. "Those are stunning!"

The heavy wooden door to the vestibule opened. Marc's eldest aunt creaked in, trailed by her brood of gangly teenage granddaughters, who looked as if they'd rather be anywhere else than in church – in scratchy dresses – on a Saturday. Marie felt herself cringe on their behalf.

"Oh, darling, look at you! You're gorgeous!" Aunt Viv gushed to her nephew's bride-to-be. "Isn't she beautiful, girls?"

The three rangy adolescents nodded and mumbled in semi-coherent agreement as Michaela retreated to the bride's prep room in deference to the elderly woman.

The woman's rickety fingers grazed the bride's lace-trimmed veil, then patted Marie's face. "I'm so delighted for the two of you – such a lovely couple!"

"You're so sweet, Aunt Viv," Marie replied, leaning to kiss her heavily rouged cheek. "It's all been such a flurry of activity – I just hope we get to enjoy the day."

"Oh, I'm sure you will. And when you get through the ceremony and reception, you've got your honeymoon to look forward to." Her eyes shone with anticipation as she gave Marie's arm a knowing pat. "Where are you going?"

Marie scratched the side of her nose with an opalescent fingernail. "We're… not." At the look of incredulity from Marc's aunt, she continued. "We can't really take time off now. Marc's just started his fall-semester classes at Yale. Besides, we already went on our honeymoon – a little early."

"What? You went on your honeymoon before you got married?" Aunt Viviane's expression grew pinched as her discontent mounted. "Is that some kind of *American* thing?" she asked with an indignant sniff.

Marie wished she hadn't said anything. In his pre-wedding primer of his family's quirks, Marc had cautioned Aunt Viv was big on her proper Norwegian heritage. "No, Aunt Viv. Marc and I had a civil ceremony a few months back, then went on a two-week honeymoon in Portugal. I'm actually surprised you didn't hear about it – it was all over the national news."

Aunt Viv made a disapproving face. "You don't need to be sarcastic."

Her chiding tone made Marie's cheeks flush. "I'm not. It really made the national news. By the time we landed in Lisbon, there were police everywhere, and the place was crawling with media."

Marc's aunt gasped and her hand flew to the glossy pink pearls at her throat. "Oh my! What happened?"

Before Marie could reply, the heavy wooden door opened again; this time, her brother Gary poked his head through. "They're ready to seat the moms. You all set back here?"

Aunt Viv looked miffed at the interruption; fortunately

for Marie, she realized his innocent-sounding question was meant to corral her back to her seat. With a last look at the bride – which Marie interpreted as *We're going to continue this conversation later* – the old woman and her cadre of granddaughters flounced back into the church to take their seats.

"Thank you," Marie said with a grateful sigh as her brother eased the door shut.

Chapter 1

(6:15 p.m., Sunday, February 7, 1993)

"Really?" Marc asked, sounding cynical. "Going over our finances? Doesn't it seem like an awful waste of a Sunday evening?"

Marie gave him a look that required no words.

He sighed in weary compliance and sank into the seat beside her at the kitchen table. "Fine. Where do you want to begin?"

"I *want* to begin with this not being an ordeal. I want us to be on the same page, that's all."

Nodding agreeably, he folded his hands on the tabletop and leaned forward. "I suppose that makes sense. Where do we start?"

"Do you have your receipts for the past month?"

"What do I need those for? They're bits of paper that would clutter up my apartment. Look around. I don't do clutter. I know what I've got coming in and I know what I spend every month. It all balances out… usually."

Marie dropped her pencil and rubbed her temples. This wouldn't be as easy as she'd thought. "Alright, let's start with that: How often doesn't it balance out?"

As she watched him, Marc's right hand began dancing along the table's edge, running scales on a non-existent piano – almost as if on its own. She noticed in the past several weeks he'd do that when he felt antsy.

"I don't know. A couple times a year." Now he began adding chords with his left hand.

She watched him for a moment. "What are you doing?"

"Practicing the piano. I do that sometimes."

"I've never seen you do it," she fibbed, not wanting to make him even more uncomfortable.

Still tinkling the nonexistent keys, Marc cast a glance in her direction before returning his focus to the careful curve of his fingers. "Then you're probably not paying attention. Either that or you're not around when I hear the melodies."

Marie gritted her teeth and sighed. "We were talking about the few times a year your budget doesn't balance out."

He concentrated on a particularly difficult configuration. After getting his fingers in the desired position, he glanced at Marie. "Right. What do you want to know?"

"Could you please stop doing that?"

Marc shook his head. "It helps me focus."

Marie rolled her eyes heavenward. "Fine. What do you do when that happens?"

He gave a noncommittal shrug. "I get creative. It's amazing what they'll let you get away with if you *accidentally* put a check for the water company into the envelope with the electric bill."

Marie flattened her hand over his to stop his finger exercises. "Marc!"

"What?" He pulled his hand free and mimed shutting the lid over the keys. "You've never had to decide which bill gets paid and which can wait 'til your next paych—" he briefly raised both hands, palms forward. "Of course you haven't. I forgot. You're a Sheldon. Money's never an issue."

Stung, she eyed him dolefully. "What's that supposed to mean?"

Marc fidgeted. "As a doctor, I imagine you're bringing down fairly good money."

"Granted. But you specifically said, 'You're a Sheldon.' What did you mean by that?"

Called on his wording, he raked a hand through his hair. "I'm sorry, honey. What I meant is your grandfather left you and your siblings pretty well set, financially. And you and Gary always seem so… spot on about money. I guess I'm feeling a little defensive." He mumbled the last part. "And maybe more than a little inadequate."

She took both his hands in hers. "Why would you feel inadequate?"

Her question wasn't antagonistic or confrontational; the softness of her tone made him do a double take. He shrugged, then pulled his hands away, raised the imaginary cover and began another series of scales. "It's stupid."

"Tell me."

Marc exhaled audibly before admitting, "Because I don't make anywhere near as much as you. Alright?"

"Well, hell's bells, Marc! What's that got to do with anything?"

"I don't know. Look, where I come from, the guy's supposed to provide for his family. I just feel like – like I'll be a 'kept' man or something." His fingers came to a halt and he smirked. "I told you it was stupid."

Where you come from?! You come from <u>Danbury</u>. She covered his hand with hers again. "It's not stupid, Marc. I think it's important we talk these kinds of issues out now, before we're married – to avoid silly arguments later on. Look, we all have our own gifts and talents."

"Right. And you're a psychiatrist, for crying out loud! You help people get their lives back in order. While I, on the other hand, play music on the radio for a living – and talk to people who aren't even there. Big freakin' deal. Oh, and occasionally I play a piano I don't even have."

"Have you forgotten you save lives? You dive into deep or dangerous water and you rescue drowning people. I've seen you do it! I could never do that."

Marc shook his head. "Not anymore."

"What happened?"

"I had to quit lifeguarding this week. I couldn't juggle it all anymore." The slump of his shoulders told her that decision hadn't been one he'd come to easily.

"So what about swimming?"

"Had to stop that, too. No time. Not with work, classes and homework." He made a wan attempt at humor. "Not to mention a high-maintenance fiancée."

"I'm not all *that* high maintenance," Marie protested mildly, acknowledging his attempt at lightening the mood. Marc's daily swim was his physical and emotional outlet. Had been for years. "Anyway, need I remind you you're also a gifted designer – who in a few years' time will be a licensed architect? And before you downplay *that*, remember this: You got accepted at Yale on your own merits. All my grandfather did was provide the means for you to go."

Marc stopped what he was about to say. He gave an acquiescent nod. "I suppose. But it still feels so irrelevant – and unimportant – when compared with what you do."

"If I were a secretary or a librarian or a waitress, we wouldn't be having this conversation. And would you love me any less? Somehow, I don't think so. Yet, because I've spent a few extra years in school and sit in an office and ask people, 'How does that make you feel?' for a living, that makes me, what? Some kind of hero? No, Marc. It's what I do for a living. I enjoy doing it and I like to think I'm pretty good at, but it's only my job."

Marie ran her hands through her hair. "I wouldn't feel any differently about you if you were a brain surgeon – or a janitor." She gestured toward him with both hands. "I love you, Marc. I love who you are and I love who I am when I'm with you. I want to build a life with you." She paused, met his gaze. "We've been through this before. I thought you knew that."

Marc reached for her hands; they were trembling. "I *do* know that, *querida*" – Portuguese for 'darling' – "But I can't help how I feel. I can't. And the truth is, I feel like my contributions toward our household expenses will be piddly compared to yours."

Marie hesitated before speaking. "Are you not going to be an equal partner in our marriage, Marc? Or will you be any less a parent to our kids?" When he shook his head to both questions, she asked, "And what does money have to do with either of those things?"

"Nothing."

"Exactly. Dirty green paper is all that is. Besides, we'll be building a marriage, not a financial merger. The fact I earn more money makes me no better than you – nor any more important to our marriage. Can we please just agree this doesn't have to be an issue between us?"

"That wasn't so bad," Marie proclaimed forty minutes later, beaming at her newly constructed balance sheet listing each of Marc's expenses, followed by hers, in a single long column. "What other monthly expenses do you have?"

With a dismissive shrug, he leaned backward, balancing his chair on its rear legs. "That's about it... except for twenty-five bucks a week for St. Joe's."

"The shelter?"

Marc nodded.

As she added the line item to the sheet, a smile lit her face. She loved this man's heart. Last week, she'd called to say she was heading to Caldor on her way home, and did he need anything?

"Can you pick up one of those ten-packs of socks and a couple packages of briefs?"

Marie scribbled the items on her shopping list. "What size?"

"One medium, one large."

Baffled by his answer, she asked, "You planning on gaining weight in the next few months?"

"They're not for me. They're for the shelter." She heard a hitch in Marc's voice. "When all you've got to your name is the clothes on your back, it's a real blessing to have clean underwear and socks once in a while."

When she arrived at his apartment with the requested items, he insisted on giving her cash to pay for them, despite her assurance it was no big deal. "Please. Don't argue with me on this, Marie. Just take it." She recalled his insistence as he foisted the unwanted twenty on her.

She hadn't understood then. Now she did. She blinked away a mist of tears. "You've been doing that every week for... what, eleven years?"

Marc gave a self-conscious shrug. "Thirteen," he corrected delicately. "Almost since I started working. It's my way of giving back. Of remembering where I ended up, and reinforcing that I never want to go back to that."

"So the underwear and socks last week...?"

"That's apart from the twenty-five bucks. I buy a package whenever I've got a few bucks to spare." He thumbed toward the bedroom. "I keep 'em in a box and go by to the shelter every few months. And whenever I'm out, I pick up a few pairs of gloves – especially if I'm in one of those dollar stores 'cause I can afford to get a lot more. When the weather starts turning, I take 'em in" – he shrugged – "you know, so Father Callahan never has to give away his last pair anymore." Marc's tone grew wistful. "He doesn't realize it, but he saved my life, Marie. I'd have been dead years ago if it weren't for him." His expression saddened as his shoulders sagged. "Of course, now I'll have to figure something else out, 'cause without that lifeguarding job" – he shrugged in hapless resignation – "I can't swing it."

Two Sundays later, while finishing dinner at her apartment, Marie beamed across the table at Marc. "I've got a surprise for you."

He tilted his head. One eyebrow arched in question. "Oh?"

Getting up from the table, she said, "I'll be right back."

She retreated to her desk and returned with a check, which she handed to Marc. "Here." She watched him expectantly.

Marc's jaw slackened, then clenched. Not the reaction she'd anticipated. "What's this?"

"It's for St. Joe's."

He stared up at her in ugly, unblinking silence for the better part of a minute. His expression grew dark, as if a cloud had crossed over it. When he could form words, he dropped the check on the table and said, in an accusatory tone, "Why would you do that?"

Marie took a step backward, feeling as if he'd struck her. "What do you mean? I thought you'd be happy about it."

His eyes turned stormy. "You don't get it. Supporting St. Joe's isn't something I do because I have so much extra money lying around. I support the shelter because I have a connection to it. I've *lived* there." He glared at Marie for a moment, then spat, "Why would you do that?" Nearly toppling his chair, Marc sprang to his feet and began to pace.

"Do what? All I did was write a check."

He whirled to face her. "Exactly my point – you wrote a check. Period."

She shook her head. "I don't get why you're so angry. I'm making a donation to the shelter."

"Yeah – one check that completely overshadows an entire year's worth of my donations." He flung his arm out in a wide arc. "I don't need you swooping in, Marie, and taking this away from me. I don't need you trying to be the hero."

Marie stared at him as ire fueled his words.

"You. Have. No. Idea. You'll never know what it feels like to live on the streets and to have to depend on that shelter for your next meal, for a place to sleep – for your *life*. You'll never know, Marie, because it's never been part of your reality. You can sit at your pretty little oak desk and write a check for fifteen-hundred dollars – like it's nothing to you. It's no big deal. You could sit there all day and dash off fifteen-hundred-dollar checks for every charity you can think of." He paused, perhaps realizing how hurtful his rant must have sounded to his fiancée. He took a deep breath and let it out slowly, to calm himself. "I'm sure you're doing it because you're a wonderfully generous and caring woman, Marie. But you will never know. You'll never understand what's involved – and what it means for me to be able to give the pittance I give each month!"

Standing between him and the table, she stared at Marc, tears welling in her eyes – both at his scalding words and because what she'd intended as a kind deed had unintentionally offended him so deeply. She gave a slight nod. "I get it, Marc," she said, wiping at tears. Her heart ached as new tears welled in her eyes. "I do. And I'm sorry. I didn't mean to intrude on your giving. In *any* way. I think what you're doing is commendable. It's giving from your heart – it's the purest form of giving. I realize it's a sacrifice for you. But when you said you'd probably have to cut it from your budget 'cause you're not lifeguarding anymore…" Marie searched his face, not sure what she was hoping to see. "I didn't want you to have to do that." One tear after another spilled over.

Marc went to his fiancée and, shushing her, wrapped her in a consoling hug.

After a long time, Marie spoke into his shoulder. "It's like the parable of the widow's mite. I get that, Marc. What I gave is from my excess, but you give from your monthly income. That alone makes your gift more significant than whatever I do. I'm not trying to upstage or outdo you. I was only trying to help…"

Her words dissolved into remorseful weeping. When she could speak again, she said, "I never intended to cast shade on you, sweetheart." Shaking her head, she pulled back a bit and looked up at him, tears still brimming in her eyes.

Putting both hands up to her face, Marc wiped Marie's tears with his thumbs. He drew her close and kissed her on the forehead. "Shh," he soothed, pulling her into his arms again. "I'm sorry, honey. I overreacted. What you did was so generous. I'm sure Father Callahan will appreciate it. I appreciate it, too." He paused. "More than I know how to appropriately express, apparently."

The words struck Marie as funny. She drew away from him again and began to giggle. As he met her gaze, Marc smiled.

Before long, both were laughing and hugging, their hurt feelings assuaged by the tender, soothing balm of mirth.

Chapter 2

(1:43 a.m., Friday, February 26)
After a long day of classes, plus an hour of production work after he got off the air, all Marc wanted was sleep. But the message light on his answering machine stopped him. More curious than weary, he pressed the PLAY button.

"Mr. Lindemeyr, this is Attorney Derek Loughton. I need to speak with you at your earliest opportunity. It's regarding your status at Yale..."

A sizeable bequest years earlier from noted New Haven-area architect Edward P. Sheldon, one of Atty. Loughton's clients, had recently enabled Marc to fulfill his lifelong dream of attending the Yale College School of Architecture.

After saving the message, Marc plodded off to get ready for bed. While he brushed his teeth, he wondered what the attorney's cryptic message meant. His status? Was there some kind of mix-up and his tuition wasn't being paid after all? Was there perhaps a problem with his enrollment? Had he waited too long to apply? Might there have been an expiry date on the funds?

When he climbed into bed, sleep swept the message – and all the accompanying questions – from Marc's mind.

In the morning, Marc dialed the attorney's number. He tried to ignore the knots in his insides as he listened to the connection going through and the phone ringing against his ear.

"Attorney Loughton, good morning," he said when the attorney picked up his direct line. "It's Marc Lindemeyr returning your call. I was at work when you phoned yesterday."

"Yes, Mr. Lindemeyr. Thanks for calling back so promptly. There's something I need to see you about. It's regarding your enrollment status."

"You mentioned that in your message. But that's about all you said," he said, a nervous hitch in his voice. "Is everything okay?" The fingers of his right hand danced across the countertop.

"Everything's fine. I didn't mean to imply any difficulty. Quite the opposite, actually," the attorney assured him. "Is there a time today you're available to meet to fill out some paperwork?"

Marc mentally reviewed his schedule. He didn't have to be at the radio station until six. "I'm in class 'til three thirty, but I'll be free later this afternoon. Where can I meet you?"

Just after 4:30, Marc found a parking space along a side street downtown. Wedging the Saab against the dingy remnants of a snowbank, he fed the parking meter and hurried along the sidewalk toward Attorney Loughton's office.

"It's good to see you again." The attorney shook Marc's hand, then ushered him into his inner office. "How are your classes going?"

"Great. It's only a month in, and I'm just taking some basics. But I'm really enjoying 'em."

"Good. Well, there's a provision of Edward's will that wasn't to be mentioned to you until after you were partway into your first semester." He motioned toward a leather-upholstered chair opposite his desk. "Please, sit."

As the attorney explained the stipulation, Marc stared at him. "Are you kidding me?"

"Not at all. Take a look." He turned the paperwork around and pointed to the section he'd referenced. "Right here."

Marc reviewed the indicated portion in astonishment. He had to read through it three times for it all to sink in.

"Are you sure?" he asked, even though he was looking at the signed and notarized document.

"You apparently made quite an impression on Mr. Sheldon, and he was insistent about this stipulation in particular. He told me he wanted you to be able to focus on your dream of becoming an architect."

For the second time in as many months, Marc arrived at work still reeling. The first was when he learned about Edward Sheldon's bequest enabling him to attend Yale.

"You okay?" Gary asked as his best friend entered the on-air studio at 6:25.

He gave a numbed nod and began slotting a stack of just-recorded commercials into vacant spaces within the cart carousel.

"You don't look okay."

As if he hadn't heard Gary's comment, Marc wandered distractedly out of the studio.

"Hi," Marc greeted Gary, still a little rattled, upon his return twenty minutes later.

"What's going on?"

Marc leaned in the doorway. "Your grandfather always seems to find ways to amaze me."

Gary didn't look surprised at his statement – although Grandpa had died nearly eight years earlier. Not only did he not look surprised, he looked amused. "How's that?"

"Apparently, paying for my tuition wasn't enough for him."

"Uh oh. What'd the ol' boy do now?"

Marc shut the door and leaned against it. His voice trembled just a bit. "He left me money, Gary – an insane amount of money," he said, sounding about as numb as he'd looked earlier.

Gary nodded. "Sounds like him. He not only insisted on paying for my tuition – and all my expenses – while I was at UConn, but he'd hide twenties in my apartment all the time, and then deny any knowledge or involvement." He checked the temperature and jotted it on the updated weather forecast. "How'd you find this out?"

"I got a call yesterday from the attorney overseeing his estate."

"Derek. He's a good guy." Gary settled his headphones over his ears and held up a finger for Marc to hold that thought as he hit the mic switch.

When Marc nodded in tacit response, he couldn't feel his head moving.

After he read the weather and mentioned Marc would be in at seven, Gary flipped off the mic and tugged off his headphones. "What'd he want?"

"He wanted to see me. I met with him just now. Your grandfather set aside money for me, for living expenses. Including during the summer – as long as I'm signed up for four courses each semester."

"That was nice of him."

"You don't understand. This isn't just a few twenties stashed here and there. It's a *lot* of money. Five hundred dollars a week!"

Gary gave a whistle of astonishment. "Sounds like something he'd do."

"That's twenty-six grand a year," Marc blurted, "just for studying to do what I love. Criminy, Gary, that's a – that's a full-time salary! On top of what I'm making here."

His smile broadened. "I'm not a bit surprised. Grandpa was wildly generous to the people he loved."

"But he" – Marc shook his head in protest – "he barely knew me…"

Gary's expression morphed to kind of a knowing look. "He knew you alright, Marc. And he thought the world of you." Nearing the end of his shift, he began gathering his things to make way for Marc behind the mic. "Grandpa had an uncanny way of reading people. He knew you had a good heart – and amazing talent for design. He'd talk to me about you sometimes. Said he saw a spark in you, 'great potential' he hoped you'd develop further. I never quite understood what he meant by that, and since it really wasn't any of my business, I never asked."

"But Gary, I can't accept this. It's too much."

"What's too much?"

"Weren't you listening? Five hundred bucks a week – just for being enrolled in four classes a semester. Gary, I can't accept that. It's way too much money."

"Not much you can do about it. The money's already allocated. And anyway, if not you, then who?"

The question stymied Marc. Money had always been something worked for, something earned – not doled out by the truckload.

"Who?" he repeated gently when Marc didn't answer after several seconds.

Marc responded with a helpless shrug.

"Like I said, we used to talk. He knew you were working two jobs to get by. He probably figured you'd have to give up at least one to go to school. This may have been his way of equalizing things for you." When he saw Marc about to protest, Gary held up a hand. "You need to understand something, Marc: My grandfather was a generous man. He was also a quietly insistent, *stubborn* man who knew how to get his way. If sending you to Yale and giving you gobs of cash in the process was his intent, then – God bless 'im! – there's no way around it. And there's certainly no sense in your objecting."

Marc's shoulders drooped and he felt himself sag. "So you're saying I should just suck it up and deposit the checks every week?"

"That's what I'm sayin'. But I've got to warn you: That stubbornness of his?" Gary shook his head and whistled. "It's an inherited trait."

"Don't remind me. Marie's stubborn streak's about a mile wide and just as deep."

The smile returned to Gary's face. "Another reason not to be weirded out by the money. You're marrying into the family, so you're officially one of his grandkids. And trust me, he did well by his grandchildren." His voice gentled. "And he would have loved that you and Marie ended up together. He'd have been absolutely thrilled about that."

From the instant Marc cracked the mic for his opening break at seven, he felt too distracted to focus. He flubbed the call letters – something he hadn't done since his second week at the station more than thirteen years earlier – and forgot to give out the request line for Seventies at Seven.

Later, as Gary locked his office door and prepared to leave, Marc called to him from down the hall.

The music director appeared at the door to the on-air studio. "What's up?"

"Could you tell me again why I shouldn't feel uncomfortable about this?"

Gary leaned in the doorway. "You really want to go through this again?"

Marc let out a deep sigh. "I don't feel right taking his money."

"Not much you can do about it. Look, Marc, the man was worth millions – many millions. Do you know what he left the three of us – Marie, Joey and me?"

Marc shrugged. "Three quarters of a million?"

Gary shook his head. "Add another zero. Each. Yeah," he affirmed, seeing the shock on his friend's face. "I wasn't real comfortable about it, either. Frankly, I'd give it *all* up to have him back. But it was his money and that's how he chose to split it up. He left tons to charities, to his parish and to Yale. Other folks got left smaller bequests. I'm sure he saw covering your tuition and living expenses as something nice to do for someone he respected and cared about.

"There was nothing he loved more than doing things for people," Gary continued. "Mostly anonymously. He never made a show of being the richest guy in town. He used to have a place in a nice section of New Haven, but he said it felt 'too ostentatious,' so he sold it. He lived in that little cottage in Milford and loved it."

"I get that. But, Gary, I don't feel comfortable accepting anything I haven't worked for. It's just not who I am."

Gary folded his arms, tried to repress a smile. "Okay. Tell you what: You argue with the dead man. Go ahead. I'll wait."

Trying to look fierce, Marc nevertheless cracked a grin. "You're enjoying this, aren't you?"

Gary nodded. "Immensely." Now he laughed. "Look, Marc, you've been given a real gift, a chance to study what you love at your dream college. And now you don't have to hold down two jobs to keep the lights on while you're studying. Where's the downside? Just smile, say 'thank you, Edward,' and run with it."

At midnight, Marc gratefully relinquished the controls to Randy Lear.

"Dude," Randy called after him, waving the unsigned program log, "you didn't sign your log pages – or fill in any of your commercial air times."

"*Batata rançosa,*" he muttered, returning to the studio to take the log and the pen Randy held out to him.

"You okay?"

Marc signed his legal name with a flourish at the bottom of each page, then flipped back through all five hours to fudge approximate air times for each commercial. "Yeah. Must've OD'd on dopey pills tonight, that's all."

Half an hour later, he dragged himself up to his third-floor apartment. He hadn't been able to think straight all night and – *dammit!* He was supposed to call Marie at 9:30. With a glance at his watch, Marc shook his head. Too late to call her now.

Trying not to dwell on the missed call – he'd have been useless at conversation anyway – he brushed his teeth and undressed, then lay awake in bed for what felt like days.

When exhaustion finally overcame Marc's restlessness,

bad dreams ran him ragged much of the night. Baseless scenarios that made no sense awakened him multiple times, leaving him jittery and ill at ease.

At last, drifting back to sleep just before six, he found himself in a rocking chair on the wide wraparound front porch of an older home, set back a bit from the street. Little traffic disturbed the tranquility of the morning. The chirp of songbirds overhead, his measured and restful breathing, and the soft creak of the rocker against the worn wooden floorboards soothed him, as did the chair's smooth forward-and-back movement.

"I only want the best for you," a voice said.

Another rocking chair shimmered into view on the porch; in it, a dignified older gentleman with white hair and a drooping mustache rocked slowly. Marc felt himself jolt backward in alarm.

"Didn't mean to startle you."

"Th-that's okay. I just wasn't expecting anyone."

The old man gave a considered nod. "I understand. It's been a rough night."

"Yeah."

"I meant what I said, Marc. I only want the best for you."

"That's what Gary said."

"But?" he prompted.

"But I..." Marc fumbled for the right words. He threw his hands in the air in frustration. "Oh, I don't know."

"You feel awkward about taking money from a dead man?" Edward's blue eyes twinkled; his mustache twitched in merriment.

"That's part of it."

The old man eyed him steadfastly. "All those years ago, when you told me you dreamed of studying architecture at Yale, didn't I say I might be able to help?"

"Well, yeah. But..."

"This wasn't the kind of help you were envisioning." It wasn't a question.

Marc shook his head. "Not at all. I thought you meant you'd put in a good word with the admissions folks. I never even got a chance to thank you. You've changed my life. Profoundly."

His rumbly laugh sounded to Marc like far-off thunder. "Well, my boy, that's the beauty of being in a position to lend assistance. You get to surprise the hell out of folks once in a while."

Marc briefly joined the old man in gentle laughter. His expression turned serious again. "I still don't feel comfortable taking your money. I mean, your paying my tuition is one thing – and that was generous enough! But that meeting I had with your lawyer yesterday really threw me."

"I figured it would. That's why I asked him to withhold that bit of information until you'd begun taking classes."

"I get that. But it's a lot of money. And I don't feel like I've earned it."

Edward rocked backward and stopped. He fixed his gaze on Marc. "Ahh, and there we have it. The heart of what's been causing your bad dreams. How does that make you feel?"

"You sound like my shrink."

He nodded, looking amused, then resumed rocking. "I know. But she's got better legs."

When Marc's grin faded, he admitted, "I don't feel like I've done anything to warrant such outrageous generosity."

"How about your being an enthusiastic and gifted designer? That day you spent in my office way back when taught me so much about your spirit and your drive. Not to mention your aptitude for design. Then, your friendship with my grandson meant the world to me; he always spoke so highly of you. And because I was in a position to help you fulfill your dream, it would have been nothing less than selfish of me not to. Got it?"

"Got it."

"And your devotion to my granddaughter makes her grandmother and me so happy." A broad smile crinkled

Edward's face. "You're so good for her! We're delighted you didn't let her drive you away again."

Not sure how to respond, Marc gave a numb nod.

"As for the weekly stipend, I knew you'd have to make sacrifices, and you might have to give up at least your part-time job to attend classes. I didn't intend for your studies to cause such financial hardship, especially since I had the means to prevent it. It was my way of acknowledging your hard work and dedication to your future career. I wanted it to be enough that if you decided to quit your radio job and go to school full time, you'd still have a way to pay the bills."

"I can't thank you enough, Mr. Sheldon."

"Don't you 'Mr. Sheldon' me, young man," Edward admonished, his eyes shining. "You're family. It's 'Grandpa.' Got it?"

Marc smiled, accepting the good-natured scolding. "Got it. Thank you... Grandpa."

"You're more than welcome, my boy. Now, when you're in a position to do likewise – and you will be – I know you'll pay it forward. In fact, you're off to an excellent start, with your weekly donations to the shelter" – his voice grew soft – "which you no longer have to worry about how to continue doing."

The two men rocked in silence for a time.

Edward glanced around, then thumped at the broad wooden arms of his chair. "Nice porch. Reminds me of the one at Gary's place in Milford."

Marc nodded. "It's a great porch. Peaceful out here."

"Yes, that's a good word for it: peaceful."

After another companionable silence, Edward spoke again. "Tell me about the house."

"This one?"

Edward nodded.

Understanding it was a test of some sort, Marc walked around the outside of the three-story structure, assessing it, then returned to sit with Edward. "On initial evaluation, I'd say it's an older construction, close to a hundred years. And it's a two-family home."

"How can you tell?"

Marc pointed. "Dual front entry doors."

The old man nodded. "Good eye. What else?"

"Asphalt roof is newer, definitely not original. There's a fireplace. Probably a walk-up attic. Given the age of the house, I'm guessing the floors and woodwork inside are all hardwood. Front rooms on both levels have great architectural appeal. Windows all look to be original; you can tell by the waviness of the glass and some tiny imperfections. Slope of the land down toward the driveway tells me there's few if any issues with water in the basement. What else would you like to know?"

Edward nodded. "I think you've pretty well covered the physical aspects. Just one last thing: Would you start a family here?"

While the question took Marc by surprise, he tried not to act startled. "Given the right set of circumstances, sure."

"Good. Glad we had this talk, Marc. Oh, and by the way, don't beat yourself up over not calling Marie last night; she got called in on a case. And while I'm thinking about it: Don't let that mile-wide stubborn streak of hers intimidate you."

Before Marc could open his mouth to respond, the old man winked and disappeared. His empty chair rocked slightly.

Marc awakened with a gasp. Blinking away sleep, he looked around his bedroom in the early-morning silence.

(10:22 a.m., Saturday, February 27)

"Sorry I didn't call you last night. It was kind of a weird night."

"That's okay; I was out on a call."

Marc almost responded, "I know." His heart thudded to a momentary stop. He didn't hear her next question.

"Marc?" she prompted. "What made it weird?"

"Uhh..." This wasn't a conversation he wanted to have over the phone. "You busy today?"

"Doing laundry this morning and washing the kitchen floor. Why?"

"Can I come over? Say, around noon?"

"I should be done by then. Everything okay?"

He hesitated. "I just need to talk to you about something that happened yesterday."

(12:03 p.m.)

When she answered the door, Marie felt her pulse quicken with worry. "Are you okay?" she greeted her fiancé, standing aside to let him in. He looked a little jittery.

"Everything's fine," he replied, smoothing her hair away from her face. "I didn't mean to alarm you."

"What happened yesterday? What did you want to talk about?" She shoved back the sleeves of her sweater and looked him over, then motioned him to the couch – the same one, she thought incongruously, where he'd proposed a little more than two months earlier.

They sat, denim-clad knees touching.

"Aww, *querida*, don't look so worried," he cooed, taking her hands in his. "Nothing's wrong. I swear."

Unappeased, she felt her insides clench. "Then what was so weird?"

He took a deep breath and exhaled slowly, likely trying to piece together his words. "I met with your grandfather's attorney. Turns out, your grandfather decided paying for Yale wasn't enough."

Marie's head tilted. She opened her mouth to speak, but no words came out.

Marc outlined the financial arrangement Edward had laid out. "I've had kind of a hard time wrapping my head around it," he finished.

"I can understand that." Marie noticed when he talked, Marc used hand gestures almost like punctuation. She thought back to their spat the week before over her donation to the shelter. This new income stream would relieve a lot of pressure for him.

"I know how adamant you are about earning money as opposed to being handed things" – she reached out a hand toward him – "but I hope you can see how this is different."

"I can. I had a talk with Gary last night and he said pretty much the same thing: I shouldn't look at it as charity, but as it was intended – the generosity of a benefactor. I realize it's an amazing opportunity, and I am tremendously grateful. It's what your grandfather wanted for me, and there's a whole lot of nothing I can do about it."

Marie watched a reticent grin take over Marc's face. "I'm delighted to hear you say that!" She hugged him. "I know it's not easy for you to accept this, honey, and I appreciate your effort. But I'm really thrilled you don't have to worry about how to keep up your weekly donations to the shelter."

Chapter 3

(7:35 p.m., Friday, March 5)
Marc was well into Seventies at Seven when Marie phoned. He looked forward to her nightly call, because it gave them a chance to share news, offload the weight of the day or just catch up with each other.

"Hey, *querida*," he greeted her. "How ya doing tonight?"

Her sigh told him it had been a long day. "I'm so ready for a good night's sleep. How 'bout you?"

"It's been a good day. Classes went well. I aced my Latin test from last week. That means so far I've got a four-oh in E.L.G."

"What's that?"

"Sorry – Elements of Latin Grammar."

"That's great, honey!"

"Yeah, it kind of balances my poli-sci grade. I feel like I'm tanking there."

"That doesn't sound good," she commiserated.

"No. I need to find a way to understand the material better. I don't want to squander this opportunity and end up disappointing everyone."

"You won't be a disappointment to anybody," Marie chided gently. "Like you said, try to do better at making sense of the course material. I'm sure you'll figure it out."

Awkward silence lingered between them. Finally, Marc broke it. "I saw Father Callahan this afternoon."

"Did you ask him about officiating at the wedding?"

"I didn't. But we'll to do that soon enough. I invited

him to lunch tomorrow. We're meeting him at the Wide Awake Coffee Shop at noon."

"Good. I can't wait to meet him!" The smile returned to Marie's voice.

(11:57 a.m., Saturday, March 6)
Marc swung his Saab into a parking space at the coffee shop. He and Marie got out and went inside to wait for Father Callahan.

A few moments later, the elderly priest pulled in and parked his battered Buick Regal, slightly askew, in the space next to Marc's car. Unusually spry for 83, he practically darted across the lot. A small bell jingled overhead as the old man entered the coffee shop.

"Hey, Father C," one of the waitresses welcomed him. "Sit anywhere you like."

He flashed a dazzling smile and gave a jaunty wave in her direction. "Good day to ye, Miss Maggie. I'm meant to be meetin' some friends in a moment" – he noticed Marc hailing him from a booth partway down the length of the diner – "oh! There they be now. Coffee, please, if you don't mind, me little Magpie."

As the priest scurried over, Marc slid out of the booth and stood to greet him.

Father Callahan wrapped him in a mighty hug. "Marcus, me boy! So good to see ye again!" He patted the young man on the back with a series of surprisingly strong thumps.

"You just saw me yesterday," he reminded the priest, sporting a broad grin.

"So I did. All the more reason to delight in seeing ye again, Marcus. Twice in as many days – this must be me lucky week!" He turned to beam at Marie. "And this is the lass I've heard so much about."

"Yes. Father, I'd like you to meet my fiancée, Dr. Marie Sheldon. Marie, this is Father Lucas Callahan, the man who saved my life." *Fourteen years ago this month.*

Marie beamed as the exuberant priest reached for the hand she extended toward him. "It's such a pleasure to finally meet you, Father! I've heard so much about you from Marc, I feel almost as if I know you already. He's spoken so often – and so highly – of you!"

Father Callahan squeezed Marie's hands. "And I am delighted to meet you, me fine miss. You're certainly a bonny lass – and no doubt ye must have the patience of a saint to put up with this scamp, this scalawag. I trust you're keeping him well in line?"

"Well, it's not exactly easy, Father," she teased, "but I'm doing my best."

"Father, please sit," Marc urged.

The priest slid into the seat across the table from Marie, who scooched over so Marc could sit beside her.

Maggie brought over three menus, along with a pot of coffee. She turned his cup upright in its saucer and filled it. "Coffee?" she asked the others.

"Yes, it is," Marc deadpanned, righting his coffee cup in its saucer.

"Please," Marie said at the same time, elbowing him as she turned her cup over for the waitress to fill.

Maggie poised her free hand on her hip. "Now, you listen here, pal," she scolded Marc, setting her coffee pot on the tabletop. "There's only room for one smart aleck per booth, and it's him." She pointed to Father Callahan, whose blue eyes twinkled merrily above his craggy smile.

"I'll keep that in mind," Marc said, accepting her playful admonition.

"You do that, dear." She patted his cheek, then pulled a stash of creamers from her apron pocket. "I'll be back in a few minutes to take your orders." Picking up her coffee pot, she drifted away, behind the counter to banter with another group of regulars.

"Miss Maggie sure is a little firecracker," Father Callahan commented, his grin lighting his entire face. "That brassy little girl's been givin' me dining companions a rough time for oh, better'n the past fifteen years or so.

"Now," he said, turning to Marie and folding his hands in front of him on the table, "I want to hear all about you, me dear. But first, I want to thank ye for the generous donation ye made to the shelter a few weeks back. When Marc dropped off the check, I was fairly well gobsmacked by it."

Marie gave the priest a sweet smile. She reached out and patted his wrinkled hand. "It was my pleasure, Father. Marc has always spoken so highly of the good work you do at St. Joseph's..." She gave a quick glance at Marc. Not wanting to embarrass him, she simply added, "All I wanted to do was help make a little bit of difference."

"Oh, that ye did, lass! And we are so grateful. As we are for every donation" – he cast a fond look at Marc – "So, you were goin' to tell me about yerself."

She shrugged. "There's not much to tell. I'm originally from New Jersey. I'm the eldest of three and I live in Danbury with my cat, Oscar. Other than that, there's not much else to say."

"There's plenty more to you than that," Marc retorted. He turned to the priest. "She's just being modest, Father. Marie's not only an award-winning therapist, she's chief of psychiatry at a private facility in Newtown. Plus, she'll seldom let you hear it, but she's got a lovely singing voice. And a magnificent sense of humor."

"And your own fan club, I see," Father Callahan told Marie with a wink.

Marie colored slightly.

"How about you, Marcus? What kind of trouble have ye gotten yerself into lately?"

"Fortunately, no trouble at all," he replied. "I've been kind of too busy for that."

"Good to hear. How so?"

"I've worked in radio since pretty much right after I got sober – and that's almost fourteen years now. Then a few months ago I got the opportunity – thanks to a bequest from Marie's grandfather, actually – to attend architecture school at Yale."

The priest's eyes widened. "No kidding! That's wonderful, me boy! I'm so delighted for ye." He looked from one of them to the other. "I imagine there was a reason you wanted me to meet ye both for lunch today."

Marc and Marie looked at each other. "That's right," Marie said, taking her fiancé's hand. She nodded toward Marc, indicating she wanted him to make the request.

"We'd love it if you would agree to officiate at our wedding."

Marc hadn't thought Father Callahan's smile could get any wider.

"I would be honored. Greatly honored, indeed, me boy." He immediately dove a hand into the inside breast pocket of his jacket and fished out his datebook. "And when is the happy day?"

"Saturday, September eleventh," Marie told him. "At ten in the morning."

Flipping to the September page, he wrote in the time in the space for the eleventh. "Where?"

"Saint Stephen's in Danbury," Marc replied.

The elderly priest gave a pensive nod. "Ah yes, St. Stephen's. Wonderful parish." He wrote that in, too.

"It really is," Marie gushed. "We love it over there!"

"We've already called the office to book the church. But I don't know how we tell our pastor we want to have someone else perform the ceremony."

Father Callahan nodded in understanding. "You leave that to me, Marcus. I've known Father Martin for quite some time. Why, we've been golfin' buddies for— well, since Jesus Himself was a wee laddie. I'd be happy to contact him and break the news to him gently.

"Now, will ye be havin' a Mass, or is it just the nuptial ceremony?"

"We wanted to have a Mass."

"Excellent. And would ye be wantin' me to celebrate the Mass or just perform the marriage rites?"

The couple exchanged a perplexed glance. "We hadn't really given that any thought," Marc admitted. "Would you be okay with celebrating the Mass?"

"Me boy, celebratin' the holy sacrifice o' the Mass is one of me favorite things to do. I would be overjoyed to celebrate yer wedding Mass."

A moment later, Maggie returned. Seeing their menus still closed, she said she'd give them another few minutes to decide. "But don't make me come back a third time," she cautioned with a teasing grin. "I don't take kindly to folks who dillydally when it comes to ordering lunch."

"She really means business, that one," Father Callahan told his companions with a twinkle in his blue eyes as Maggie retreated again. "And I've only seen it happen the once, but if you push her beyond her breakin' point, she'll be comin' out here swingin' a cast-iron skillet at ye. And fer sure ye don't want to be on the receivin' end o' *that*, me friends. She's got a mighty good aim."

When Maggie returned again, they were ready to order.

Over their lunch platters, the three chattered easily together, like old friends.

Father Callahan invited them to come by to the shelter after lunch to see firsthand some of the improvements he'd been able to facilitate through their contributions.

They accepted gladly.

After lunch, Marc and Marie followed Father Callahan to St. Joseph's, where he gave them a tour of the expanded facility, explaining they now had the capacity to feed and provide sleeping accommodations for nearly eighty men a night.

A little shudder ran through Marc as he recalled his last night in the shelter – how he and Father Callahan had talked for so long while they cleaned the dining hall after supper, then washed the dishes together, broke down the tables and made up cots for sleeping. Back then the old shelter only had space for about three dozen cots. He'd told the priest about the shambles he'd made of his life, and how ashamed he was of the awful things he'd done to hurt the people closest to him.

Moved with pity for the young man – Marc was scarcely twenty at the time – the priest had spontaneously offered him absolution for his many transgressions; then he drove him, more than half an hour out of his way, back home to his parents.

A mist of tears clouded Marc's vision as he recalled the emotional reunion with his parents and Emily, who was barely a teenager.

Father Callahan's voice jolted Marc out of his contemplation and back to the present.

"Marcus, ye'll never know how much it's meant to me over the years to get yer donations every week," the priest said as they walked through the shelter dining hall. "Ye may not think so, but it makes such a difference. I can probably count on one hand the number of shelter alumni who've given back when they were in a position to do so. Fer that, me boy, I am profoundly grateful to ye."

Chapter 4

(Saturday, March 27)
Now that their daughter Felicity was three months old, Marc's sister Emily and her husband Clive finally felt comfortable welcoming people into their home to see the baby.

Marc and Marie leapt at the Petersens' weekend brunch invitation. When they arrived, Marc carried the apple pie he'd baked that morning; no family gathering was complete without one of Marc's pies. He handed Marie a small pink bag with polka-dotted ribbon handles.

"What's in here?" she asked, peering into the carefully arranged clusters of pale-pink tissue as they made their way up the front walk.

"A gift for Felicity."

"What is it?"

Before he could respond, Emily threw the door open and rushed out onto the porch. She clapped her hands in glee. "It's so good to see you!"

As their guests entered the modest Cape Cod-style home, Emily took the still-warm pie from Marc and handed it to Clive, then hugged her big brother enthusiastically. "I've missed you!"

When she released him, Emily wrapped Marie in a similarly exuberant hug. "What's this?" she asked, indicating the bag dangling from her future sister-in-law's fingers.

"It's a little something for Felicity."

"Oh, how sweet! What is it?"

Marie shrugged. "I have no idea. You'll have to ask

Marc – or wait 'til Felicity opens it."

Emily herded them into the living room and took their coats. "I'm glad you two came. It's so nice to interact with grownups again!"

As his wife hung their coats in the hall closet, Clive led them into the kitchen, where he was still cooking. "She's not kidding," he said, breaking into a broad grin. "I swear she waits by that door for the mailman every day. She buys all this mail-order stuff; she says it's for the baby, but I'm pretty sure she only does it to lure the UPS guy to our door." Emily went to her husband, who slid an arm around her shoulder and kissed her on the temple. "My sweet wife even engages telemarketers when they call – to the point *they* look for an excuse to end the call."

Marc laughed at his brother-in-law's comment. "You're making that up."

"No, he's not," Emily admitted with a self-conscious giggle. "I've actually started doing that. It makes 'em so uncomfortable. I had one poor guy on the phone for about seven minutes the other day – he'd called to try to sell us a kitchen remodel. We don't need any work done, but it sure was nice to carry on an adult conversation."

"I'll say you don't need any remodeling," Marie commented, looking around at the gleaming appliances and expansive counter space. "Your kitchen is lovely. I almost envy you those calls. Then again, we don't even have a place to call our own yet." She shot a petulant look at Marc.

He pretended not to notice. "Where are you hiding my adorable niece?" he asked, changing the subject.

"Thought you'd never ask. C'mon – you too, Marie! She's just about to wake up from a nap. I can't wait for you to see how big she's gotten!" Emily grabbed her brother by the arm and pulled him upstairs to the nursery, with Marie following behind.

As they returned downstairs twenty minutes later, Marc held his just-fed and freshly diapered niece in his arms. The women trailed behind, chatting about how wonderful he was with kids – and what a fantastic dad he would be one of these days.

"Now that she's awake," Marc asked, "can she open her present?"

"Of course!" Emily retrieved the bag from the coffee table and settled onto the couch beside her brother. "I doubt she's got sufficient agility," she said with a giggle. "May I open it for her?"

"No," Marc deadpanned, joggling the infant on his knee. "You have to wait 'til she's got the manual dexterity to do it herself." He grinned at his little sister. "Of course you can open it, ya big goofball."

Bubbling with delight, Emily poked a hand into the bag and felt around amid the folds of pink tissue-paper filling. Inside something felt soft. She pulled it out and peeled away the layers of tissue wrapping that swathed the gift itself.

She gave a delighted squeal. "Oh, Marc... it's perfect!" Clutching the realistic-looking white plush bunny in one hand, Emily hugged her brother. "And so appropriate, coming from you."

Until their trip to the orchard last fall, Marc had never told his sister why he'd harbored such deep-seated terror of rabbits. His last time going through alcohol withdrawal, almost fourteen years earlier, he'd hallucinated being swarmed and attacked by enormous, vicious rabbits. Even an image of one on television gave him palpitations. He'd finally faced his fear five months ago. And at Em's urging, he had even held Esmeralda, a sweet little bunny, in the orchard's petting enclosure.

Emily inspected the stuffed animal's tiny pink nose and matching eyes. Her face lit up when she noticed the name embroidered in white script inside the pink lining of the bunny's left ear. "It's Esmie!"

Marc nodded. "Yep. And look: No parts that can come loose – all her features are sewn."

Sitting at Marc's other side, Marie smiled at her fiancé's attention to the tiniest details.

"You're so thoughtful, Marc," Emily said, handing the toy to Felicity. Gurgling happily, the infant pulled it close and sucked on one of its ears.

"What's that, sweetie?" Emily leaned toward her baby daughter. "I see. Oh, I'll tell him." She looked at her brother, beaming. "She says, Thank you, Uncle Marc; it's delicious."

"It's adorable," Clive said, watching over his wife's shoulder. "Thank you, Marc. Apparently, she already loves it." He motioned toward the kitchen. "Meanwhile, I don't want to be antisocial, but if we want to eat sometime today, I'd better finish cooking. You guys are welcome to join me."

Aromas of baking bread, poached salmon and frying bacon wafted from the kitchen.

"It smells wonderful in here," Marie remarked, entering the room, with the others following close behind.

Clive stood at the stove, sprinkling his pan of scrambled eggs with cheese and herbs.

"Sure does," Emily agreed, going to hug her husband. "Clive's a wonderful cook!" The petite blonde gazed up at him in adoration. "Just wait 'til you taste the dilled salmon; it'll knock your socks off!"

A cut-glass vase of pink and yellow tulips graced the center of the dining-room table, which was laid with the Petersens' good china and crystal, most of it wedding gifts.

"The table looks lovely, Em," Marc observed. "You've got such a good eye for design."

Emily beamed. "Thank you! I can't see the point of having pretty things if we don't put them out, where we can enjoy them," she said. "I mean, so many people we love gifted us all these beautiful items. Why on earth would we want to hide them away?"

She glanced about the room and smiled. "It makes me

so happy to look around and see all the beautiful things folks have given us – and isn't that the whole idea? To think about the people we love as we enjoy their thoughtful gifts?"

Marie nodded. "That's exactly how I feel. Why not use the 'good' china even when it's just the two of you? You deserve to enjoy your pretty things. And the table really does look beautiful!"

Emily glowed at the compliment. "Thanks. Speaking of good china, are you guys registered anywhere yet? September's practically around the corner."

Marie shook her head. "That's another of the things we haven't had time to do."

Taken with cuddling Felicity – who was still gumming her new bunny – Marc seemed to take no notice of Marie's comment.

"Anyway, we've both lived on our own for so long, we really have everything we need. But folks keep asking where we're registered," she added. "And we honestly haven't got time for that, between both of us working and Marc in school... and studying. Honestly, I'd be thrilled if everyone came to the wedding to enjoy themselves and no one gave us a darn thing."

"Wow!" Emily exclaimed, retrieving the salad from the fridge. "Marc must love that – a low-maintenance fiancée!"

Looking up, Marc gave a throaty laugh and rolled his eyes.

Emily turned to glare at her brother as Marie snickered. "Oh, I never said that – and neither would *he*... trust me! All I meant is, we just want our friends to celebrate with us. That's all."

When Clive announced brunch was served, Marc reluctantly relinquished Felicity, depositing his niece in the arms of her daddy. Clive laid the infant in her bassinet in the living room, where they'd still be within earshot in case she needed something.

During brunch, Marie again remarked how beautiful their house was, pointedly mentioning how nice it would be once she and Marc had a common address to call home.

"Stop it," Marc hissed, firing a momentarily fiery glare across the table. The look of intense displeasure that followed warned her not to bring it up again.

The rest of the afternoon passed amid largely amicable conversation and extensive cooing over Felicity. Emily admitted she was so enamored of their little girl, she scarcely noticed she hadn't set foot in her studio since the day before Felicity was born. Nor had she especially missed painting.

"And she's such a good baby – hardly ever cries or fusses. Isn't that right, smoochie-poo?" she said, snuggling her infant daughter.

Felicity broke into a drooling grin and let out a giggle.

"She's even sleeping five or six hours at a time, so we can get almost a full night's sleep."

"That's unusual for her age," Marie said, "right?"

"It's not unheard of, but her pediatrician said it's not the norm. Fortunately, Felicity's in the eighty-fifth percentile of weight for her age, so Doctor Van Helm's not really concerned about it. But, ohh! When she wakes up, she's hungry like a bear coming out of hibernation."

(4:15 p.m.)

Back at Marie's apartment, Marc trailed his fiancée into the kitchen. He leaned against the counter near where she was preparing supper. He watched her in silence for several seconds. "I hate it when you play games with me, Marie. Especially around other people," he said in a matter-of-fact tone. "You should have known I wouldn't respond to your passive-aggressive barbs at Emily's house. If you've got something to say to me, say it."

Marie dropped her peeler and thumped the carrot in her hand onto the cutting board; she pressed her fingertips to her pulsing left temple. She knew her comments at his sister's house had set Marc off. Truth be told, she had deliberately provoked him.

While they managed to curtail the bulk of their hostilities during their visit, their bickering had resumed in his car on the way home – and it intensified once they got back to her apartment.

"I wasn't being passive-aggressive, Marc; all I said was we should start thinking about getting a place together," she replied. "But any time I bring it up, you get all floppy. Face it, honey, at some point we're gonna have to move in together – unless you intend to keep separate apartments after we're married." She selected the eight-inch chef's knife from the block of knives on the counter.

Marc fumed for several long, unsettling seconds. He looked like his head was about to pop off. When Marie thought he couldn't possibly look any more irritated, he shook his head slowly and muttered, "*Batata rançosa.*"

Marie thumped the knife down onto the cutting board. Advancing toward Marc, she glared at him, hands on her hips in a challenge posture. "What did you call me?"

Marc met his fiancée's gaze. In as measured a tone as he could muster, he replied, "A rancid potato."

She sputtered momentarily and then burst out laughing, her anger evaporating. "Why on earth would you call me *that?*"

Irritation still clouding his expression, he now looked uneasy. "I accidentally said something inappropriate in front of Mandy a couple months back; so Micki, being Micki, politely ripped me to six thousand neat little ribbons that instant and suggested if I ever wanted to see their kids again, I'd best be watching my language."

"Can't say as I blame her," Marie said with a shrug. A little smile tugged at the corners of her mouth. "I wouldn't want *our* kids cussing like sailors." She picked up the knife again and began slicing the carrots into coins.

"True," Marc conceded. "What's worse is now Mandy will blurt it out at really inopportune moments – not that there's ever a *good* time for a toddler to say 'shit.' She calls it 'talking like Unca Mahc' – which, as you can imagine, endears me to Gary and Micki not at all."

She chuckled. "So you're replacing English curses with Portuguese nonsense?"

Marc grinned – one of those silly grins Marie loved. "Pretty much."

"And now I'm a rancid potato?"

"Only sometimes. But today, definitely. Just don't make me call you a wasted giraffe," he warned.

Marie's headache was gone, she noticed. Her irritation had also evaporated and the corners of her mouth turned upward in a playful grin. She cocked her head. "How's that sound?"

"*Girafa desperdiçada.*"

She gave an exaggerated shudder. "Yikes! I'll certainly try never to get you that angry, then."

Marc nodded in assent. "I'd appreciate that."

When their smiles began to fade, Marie carefully steered the conversation back toward what started their disagreement. "We still need to start looking for a place to live." She held up her hands as she saw him about to balk. "I don't want to rip the scab off the argument, Marc. All I'm saying is we're getting married in five months. I don't want to deal with packing, moving and *un*packing while we're trying to finalize wedding plans. Or when you should be studying for finals."

Marc nodded at her last sentence; as he did, some of his intensity seemed to abate.

Marie had figured his resistance had a lot to do with anxiety over his classes. She didn't want to cause him undue stress – and now she regretted having baited him. She laid aside the knife again and went to him. Slipping her arms around him, she rested her head against his chest. "I'm sorry I antagonized you. I admit I went about it the wrong way. I know you want to do well in school. I want that for you, too." Pulling back from her fiancé, she steered him toward the table. "Look, I found some places I thought you might like."

Together they sat to review the newspaper listings

she'd circled.

"I was thinking we should rent for now, somewhere between both our jobs and Yale. Then, after you graduate, we can buy – or build something you'll design." Her words gathered momentum. "I didn't think it made sense to buy a house now, especially one with a yard that has to be mowed. Granted, we're not building any equity, but we're also not responsible when the water heater goes kaflooey. This way, we can take our time and look for an area we both like – one with good schools, parks and other amenities."

Marc's expression relaxed into an admiring smile. "You've given it a lot of thought, haven't you?" He leaned in and kissed her. "You're so methodical. I love that about you."

Marie's cheeks tinged pink at his compliment. "I was thinking about Seymour."

He feigned offense. "We're not even married and you're already thinking about other men?"

Marie balled up a fist and socked him in the arm. "The town, you *batata ramposa*."

Marc chuckled. "It's *rançosa*. If you're going to insult me, at least pronounce it right."

"Okay, you little *shit*." She grinned. "Is that better?"

He kissed the end of her nose. "Much better. But don't let Michaela hear you say that. Or Mandy."

Four days later, Marie told Marc, "I've got some bad news... and I'm afraid you're going to call me a stumpy antelope or something."

"You mean a wasted giraffe?"

"Yeah, that."

Marc's grip tightened on the phone receiver as he scanned the program log for his next set of commercials. "Why's that?"

"I won't be around for your birthday. I'll be in Houston for a symposium. I just found out about it. I fly out on the sixth and won't be back home until late on the night of the twelfth."

Marc noticed the calendar on the wall and exhaled aloud. "Let me guess: This is your lame attempt at an April Fool's joke."

"N-no." Marie faltered. "It's not. That'd be a lousy thing to joke about, Marc. I really have a convention in Houston that week."

"That sucks. I guess we'll just have to have the wild rumpus before you leave, then."

"What wild rumpus?"

"The celebratory surprise birthday rumpus you were planning with all my friends."

"Oh, the big thirty-fifth birthday bash! No, I had to call that off," Marie teased. "Neither of them could make it."

"Ouch! You sure know how to hurt a guy," Marc grumbled playfully. "Cut me right to the quick, why don'cha?"

"Well, someone had to," she parried right back. "Tell you what, I'll make it up to you."

Marie could hear the beguiling smile in his voice. "Oh yeah? How d'you plan to do that?"

"By taking you to lunch for your birthday before I leave. Just the two of us. Wherever you want to go."

"Carpaccio?"

It was his favorite restaurant. He'd taken her there for their first date. "What did I just say?"

"Man, you can be downright testy when you're buying lunch."

Marie grinned at his playfulness. "Oh hush. I figured you'd want to go there. I already made reservations."

Chapter 5

(9:45 a.m., Saturday, April 11)
"You ready?" Marie asked when Marc answered the buzzer.

"Be right down."

Two minutes later, Marc burst through the front door and down the steps. "Hi," he greeted her as he reached the sidewalk.

"Hi there. You seem to have taken your cheerful pills today."

Marc gave her a kiss. "I did, indeed. You ready to go look at some apartments?"

Forty minutes later, Debbie May, the rental agent, greeted them at the first of the six places they intended to look at. The quaint, fully applianced ranch-style home had a standard-size fenced city lot and an in-ground pool. It was available immediately. She said the owner wanted it occupied as soon as possible and no, he wouldn't rent to someone with pets.

"I've checked all your references and your financials. Your credit scores are both, in a word, enviable. Everything looks good," Debbie said. "There's no reason we shouldn't be able to get you into this, or any of these properties. So, what are your thoughts about this one?"

"It's nice," Marie said with optimism, enjoying the feel of Marc's hand holding hers.

"It *is* nice," Marc agreed, stroking the back of her hand with his thumb. "But it's a no go."

Marie stared at him. "But, Marc… it's got a pool," she said. "I thought you'd like that."

"I do. But what good is that if they won't let Oscar live here?" He turned to the rental agent. "We need a place that will accept a well-behaved cat. That's not negotiable."

Debbie scanned the rest of the addresses on the list. "Well" – she tapped a manicured finger to her lips – "most of these places are prohibitive about pets. I'm sorry. There's nothing I can do."

"Even with a sizeable deposit to cover any expenses incurred?" Marie asked hopefully.

The realtor shook her head. "I'm afraid most of these owners are insistent – no pets."

"So you won't even ask them?" Marc asked evenly.

She squared her shoulders as she turned to face him. "I don't see what good it would do."

Marc didn't care for her snippy tone. "Then we'll find an agent who's actually willing to go to bat for us. Thanks for your time." He squeezed Marie's hand. "You ready to go, hon?"

Marie gaped at him.

"But sir, these – these property owners are adamant about pets," the rental agent sputtered.

"I understand," he replied calmly. Releasing Marie's hand, he folded his arms. "So am I. Adamant about our pet. Now, either our excellent references and *enviable* credit scores are sufficient for us to live in one of their vaunted rental properties *with our cat*, or we'll look elsewhere. You decide. What's it gonna be?"

Debbie's mouth dropped open as she stared at him.

Refusing to back down, he met her gaze and held it.

Marie took hold of his arm.

Marc patted her hand but did not break eye contact with the rental agent.

Finally, the woman caved. She shifted foot to foot. "Very well. I'll see what I can do."

"Great. Once you've got a favorable answer from one

of these owners, Debbie, you know how to reach us. Thanks so much for your time." He offered a perfunctory handshake.

Back in the car, Marie was still staring at Marc in numb astonishment.
"What?" he asked at last.
"That was masterful! I've never seen you play hardball."
"That was nothing. They're crazy if they think we'll rent a place that won't let us keep Oscar. Besides, they need us more than we need them." A slight smile crept across his face. "Now, seeing as we've unexpectedly got the rest of the morning free, where would you like to go for breakfast?"

Over bacon and softly scrambled eggs at the 67 Family Diner, Marc and Marie reviewed the for-rent listings in the *Post*.
As they lingered over refills of coffee, Marie gasped. "Listen to this!" Pointing to a for-rent listing, she took up the paper and read the ad aloud. " 'Sunny six-room apartment. Second floor of two-family house in an area of well-maintained older homes. Hardwood floors. Large kitchen with all appliances. Resident landlord. Cats welcome.' It sounds perfect!"
Marc set down his coffee. "So what are you still doing talking to me? Call them," he urged.
Marie dug her phone from her purse, dialed the number listed in the ad and went outside to place the call. Three minutes later, she returned, a triumphant smile lighting her face. "They're home and they said it'd be no problem for us to come and see the place this morning."

At 11:15, they pulled up outside 27 Washington Avenue. Marie drew in her breath as Marc shifted into park and cut the engine. "Oh, Marc!" she breathed barely aloud, clutching his arm. "I can totally see us living here. Look at that front porch… it's beautiful!"

Marc silently admired the wide wraparound porch. Something about it felt familiar. He drew in a sharp breath. All that was missing was the wooden rocking chairs. "It is. But let's see what the apartment looks like inside before you go berserk over it, huh?"

In his head he heard Edward ask, *Would you start a family here?*

Marie shook her head. "You are such a rancid potato," she muttered, grinning.

"Good morning," a fair-skinned woman who looked to be in her mid 30s greeted them as they approached on the sidewalk. Her dark eyes met Marie's. "Marie? I'm Val Quindlen. We spoke on the phone. This is my husband, Tim."

Marie greeted Tim, then introduced him to Marc.

"Pleased to meet you both," Tim said, extending his hand to Marie and then Marc. "Shall we go inside?"

"Like the ad said, it's the second-floor apartment," Val said as they headed upstairs. "It's got hardwood floors throughout – except for the kitchen; that's got linoleum. It's got a ton of space and plenty of closets. And lots of light. It's a great apartment!"

"The woodwork is gorgeous," Marc commented, looking around. "All original?"

Tim gave a slight nod. "Mostly."

While Val showed Marie around – pointing out various features, including the laundry area, pantry, closets and built-in cabinetry and shelving – Marc continued his exploration to assess its structural soundness. He checked the ceilings, and the floors immediately surrounding each window and radiator, for evidence of water stains, then examined the kitchen and bathroom fixtures for any signs of leakage. Finding none, he asked about the plumbing and electrical systems.

"We updated just about everything when we bought the place last July," Tim said, ticking off items on his fingers. "Plumbing, electrical, insulation, roof. Not the windows yet, though."

"It all looks sound. And you did a nice job refinishing the woodwork," Marc observed with an approving nod. "I can hardly tell where you had to replace that bit of molding over the window in the living room. It's almost an exact match to the original."

Tim nodded in appreciation. "You've got an excellent eye, Marc. We had that piece custom made. You a contractor?"

"Nah. Just always been fascinated by architecture."

The two men returned to the living room to wait for the women.

"I love these pocket doors!" Marc ran a hand admiringly over the wood surface. "Too bad they don't put these kinds of details in houses anymore."

"Aren't they fantastic?" Val bubbled, reappearing with Marie. "We've got 'em downstairs, too. They add such charm!" She chewed her lip as she studied Marc. "I don't mean to pry, but... your voice – it sounds so familiar. Why do I know your voice?"

"I work in radio," he replied. "I go by Marc Lindsay on air."

"*That's* where I know it from!" Val exclaimed, snapping her fingers. "You do that Late-night Love Songs program. That must be such an exciting line of work."

Marc shrugged. "No more than anything else, I expect. What do you folks do?"

"I'm a police detective."

"And I'm a veterinarian," Tim said.

"Interesting. So, the remodeling...?"

"Like you – just a fascination. Well, more of a hobby,"

After a few more minutes of perusing the apartment, Val and Tim retreated to one of the smaller bedrooms, to let the other couple discuss their findings privately in the living room.

When they were ready to go, Marc and Marie went to find the landlords.

As they headed downstairs to the Quindlens' apartment to talk further, Marc asked Tim, "What's a typical month's expense for utilities?"

"I'll have to check the exact figures," he replied as they settled in the living room, "but based on what we pay here, which I'd think would be comparable..." he cited numbers for what they were paying. "Of course, your heating bill would necessarily be lower, being on the second floor."

"Granted," Marc replied with a nod. "Overall, though, that doesn't sound bad."

"You told me on the phone the apartment would be available in late August," Marie said. "Is there a reason it's not available 'til then?"

"We have a few things we wanted to do: refinish some of the woodwork, wax floors, paint... that kind of thing," Val said. "It's not a lot, but since we're doing it ourselves, we have to work on it as we have time. Which, frankly, isn't all that often. It probably won't take all that long to do, but we figured we should allow extra time, just in case. I may as well ask: What color would you like your kitchen walls?"

Marc and Marie glanced at each other. Marie voiced the question on both their minds.

"Don't you need to check our references first? Or at least our credit?"

Val shook her head. "We're both pretty good judges of character. We think you'll be a good fit. The apartment's yours if you want it." She grinned. "Plus, now your fingerprints are all over everything – if I really wanted to, I could run them and make sure you don't have criminal records."

Marie snickered.

"And you're definitely okay with us having a cat in the apartment?" Marc clarified.

"Of course," Tim said. "What kind of vet wouldn't be okay with pets?"

Marc nodded. "Good point."

Marie glanced at the Marine memorabilia adorning the walls. "Which one of you was in the Marines?"

The Quindlens exchanged a glance. "Both of us," they replied in unison.

"Oh," Marie said. "That must have been interesting. How long did you serve?"

"Twelve years," Val said.

"Four for me."

"Is that where you met?" Marc asked.

Tim gave a headshake. "Negative. We grew up together in Naugatuck. Next-door neighbors."

"Did you serve together?" Marie asked.

"Negative on that, too," Val replied. "I was already a sergeant when Tim enlisted."

"She left active duty as a captain," Tim added, reaching to take his wife's hand. He gave her a fond smile. "I left as a sergeant. So, yes, she's my superior."

"In every regard," Val added with a trace of a grin.

"And she reminds me of that at each opportunity," he parried back with an exaggerated sigh.

"So if you didn't cross paths in the service, when did you reconnect?" Marie asked.

"Several years ago," Val replied, "when Casey, my golden retriever broke his leg chasing a rabbit. I brought him to the emergency clinic and guess who was on duty?" She squeezed Tim's hand.

Tim picked up the story from there. "I set his broken tibia, reassured his fretful owner he'd be fine, then asked Val to go out that Friday. We went out three more times and realized there was more between us than a passing interest in catching up with a former neighbor. We were married about six months later."

"How did you two meet?" Val asked.

"That was my brother Gary's fault," Marie replied glibly. "He works with Marc at the radio station and they became friends. Such good friends that he and his wife asked Marc to be godfather to my niece. And from there, he managed to weasel his way into pretty much every party and family function, so there was no escaping him."

"This is true," Marc confirmed, smiling and taking her hand. "She hated me. Fervently. And made no secret of it, either. In fact, she seemed to make it her life's ambition."

Marie grinned. "Only because you insisted on showing up at every party flaunting a different gorgeous woman."

"Well, there's that," he conceded. "But don't let her fool you; that wasn't the only reason. She hated me on general principle. Fortunately, my charisma and good looks wo—"

Now Marie guffawed. "Let's not forget modesty."

"Yes, that," Marc added with a laugh. "Those things all finally ganged up and won her over. Plus, I *really* impressed her by saving her boyfriend from drowning. So it only took, what, ten years for you to go out with me?"

"Something like that."

Val laughed. "Sounds more like a horror story than a courtship."

"Oh, I wouldn't exactly call it a horror story," Marc demurred.

"Maybe not, but it's had its moments," Marie replied, giving his arm an affectionate pat.

"When are you getting married?"

"September eleventh," Marie said.

"Do you have your colors picked out?" Val asked.

"Uh oh, they're gonna start wedding talk." Tim gestured toward the porch. "C'mon, Marc, that's our cue. If you're wise, you'll stay as far away from that mess as possible."

He planted a kiss on his wife's forehead. "We'll take Sebastian for a walk while you get that wedding stuff out of your systems."

Chuckling, Tim took the leash from its hook in the front hall and whistled for their cocker spaniel puppy. Marc followed him out into the still-chilly April sunshine.

"Your husband's a riot," Marie told Val.

"He is that," she agreed. "Fortunately, he's also pretty easygoing. You and Marc seem well suited, too – like you've got a really solid relationship."

"We've had our issues, but we're getting better about talking them out."

"That's important, maintaining good communication between you. It's not always easy, but it's so worth it." Val cocked her head. "We've talked about what Tim and I do, and what Marc does. What about you?"

"I'm a therapist. I specialize in pediatric psychiatry, but I also see adult patients."

"Wow – that's unusual. It must be exciting. And sad sometimes, I'll bet."

"It can be. I try not to bring it home. But even if I do, Oscar doesn't mind much."

"Oscar?"

Marie's face relaxed into a smile. "He's the sweetest little tuxedo cat. I've had him about four years."

"That's why Marc was so persistent about our accepting cats. They must get along well."

"They do now, since Oscar established some boundaries. He bit Marc once. Right out of the blue. One minute he's sprawled on his back in Marc's lap, purring up a storm; next minute he's had enough attention and chomps Marc's index finger. Blood everywhere. I never saw a puncture wound bleed like that!"

Sebastian tugged Tim along the sidewalk, sniffing at every clump of grass in sight.

"This is a great area," Tim told Marc as the spaniel puppy stopped to inspect an intriguing shrub. "For the most part, it's pretty quiet. The neighbors have been really welcoming. All their kids love playing with Sebastian. I mean, what kid wouldn't love a puppy, right?"

Marc nodded in agreement.

They walked in silence for a time.

"That church over there" – Marc pointed up the road – "Catholic?"

Tim's face broadened into a full-blown grin. "Yeah. St. Augustine's. Terrific parish! We love it there."

"Good to know. I mean, we like our current parish, but once we move, it'll be forty-five minutes away. Kind of a long haul."

"Oh, it's so convenient, living three doors up," Tim said, "especially when you wake up and realize Mass starts in fifteen minutes."

Sebastian tugged him along to the next set of bushes.

They continued on in comfortable silence for another half block.

"How long a drive is it to New Haven?" Marc asked.

"Little over twenty minutes. Why?"

"I need to know how long it'll take to get to class."

"What are you studying?"

"Ultimately, architecture; but for now, just basic classes. Core requirements, I guess they call them."

"Where? UNH?"

Marc shook his head. "Yale."

Tim stopped walking. "No shit! That's awesome. When did you start?"

"January. No actual design classes yet, 'cause they don't let you declare an architecture major 'til second year. Plus, since I just started, it'll be my first full year, coming up in the fall."

"So the radio gig is just, what, killing time?"

"Something like that."

"That's great. Hey, I'd love to pick your brain about building ideas sometime."

"I'm not sure what help I'll be at this point, but sure."

By the time the guys returned with Sebastian, Val and Marie had moved on from talking about weddings to gardening. Val had brought out her notebooks, filled with color sketches and ideas for the annual flower beds out front, raised-bed vegetable plots for the small back yard and even a modest grape arbor. She and Marie were huddled on the couch in the living room, looking through a notebook and discussing colors, textures and heights of various flowers when Sebastian barreled into the room, leaping into Val's lap.

"Sebastian!" she exclaimed, raising her head to escape licks from the puppy's exuberant pink tongue. "Get down, sweetie." She lifted the pup and set him on the floor, where he squirmed about, squatted and immediately piddled at Val's feet, then danced through the puddle of pee.

"No," Val wailed. "Not again!"

"I'll get it." Tim scooped the squirmy puppy into his arms. "Watch your feet, Val."

As he carried the dog out of the room, he said, "Sebastian, we've got to work on that, buddy. You can't go excitement-peeing all over the floor *every* time we come home from a walk. It's gonna stop bein' cute pretty soon, pal."

Minus the puppy, he came back into the living room, carrying a roll of paper towels and a bottle of disinfectant spray, then set about cleaning up the remnants of Sebastian's enthusiasm.

Val got up from the couch, steering clear of the small puddle at her feet. She led Marie and Marc back into the kitchen while Tim worked.

"You want to stay for lunch?" Tim invited, returning to the kitchen to wash his hands when he finished cleaning the living room floor. "Nothing special, just my homemade chicken soup and some grilled-cheese sandwiches. But Val and I would love to chat with you folks some more."

Marc and Marie exchanged a brief look.

"That'd be great," Marc replied. "What can we do to help?"

Tim deferred to his wife on that question.

She shook her head. "Not a thing. Unless you'd care to pick which kinds of cheese you want. There should be American, Swiss, provolone" – she ticked varieties off on her fingers as she went – "muenster and probably cheddar in the fridge. Would you get them out, please, Tim?

"I usually go with a blend of American, provolone and

muenster," she added, "because I like the way that particular combination tastes when they melt together. But you may prefer something different."

"Bonus!" Tim crowed, his head still inside the refrigerator. "Aside from the usual selection, today we've also got asiago, gruyère and mozzarella." He pulled out the full assortment of cheeses, along with the butter dish and a loaf of sourdough. Then, reaching into a cupboard near the stove, he brought forth a box grater.

"I never thought of using anything other than American for grilled cheese," Marie admitted, assessing the various cheeses before her on the counter.

"No? We always have at least three options. Frankly, I wouldn't have it any other way," Val replied as she reached into one of the cabinets for her griddle. "I guess I'm just spoiled."

Tim gave an exaggerated nod, rolling his eyes skyward for emphasis.

Val elbowed him good-naturedly in the ribs.

"Ooh, I feel like such a rebel," Marie exclaimed with glee.

Tim chortled. "Marc, your fiancée is a hoot."

"That's one word for her," he agreed with an amiable grin.

Over lunch, the two couples talked about the work the Quindlens planned to accomplish on the upstairs apartment before their new tenants moved in. They also discussed gardening, and Tim told Marc and Marie they should feel free to take advantage of the access to the garden plot.

"I'm afraid I've got the original black thumb," Marie quipped. "I'd be useless in a garden."

"And I'm either gonna be in class or at work most of the time," Marc added. "Or studying. So gardening really wasn't even on my radar."

"That's fine. At any rate, I'm sure we'll have plenty of produce, so don't be surprised if you come home sometimes to find a carton of tomatoes and zucchini on your back porch," Tim warned.

"That would be heaven," Marie said with a full-on smile. "I remember my grandmother used to fry up the zucchini flowers."

"I've heard of that, but I've never tried fried zucchini flowers," Tim commented.

"But if you take the flowers, you won't end up with any squash," Val said, looking horrified. "And I love zucchini! I couldn't imagine planting them just to take their blooms."

"They'd have a dozen or more zucchini plants running all over the place," Marie recalled, "so her taking a couple dozen flowers didn't really have much of an impact on their harvest. Nonna was the quintessential green-thumbed Italian grandmother, so there were always plenty of veggies."

An hour and a half later, Marc and Marie headed back to Danbury, with a signed lease in Marie's purse, eager to move into their new apartment – Oscar and all – at the end of August.

Marie took Marc's hand. "Hard to believe we just met them a few hours ago, huh?"

He glanced over at her. "Yeah. They both seem really nice."

After another brief silence, she asked, "Are you excited about moving in?"

"A little. I'm not looking forward to the packing or the unpacking. But I'm glad we found a place we both like, that's convenient to both of our jobs and Yale."

"Hmm," Marie acknowledged in a noncommittal sort of way.

After that, they fell silent again, each tending to their own thoughts.

In the quiet, Marc heard Edward's voice in his head. *Would you start a family here?*

Yes, he answered silently. *Without a doubt.*

Chapter 6

(9:15 a.m., Sunday, June 13)
Marie was almost finished getting dressed when the doorbell rang. Marc had asked her to be ready to go by 9:30, because he had a surprise destination for her.

"Dress casually. And wear comfortable shoes; sneakers are fine. We'll be outside and doing plenty of walking," he'd said the previous evening. "Feed Oscar before we leave, 'cause we won't be back anytime soon."

She'd pressed him for clues, but he refused to reveal any more.

Wearing a floral-print skirt and blue short-sleeved top, but still barefoot, Marie hurried to answer the door. She broke into a grin when she saw her fiancé on her porch. Wearing khakis, black sneakers and a short-sleeved green polo shirt, Marc looked so handsome her initial impulse was to scrap their plans for the day and just drag him inside.

"Hi. C'mon in. Sorry, I'm not quite ready." She looked at her watch, her brow furrowing. "Wait, you're too early. I wasn't expecting you for another fifteen minutes." She gave brief consideration to whether there was time for a quick tumble in the sheets.

"I know. I'm a little ahead of schedule. I couldn't wait to see you."

At his admission, a shy smile overtook Marie's face. Now she noticed he was holding a gift bag that sported pretty green tissue paper poking out from the top. She stood aside. "C'mon in."

Marc held out the enticing gift bag to her. "*Feliz dia de Santo Antônio,*" he greeted her.

"What's this?" she asked as she accepted the present.

"Gee, it looks suspiciously like a gift bag to me," he replied, his grin impish. "My guess is you should open it and find out what's inside. That's generally what people do with gifts."

Marie grinned at Marc's teasing. As she pushed aside the tissue paper to look in the garden-themed gift bag, she recognized the sweet-spicy aroma. Basil. Inside was a small potted basil plant, full and bushy, with plenteous bright-green leaves. In its center was a bright-yellow tissue-paper flower crudely wired to a chopstick. She pressed her face into the fullness of the plant's greenery and inhaled its scent deeply. "Mmm! I *love* basil! Thank you, sweetheart." She reached upward to kiss him. "But why are you giving me this?"

"Tradition." He slipped his arms around his beloved and drew her close for another kiss. "Today is the feast day of Saint Anthony, and it's a custom in Portugal for a single man to give a potted basil plant to the woman he hopes to marry."

"How sweet!" Marie bubbled. "So this means you're still planning to marry me, huh? That's good to know."

"For the moment, yeah," he teased.

She giggled, then kissed him. "Is this kind of like a Portuguese backup plan to sweep the woman off her feet? You know, in case the engagement ring didn't quite do the trick?"

Marc shook his head. "Not exactly. It's normally done the other way around: basil first, then diamonds." He gave a little shrug. "But I figured it couldn't hurt. Besides, it helps the *agricultores* boost late-spring sales before their basil plants start getting all leggy and sparse."

Marie loved it when he dropped in the occasional word or phrase in Portuguese. She also found it endearing that Marc was still wooing her. She lifted the plant from the gift bag, then set the bag aside to take a closer look at the plant. He'd presented it in a cheerful yellow ceramic pot with blue stripes at the top and bottom, green dots at the top edge and perky roosters painted around it. And tucked into the soil was a miniature statue. Saint Anthony, she guessed.

"What are these?" she asked when she noticed a trio of rolled-up papers nestled amid the plant's dense foliage.

"Ah." Marc took the pot from her hands and set it on the coffee table. "Those are for you to read when you're alone."

"But...?"

He planted a kiss on the end of her nose. "No buts. You need to finish getting ready to go."

"Are you going to tell me where we're going?" Marie asked once they were underway.

"We're going to Mass."

"Outside?"

"Hush," Marc commanded playfully. "You ask too many questions."

He took her hand in his, drew her hand to his lips and kissed it. "You look pretty."

"Thank you," she replied, blushing a bit.

He released her hand when he had to turn onto Route 53, then reached for it again as they navigated the gently winding stretch of road.

"I know we're headed south," Marie said, hoping to dislodge a bit of information from him.

"Correct."

When he offered nothing further, she began to drum her fingers against the arm rest.

Before long, they turned left onto Great Pasture Road, which later became Wooster Street.

"Any more observations?" he asked mischievously.

Marie drew her lips into a tight line. "Still headed south... pretty much."

Marc nodded. "Yep."

At last they turned right onto Route 58. And still they continued south until the road merged with Route 59 at the Easton fire station.

"Care to venture another guess?"

"You're looking for somewhere to bury the body and you figured Bridgeport was the place to do it?" she kidded.

"Bury what body?"

"Mine."

He laughed aloud. "Why would I be wanting to bury you, *querida*? Didn't I, not an hour ago, give you a potted basil plant and explain to you its significance?"

She gave him a sideways glance. "You did." Her tone remained guarded.

"So what in heaven's name would lead you to believe I was looking for a place to ditch your body – after I've somehow managed to dispatch you?"

Marie played with her hands in her lap. "Paranoia?" Her nose crinkled the slightest bit.

"Silly girl. If I were going to do that, I would not have invested in the basil plant. Let alone that rooster pot it's in. Do you have any idea the trouble I went to in order to find that particular pot for you? Do you?"

He turned left onto Suburban Avenue.

Suburban Avenue. She grinned. Such a pleasant name for a lovely residential section of town. No way would he plan on ditching her body around here.

Suburban Avenue terminated at Park Avenue. Marc turned right and advanced slowly.

Cars lined both sides of the street as far as Marie could see. Something big must be going on.

A few hundred feet along Park Avenue, Marc stopped. The wooden sign posted in front of the property read, SAINT MARGARET'S SHRINE – AN OASIS OF PEACE.

It didn't resemble anything the slightest bit peaceful, Marie observed. The grounds buzzed with activity – men and women in bib aprons scuttled back and forth across the driveway with large serving pans covered with aluminum foil. Announcements blared from loudspeakers. Makeshift tents had been set up along the parking lot's perimeter... and was that a Ferris wheel in the distance?

"We're here," he announced. "I hope you're ready for some walking, because it doesn't look like we'll be able to park anywhere close."

The nearest parking space turned out to be a block and a half away.

As they headed, hand in hand, back toward the bustling activity at St. Margaret's, Marc explained what was going on. "St. Anthony is as big a deal for the Italians as he is for the Portuguese. I'm kind of surprised you didn't know about him."

"I know a little about him," she responded, feeling a bit foolish.

"He was a Franciscan priest who came from a wealthy family in Lisbon."

"I thought he was called St. Anthony of Padua. Isn't that in Italy?"

"It is, and that's where – as I understand it – he served as head of his order."

"But he was Portuguese?"

"Mm-hmm. And aside from being best known as the patron of lost items, he's revered as the patron of Lisbon."

"So why are we at St. Margaret's Shrine if we're here to celebrate St. Anthony?"

"Because every year they host a festival in his honor. I've never been to it here, only heard about it." Muted excitement surfaced in his voice. "And I wanted to share it with you."

Marie smiled at his enthusiasm, however understated. "So what happens at this festival?"

"From what I understand, it starts with outdoor Mass at eleven, followed by a procession, and then the festivities begin," he explained. "It's billed as the 'original' feast of St.

Anthony. I'm not sure what to expect. But we'll find out soon enough."

They made their way through the crowds and staked out a patch of lawn in the shade of a maple tree, near where the Mass would be celebrated. An altar had been erected beneath a pop-up canopy at the far end of the parking area, next to the church building; and, from their vantage point, they had an excellent view of the festivities.

After Mass, Marc and Marie remained at the periphery of the crowd as the procession, led by the priest, deacons and two teens bearing banners, made its way around the grounds. Four strapping men, preceded and followed by musicians, conveyed a wooden statue of St. Anthony on a litter held aloft by poles carried at shoulder height. People surged around them, cheering and waving brightly colored tissue-paper flowers, like the one Marc had tucked into the pot of basil he'd given Marie.

When they arrived at the site where the statue would rest, the men lowered the litter onto a plinth and removed its carrying poles. As the men moved away, eager onlookers swarmed around, touching the feet and robes of the statue and crossing themselves; some pinned dollar bills to the statue's base.

"Why are they doing that?" Marie asked, comfortable with her hand in Marc's.

"Some of them are making offerings to St. Anthony in return for prayers answered. And others are petitioning his assistance." He shrugged. "People have all sorts of reasons."

"What happens now?"

"I think we're about to find out." He indicated a man with a loudspeaker who looked ready to make an announcement.

The man announced the festival was officially underway and the various carnival rides and food booths were now open. He reminded the crowd admission to the festival was ninety-nine cents and children under twelve were admitted free. He pointed out the location of ride-ticket booths and made a point of reminding festival goers that all-day ride bracelets were available for twenty dollars.

Marc and Marie made their way in to the festival with the other revelers, but hung back while crowds of people flocked to the fried-dough and sausage-and-pepper booths. She watched how the look of gleeful anticipation on his face dissipated as they made their way through the festival.

"What's the matter?"

"I'm not sure," he mused, his expression seeming too somber for the festive atmosphere. "I guess I hoped it'd be a little more like I remembered it in Lisbon."

"Maybe next year we can go there," Marie suggested hopefully. "Your classes will have ended by then and if you don't take any summer courses, we should be able to get away for a week or so."

Marc squeezed her hand. "That sounds nice."

"In the meantime, we're here, so let's enjoy the festival for what it is. C'mon, want to go on the Ferris wheel?" She flashed a coy grin. "I might even let you kiss me when we reach the top."

Now he broke into a broad grin. "Well, that's an offer I can't resist. Lead on, McDuff."

On the drive home, Marie looked over at Marc. He'd gotten quite a bit of sun and his face and forearms were tanned – almost to the point of being ruddy. On a long straight stretch, she took his hand. "Are you okay?"

Marc seemed surprised. "Of course. Don't I look okay?" He flashed a jack-o-lantern grin.

"Not really," Marie pressed gently. "You were really looking forward to the festival on the ride down. But once we got there, you seemed… disillusioned. Didn't you have a good time?"

"Sure I did. Anyway, my main goal was spending the day with you. So that's what matters." He kissed her hand, then gave her a sideways glance; the corners of his mouth twitched into a grin. "That, and sneaking in a few smooches at the top of the Ferris wheel."

"Well, for me, the high point is that you didn't dump my carcass in Bridgeport."

Marc thumped the heel of his hand against the steering wheel. "Darn it! I forgot to look for a decent spot." A playful smile lit his countenance. He gave an exaggerated sigh. "I guess we'll just have to turn around and go back."

Chapter 7

(Saturday, July 3)

"It's a perfect beach day!" Michaela exclaimed, entering the kitchen with Amanda balanced on one hip. "Too bad Erin's in Cleveland – she'd have had a blast playing with Tanya's kids."

Erin was Gary's daughter by his high-school girlfriend. The ten-year-old came to live with her father and stepmother last summer, after her mother died the year before.

"I know." Gary had his head in the refrigerator and was rummaging around. "We couldn't have asked for a better day. But they always spend Fourth of July with her great-grandparents."

After unearthing the platter of Michaela's extra-thick hamburgers and a zip-top bag of marinating drumsticks, he shoved the door shut with an elbow. He leaned to kiss his wife and toddler. "Hello, baby."

Michaela ruffled Gary's hair. "Hi, yourself."

Now he laughed. "What makes you think I was talking to you?"

Grinning, Michaela took the bag of chicken from her husband's grasp with her free hand.

Amanda reached out to her dad. "Dah! We having pahty today. All my fwiends comin'. We gonna pway in da wohta. An' I gots my baving zuit on. See?" She lifted her shirt to reveal a brightly colored floral swimsuit.

"I see," he said. "You're gonna be the prettiest little girl at the party." Gary set the plate on the counter and reached for his daughter. "Come here, *chiacchierone*."

Amanda giggled at the silly-sounding Italian word for "chatterbox."

Michaela leaned against the counter in the cottage's little kitchen and watched her husband snuggling their little girl.

Before long, Amanda caught sight of Attila skittering through the room. She wriggled and squirmed and demanded to get down. Gary complied.

As the toddler scurried into the living room after the little tabby cat, Micki returned to their previous topic of conversation. "It was nice of you to cover the cost of their trip."

Gary shrugged. "It was the least I could do. After all, when Erin lived in Jersey, they could make the trip in about eight hours. But having to pick her up here adds another three and a half. And that wasn't fair to them. Now they can spend more time together – and that's the whole point."

"I suppose." Micki slid her arms around her husband. She knew Gary had learned long ago the art of quiet generosity from his granddad. "They were so grateful!" she added, thinking back to Monday afternoon, when she picked up Erin's grandparents, Bob and Christina Farricelli, at the train station. As she greeted them, Michaela pretended not to notice the tears in Christina's eyes.

After breakfast on Wednesday, Gary had driven Erin and her grandparents to Tweed New Haven Airport for the ninety-minute chartered flight to Burke Lakefront Airport.

About to embark on her first-ever plane ride, Erin ran to the wall of windows, her eyes wide with wonder, as aircraft approached and departed. She clung to the *Ramona* books her stepmother had given her to read on the flight.

Erin gasped when her dad pointed out the small jet that would carry her grandparents and her to Cleveland. "That's our plane?"

Crouching beside his daughter, Gary stroked the little

girl's dark, silken hair. "Sure is."

"It's so big! Who's going to be on it?"

"Well, there's the pilot and copilot, probably a couple flight attendants and other crew, and you and your grandma and grandpa."

"That whole plane just for us?"

He touched her nose. "Just for you."

Erin's mouth fell open. "That must have cost half a million dollars!"

He smiled gently at her exclamation. "Not nearly as much as all that." He smoothed her hair away from her face. "When you get back, I want to hear all about your trip. Promise?"

Erin hugged him. "Okay, Daddy!" She let go as her grandparents approached. "Are we going now?"

"In a few minutes, sweetheart," Mrs. Farricelli told her.

The child ran to the other side of the airport, where a single-engine plane was preparing to take off. Her eyes widened as the plane gathered speed and finally hopped off the ground and into the air with a roar of its engine. "Daddy, look!" she exclaimed. "Grandma, Grandpa, look – it's flying!"

A few minutes later, just as the trio grabbed their bags to enter the jetway, Gary took Robert Farricelli aside. "Call before you leave next week, so we'll know when to meet your flight."

Gary kissed Michaela on the forehead. "I hope they're having a good time."

"I'm sure they are." Patting his arm, she motioned toward the meat on the counter. "C'mon, you'd better get those on the grill. And I've got to put together the macaroni salad. People are gonna be here before we know it."

"Yes, ma'am. Right away, ma'am," Gary said, grabbing the bag of drumsticks and heading out the door.

"I'm so glad you guys came," Gary greeted Marie and

Marc three quarters of an hour later as they made their way up the driveway. He thought back to last year's Independence Day party – Marc was dating that leggy redhead and Marie showed up with that awful cop. He shuddered. The day had been tense right from the start, and it had ended horribly. Dispelling the memory of driving Marie to Milford Hospital behind the ambulance carrying her nearly drowned boyfriend, he motioned toward the enormous bowl in his sister's arms. "That better be your potato salad."

"You think I'd dare show up without it?"

"If you did, he'd probably send you home," Marc teased.

"There's no 'probably' about it, Marc," Gary asserted. "She'd be goin' back to get it, for sure. You made it with the eggs, right?"

"Of course. You didn't say anything about Tanya being pregnant again this year."

Tanya had been Gary's college girlfriend; over the years, the two had remained friends.

"Hey!" Feminine laughter filtered over to them on the humid July air. "I thought I heard my name being bandied about in a disparaging way."

Marie relinquished the coveted potato salad to her brother. "So good to see you again," she squealed, hugging the blonde in the cutoffs and sea-green top who'd sashayed over.

"Same here – you look fantastic!"

"Not nearly as good as you – and I didn't just have my fourth child!" Marie replied. "Speaking of which, where *is* the littlest St. Pierre?"

Tanya flipped her tawny mane back over one shoulder as Gary retreated to the picnic table with the potato salad. "Michaela's got her. She took one look at her and snatched her away. She's a sucker for a new baby."

Tanya greeted Marc with a broad smile and a quick hug. "It's so nice to see you again!" She looked from Marie to Marc and back again. "Gary wouldn't tell me what it was, but he said you've got news. I'm hoping it's something good…?"

"It is," Marie reached for Marc's hand. "We're getting married. In September."

"No way!" Tanya hugged her again. "That's fantastic!"

"What's fantastic?" David St. Pierre asked, coming around the corner of the house.

"Marc and Marie are getting married," Tanya said, sliding an arm around her husband as he joined them. "Isn't that wonderful?"

"Congratulations!" He smiled broadly and gave Tanya a loud kiss on the temple. "Marriage is terrific. Once you find the right woman, that is."

Marc put an arm around Marie and drew her close. "I think I've got that covered."

As noon approached, people began arriving in greater numbers; among them, one stood out. Gary couldn't recall the last time he'd seen Micki's dad in anything other than a suit. Then again, he figured, it came with the job. Michael Conwaye was State's Attorney for Waterbury.

"Hey, Dad," Gary hailed the other man, meeting him by the volleyball net. "Good to see you!"

"Thanks for the invite." The two men hugged briefly, thumping one another on the back. "I didn't want to subject anyone to my woeful lack of culinary skills, so I figured I'd play it safe with these." Michael opened a grocery sack to reveal several bags of chips. "There's salsa and onion dip in there, too," he added as Gary accepted the paper bag from his father-in-law.

Michaela hurried over. "Daddy! You made it!" She gave her father a hug and a kiss and let him take Amanda from her arms. "I'm so glad you were finally able to come. You've missed some amazing beach parties these past few years."

"Speaking of missing…" Michael looked around. "I seem to be down one granddaughter."

"She's with her Jersey grandparents – visiting family in

Ohio," Gary replied. "They go for a week every July."

"Oh, that's right. You mentioned that." Michael's brow furrowed. "Sorry I missed her."

"Yeah. It's way too quiet around here without her. But it means so much to her family, especially now, getting to see her every summer." He recalled Erin's mother's death almost two years earlier. "Besides, they've already lost so much; I'm not going to take that from them, too."

Nodding, Michael clapped his son-in-law on the shoulder. "You're a good man, Gary."

The younger man scowled. "Don't let that get out," he said gruffly. "I've got to protect my reputation as a colossal jerk."

"Hah! No danger there."

Gary looked in the direction from which the teasing barb had come. "Who invited you?"

Joey Sheldon's lopsided grin mirrored his big brother's. "As I recall, you did."

Chapter 8

(Tuesday, July 6)

"Better hurry up," Marc cautioned, glancing at his watch. "We don't want to be late."

Marie emerged from the bedroom, her heels clicking on the hardwood floor. "I hate that we're going to be apart for your birthday."

"A year ago you couldn't have thought of anything you'd like better."

Her gaze darted away as her cheeks tinged pink. "What a difference a year makes, huh?" She ducked into the bathroom.

"I love that dress on you," Marc said as she returned with a bottle of rosewater body lotion to stow in her carry-on bag. "The color really brings out your eyes."

She straightened, delighted that he'd noticed. The topaz earrings he gave her last Halloween winked demurely. "Thank you. I wanted to wear something nice to take my oh-so-wonderful fiancé to lunch for his birthday."

As Marc crossed the room, she looked him over and smiled in approval. His neatly pressed shirt was a single white cloud in a charcoal-grey linen sky.

Marie fingered his tie with approval. "Looks like we both got the blue memo."

"Thought you'd approve."

She slid her arms around him. "You look so handsome. I wish we had more time before we had to leave."

"Don't you be starting something we don't have time

to finish," he warned as she kissed the side of his throat.

Pouting slightly, Marie broke from him. "Oh, alright. Guess we'll have to see if it's really true what they say about absence."

Marc shook his head. "My poor dear. You're just a little sex kitten, aren't you?"

She gave him a coy wink. "Meow."

"Speaking of kittens, where's Oscar?"

"Over at Gary and Micki's."

"Didn't trust me to watch him?"

"You're not supposed to have pets. Anyway, he'd have driven you crazy by tracking litter all over the floors."

"Excellent point. Here, let me take this out to the car" – he reached for her suitcase – "Good lord, this thing's heavy! Did you pack for six days or two weeks?"

At his words, Marie's heart skidded to a momentary stop.

After checking her purse to make sure she had the airplane tickets and all the necessary documentation, she pulled the door shut, locked the deadbolt and hurried to catch up with her fiancé.

After stowing her suitcase in the trunk, Marc unlocked the passenger-side door of his '78 Saab and helped her inside. Going around to the driver's side, he got in and turned the key in the ignition. At first, the car made a ticking noise, but refused to start. He turned the key again. Nothing.

"C'mon," he urged. He tried a third time. None of the dashboard lights even came on. "*Tomate quadrado* – of all the times for this to happen," he muttered, thumping the steering wheel with the heel of his hand.

"Let's just take my car," Marie suggested, touching his arm. "No sense fretting over it now."

Marc sighed. "I guess you're right." He went to retrieve her bag from the trunk.

Marie headed him off. "I'll get it." She unlocked the trunk and handed him her keys. "Here, you drive."

Reaching inside the trunk, she tugged out her bag.

Shoving it into the trunk of her Volvo, she thumped it shut and climbed into the passenger's seat.

Heading toward Carpaccio, Marie suggested they stop at City Hall. "It's on the way. We can pick up our marriage license."

"We'll have plenty of time to take care of that later," Marc countered, glancing at his watch yet again.

"But we're going right by there. Anyway, I tried to get it last week and they said we both need to show up. When else will we be near here at the same time?"

"Okay," he replied amiably. "City Hall it is."

It was almost 11:40 when they arrived at Carpaccio. A hostess greeted the couple and led them to the open-air patio. At the far end, against the picturesque backdrop of Hazen Lake, stood a tulle-swathed archway festooned with white flowers. A light breeze stirred the air, swaying the filmy material.

When Marc lagged behind, Marie gave him a questioning look.

"Looks like we're intruding on somebody's wedding," he worried, hesitation evident in his voice as they crossed the cobbled surface.

"The patio's way too small for that," she countered dismissively. "Besides, who gets married on a Tuesday? Anyway, if that was the case, why would they have seated us here? It's probably just there for ambiance."

"I suppose," Marc replied as the hostess laid menus on a table set for two.

While he was still pondering her words, Marie took the seat facing the restaurant.

Marc settled into his chair opposite her. He picked up his menu. When Marie did likewise, she pretended to review its offerings; instead she glanced over Marc's right shoulder as a tall man in a dark suit approached.

"Are you Marie?" he asked.

Marie looked up from her menu. "Yes."

"Are we ready to proceed?"

Catching sight of two well-dressed couples stepping onto the patio, she nodded. "Yes, sir."

Looking up to see who she was talking to, Marc saw a man he didn't recognize holding a leather-bound book. His apprehensive gaze returned to Marie. "What's going on?"

The guarded hesitation in his voice made the back of her neck prickle. Her smile fled.

She fidgeted with her napkin. "Well, it's like this... I couldn't bear to be away from you all week and not know I was coming home to my husband," she confessed. "Marc, I want us to get married before I leave. Today. *Now.*"

He stared at her blankly. "I-I'm sorry, what?"

"We'd still have the church wedding in September," she blurted, her words picking up speed. "With all the family and friends. But this way we'll already be married. It'll be our own little secret. And all the pressure will be off us that day, so we can just enjoy ourselves..." Twirling a lock of hair, Marie trailed off to uneasy silence as her anxiety mounted. *Please?* She bit her lip; she had hoped it would be more of a happy surprise for Marc. She motioned toward the other man. "This is Terence Baxter, the justice of the peace who'll be doing the ceremony... if you say it's okay. Please, Marc?"

Marc stood to shake the other man's hand. She couldn't read his expression. If he was opposed to the idea, or upset by it, he didn't let on.

"I guess it *was* set up for a wedding after all," Marie said, gesturing toward the arch, hoping to defuse whatever might be simmering beneath Marc's placid façade. "I hope you're not angry with me, sweetheart."

Astonishment replaced suspicion. "Of course not!" Marc's hand reached for hers. "You are amazing, Marie. Sneaky, but amazing. I did *not* see this coming. I think it's a wonderfully romantic idea. And yes, *querida*, I'd marry you any day of the week."

"Even on a Tuesday?"

He kissed her hand. "Especially on a Tuesday."

At his words, Marie's smile returned.

"But don't we need witnesses?"

She gave a sly nod. "We do, indeed."

Footsteps approached from behind him.

"About time you two showed up."

At the sound of his best friend's voice, Marc whipped around.

Gary and Micki, Emily and Clive stood in a semicircle behind him.

"Yeah, it's about time," Emily echoed, stepping forward to hug her startled sibling.

"You were in on this?" Marc stammered.

She gave his cheek a playful pinch. "Of course. It's all a grand conspiracy, ya big doofus."

Gary chuckled as he embraced his soon-to-be brother-in-law. "She's right. I'm afraid you just can't trust anyone anymore. We're all out to get'cha... *married.*"

Terence Baxter asked everyone to take their places for the ceremony. Marie and Marc stood beneath the tulle-adorned pergola, with Emily and Gary flanking them.

"We're gathered here this glorious Tuesday to join this befuddled man and this sneaky woman in matrimony," he began. "Marc and Marie, you have come here today in full willingness – even if in a bit of a surprised stupor – to be married. Yes?"

Both nodded and murmured their assent. Marc heard Gary snickering quietly behind him.

"Excellent. Now, before you declare your vows to one another, I'll ask you to officially affirm it is indeed your intention to be married today, forevermore. Marie, do you come here freely and without reservation to give yourself to Marc in marriage?"

"I do," she replied, her blue eyes more intense than

Marc had ever seen them.

"And Marc, do you come here freely and without reservation to give yourself to Marie in marriage?"

Smiling warmly at his beloved, Marc gave a slight nod. "I do."

"Good. Now, Marc and Marie, please face one another and join hands."

Marie gazed at Marc as he took her hands. She briefly worried whether he'd harbored any reservations or misgivings about this impulsive escapade; but when she looked at him, the love she saw shining in his deep mahogany eyes erased all doubt.

At the officiant's prompting, she stated her vows. "I, Marie Claire Sheldon, take you, Marc Willem Lindemeyr, to be my lawful husband. I promise to be true to you, for better or worse, in sickness and in health, in good times and in bad, for richer or poorer, forsaking all others, all the days of my life."

When she was finished, the justice of the peace led Marc through stating his marriage vows.

"I, Marc Willem Lindemeyr, take you, Marie Claire Sheldon, to be my lawful wife." As he spoke, he felt the warmth of her hands in his and knew he was making the wisest decision of his life. "I promise to be true to you, for better or worse, in sickness and in health, in good times and in bad, for richer or poorer, forsaking all others, all the days of my life."

When they finished, Terence turned to Gary. "Do you have the rings?"

In the instant during which Marc wondered how he'd gotten them, Gary pulled the wedding rings from the breast pocket of his suit and handed them to the officiant. As Terence began to speak again, the unvoiced question fled from Marc's mind.

"I understand these rings had belonged to Marie and Gary's grandparents, and were willed to them upon their grandfather's death. When Marie became engaged to her brother's best friend and wore her grandmother's ring as a symbol of their engagement, Gary entrusted his grandfather's ring to Marc. I can't think of a more beautiful legacy for these two rings – the outward, visible sign of the unseen inner bond that already unites this couple."

The officiant handed Marie's ring to Marc and guided him through the words of the ring ceremony.

"Marie, take this ring as a symbol of my love and fidelity," he repeated solemnly. "When you wear it, be reminded of my singular, unbreakable love for you, and the eternity of our bond of marriage."

Marc slid the ring onto Marie's finger. "With this ring, I thee wed."

When it was her turn to repeat the ring-ceremony wording, Marie's hands trembled fiercely. After stammering her way through the words, she managed to slip Grandpa Sheldon's gold wedding band onto Marc's finger without dropping it.

The justice of the peace looked from one of them to the other. "You two have declared your intentions to each other – before witnesses. And now it's official," he said. "But before we conclude, I'd like to share some words of wisdom from the American poet Ogden Nash, who said, 'To keep your marriage brimming, with love in the loving cup, whenever you're wrong, admit it; whenever you're right, shut up.' "

While the others laughed, Marc and Marie exchanged a private glance and a hand squeeze.

"Now, in accordance with the laws of Connecticut and by virtue of the authority vested in me by the law of the State of Connecticut," Terence concluded, "I do pronounce you husband and wife." He turned to Marc. "You may kiss your bride."

Leaning in toward Marie, Marc took her face in his hands, in full awareness he was cradling a treasure of inestimable value. The world slipped away as Marie's arms slid around his waist. He met her clear blue gaze and murmured, "Hello, wife." A moment later, he bent his head toward her upturned lips. As they kissed, his hands slid into the softness of Marie's loose auburn curls. Marc felt his wife's body tremble; a nearly audible sigh escaped her lips and she drew him nearer.

At last, remembering they were in a public place, Marc eased back from Marie, planting a series of quick, soft kisses on her lips before drawing away from her.

After a celebratory lunch, the others bade Marie and Marc farewell, sending them on their way with hugs, kisses and best wishes.

(2 p.m.)
"Job interview?"

Gary leaned in the doorway to his boss' office and gave him a lopsided smile. "That's next week."

"So what's with the suit?"

He came in and sat down. "Marc had no idea he was getting married today."

"That's right," Pete said with a nod. "How'd it go?"

"Fine. He reacted well when he found out. No struggle to get away, no howling or baring of teeth. Nothing too embarrassing."

"That's kind of encouraging."

"He didn't even forget her name or drop the ring," Gary said, sounding a bit disappointed. "Tell you the truth, it was kinda boring."

"Sorry to hear that. They got off on their trip okay?"

Gary shrugged. "Far as I know. Last I heard, Marc still thinks he'll be on the air at seven."

Pete chortled. "It'll be quite a shock when he learns otherwise. That sister of yours is pretty conniving. She told me Friday she planned this whole thing right under his nose. I guess the final detail she needed to figure out was some way to disable his car this morning."

"I took care of that; disconnected the battery."

"You're just as conniving as she is."

Gary shook his head. "Not even close. I'm just the Prince of Prevarication. She's the Diva of Devious."

(3:27 p.m.)

Marie exited the highway and began the creeping trek toward JFK. She had to suppress the beginnings of a smile when Marc glanced at his watch for about the thirtieth time in the last twelve minutes.

"What's the matter?"

"I should've allowed more time" – he shook his head – "or just taken the night off. I'll never make it back before seven."

"So Gary'll fill in for a few minutes," Marie replied with a shrug, knowing her answer would make her husband bonkers; he hated being late for anything. He must have been practically crawling out of his skin when they showed up eight minutes late for their lunch reservation.

"That's not the point," Marc said, his voice getting that little warble to it.

She reached over and took his hand.

After a moment, he pulled it away. "Both hands on the wheel, please." His tone held the same tension she'd felt in his fingers.

Marie glanced over at her husband and placed her right hand back on the steering wheel with a quiet sigh.

They drove in silence for another few minutes. During that time, she noticed, he checked his watch three more times.

"What are you doing?" he exclaimed when she veered left toward a parking area.

"What?"

"You took the wrong turn – this takes us to *long*-term parking." He pointed in the opposite direction. "Short term is over *there*. Turn around."

"Turn around where?"

"I don't know. Anywhere – just find a place and go

back." His sigh couldn't have sounded any more exasperated. "Why didn't you let me drive?"

Marie continued along, showing no indication of even looking for a place to turn back.

Marc's hands tightened into fists, loosened, then balled up again. "Why are you still *driving*?" he blurted as his frustration found words. "Turn around!"

After driving for another minute, Marie pulled in to a parking space and shifted into park.

"You're going to miss your flight," he grumbled, his teeth gritted.

"Yes. And you'll be late for work. I know." She watched Marc's left eye twitch as his tension mounted.

At last, when she felt it would be cruel to torment him further, Marie killed the engine and turned toward her nearly apoplectic husband. "There's something else I know. But first, I've got a confession to make."

His face morphed from anger to disbelief to worry in the space of about two seconds. His mouth opened, then shut. "Wh-what? What?!"

Marie waited another moment to let him get the wrong idea. She took his hand. "I'm not going to Houston. There is no conference."

Marc looked at her. "What?" His breathing quickened. His blink rate increased so much she swore she could feel a breeze. "Then what are we doing here?" His controlled tone and the set of his jaw revealed he was well past frustration and on his way to fury. "Normal people don't usually drive two hours into New York City, Marie, fighting traffic the whole way, to get to airports unless they're planning on going somewhere."

"I know." She knew she sounded a little too patronizing and psychiatrist-y for Marc's liking. "But I never said we weren't going somewhere."

As he impatiently waited for her to continue, Marie reached above the sun visor, took down an envelope and handed it to him. She watched in something bordering on glee as he opened it.

His brow wrinkled as irritation dissipated and confusion took its place.

"You're not going to be late for work, sweetheart," she said. "You're not working tonight."

Her words buzzed around in Marc's head. He stared at her for several moments. "I'm sorry, what?" he said at last. His lips felt thick and ineffectual.

"*I'm* not going anywhere," she clarified. "But *we* are. *We're* going on our honeymoon."

"But..." After the first word, Marc's mouth fell uselessly open as he stared at her.

Marie gestured with one hand. "Go on – look."

He eyed the tickets in his shaking hands. Then he looked up at his wife.

"I don't think I've ever seen you speechless," Marie crowed, sounding equal parts powerful and impressed.

Marc found his voice. "How... how did you manage this?" He cradled Marie's face in his palm. "And how could I have been so clueless?"

"It was actually pretty easy. I snooped around in your stuff a month or so ago 'til I found your passport, so I'd know where it was. While you were at work on Friday, I went in, packed your suitcases and stowed them in my trunk."

"No wonder I couldn't find my green shirt yesterday." He shook his head. "What a sneaky little wife you've turned out to be!"

"I know. I'm just awful," Marie said, shaking her head sympathetically. "And this morning, I just distracted you while Gary disconnected your battery, so we'd have to take my car."

Marc sighed aloud. "That's all that's wrong with it?"

"That, and a scheming brother-in-law. So you can quit worrying."

"Hey..." Suspicion rose in Marc's voice. "How did

Gary end up with the ring? Last I knew, it was tucked away in my bureau..."

Marie laid a calming hand on his arm. "That was all my doing. You said it yourself, Marc: I'm a sneaky little wife. And now I've got a reputation to live up to."

"You're certainly off to a good start."

Her grin seemed to overtake her entire face. "I know." She leaned in to give Marc a quick kiss. "We'd better get moving; we've only got three hours 'til our flight leaves."

The newlyweds retrieved their luggage from the trunk and hurried toward the international departures check-in counter at Terminal 7.

Two hours later, as the airline staff announced first-class passengers for PortugAir Flight 720 to Lisbon were being permitted to board, Marie stood. "That's us."

When Marc gave her a questioning look, she said, "Did you think we were going to spend eight hours in business class? I don't know about you, but cramped seats with zero leg room doesn't sound like my ideal for how to start married life."

Marc gave a solemn nod. "You're right. I'd rather it started with deceit and obfuscation."

If Marie hadn't been looking at him, she'd have missed the twinkle in Marc's eyes. She nudged him in the ribs and kissed him. "You're cute when you use big words." She picked up her carry-on and tugged at his hand. "C'mon. We don't want them to leave without us."

As they waited for their plane to taxi to its departure position on the runway, Marc looked up from the book he was reading and nudged his bride. "Hey. Wife."

Marie looked up from her own book, smiling at his form of address. "Yes, husband?"

"There's something I don't understand."

"I'm sure there is," she replied, a teasing sparkle in her eyes.

"Why'd you bother dragging me to City Hall today to get a marriage license when you knew good and well we wouldn't be getting married in Danbury?"

She shrugged. "I had to make you think we were. You bought it, though, right?"

"Yeah." He gave a reluctant nod. "That's the last time I believe anything *you* say."

She reached over and tousled his hair. "Oh, stop being grumpy. You're far too young to be such an old curmudgeon."

He went on, undeterred. "Anyway, how'd you get a marriage license in Redding by yourself? I thought we were both supposed to show up to apply for it."

"Yeah... about that," Marie replied, twisting her hands together in her lap. "I'm afraid that was more deceit and obfuscation."

Chapter 9

(7:55 p.m.)

"I'm so glad you're home," Michaela exclaimed as Gary pulled his key from the front-door lock.

Delicious aromas filled the house. He inhaled deeply, his mouth watering as he identified the smells of warm bread and Grandpa's beef stew. He'd long ago shared the recipe with his wife and, over the years, she'd done well by it.

He leaned to kiss Michaela and smiled as she drooped into his arms. "You look positively frazzled. Mandy been keeping you on your toes?"

"Not just Amanda. The cats."

"Ahh, the cats." Gary's expression turned to worry. "What happened?"

"Nothing... yet. But Ginger and Attila are plenty pissed about having Oscar around. Lots of grumbling and angry tail swishing. And some hissing over the water bowls. At the very least, they're gonna need some time to adjust to their houseguest."

He pocketed his keys. "Let me guess: By the time they do, Oscar'll be going home."

Michaela sighed. "It's gonna be a long two weeks."

"Are you regretting offering to keep him while they're away?"

"Regretting, no. I just wish I'd been a bit more prepared, that's all."

Gary led Michaela to the couch and coaxed her down

beside him. "Come sit down. Let's talk."

"Dinner's ready," she protested, gesturing toward the kitchen. "I warmed it up for us a few minutes ago."

He shrugged. "It'll keep. How often do we get a quiet house all to ourselves?"

"Not often enough," she concurred; she cuddled against her husband's chest, relaxing into the comforting security of his arms.

"You were going to tell me about those darn cats," Gary reminded his wife, kissing the top of her head.

"Oh, yeah… that. I guess I should've introduced them a little more slowly," Michaela began meekly, "instead of just letting Oscar out of his carrier in the living room when I got him here."

"Aha!" He gave her nose a playful tweak. "So it's *your* fault. Twenty lashes with a wet noodle for you, my love." Seeing her unamused expression, he abandoned his light-heartedness. "How did they react?"

"Plenty of hissing, spitting and growling, and some scrambling to get away. Even a bit of knocking things over."

"Anything break?"

"Nothing that can't be repaired."

He snugged his arms around his wife. "I'm sure tomorrow will be better."

"I hope so. Meanwhile, Amanda's utterly taken with the idea of having a new cat in the house. She followed Oscar around all afternoon, going, 'kitty-kitty cat, kitty cat, kitty cat' – until he climbed the bookcase in your study just to get away from her. He stayed up there 'til after she went to bed." She looked around. "Now he's in hiding somewhere."

"Can't say as I blame him. I might've done the same."

Micki giggled. "Me too. Today was one of those days I wished *I* could do a six-foot vertical leap."

A grin crept across Gary's face, as if he were envisioning it. "I'd have paid to see that. You'd look pretty funny perched on my bookcase." He paused. "But then again, I could legitimately tell people you're my trophy wife."

Michaela ruffled his hair. "What do you need with a trophy wife? Besides, I'd have to be mounted on the wall," she said, wrinkling her nose. "And I wouldn't much care for that."

He nuzzled her throat. "No? So where *would* you like to be mounted?"

Micki gasped and thumped him in the shoulder with the heel of her hand. "Out of sight of the children, preferably."

Still my blushing bride, I see. Chuckling softly, he got to his feet and scooped her into his arms. "That can be arranged. C'mon, woman."

"Gary!" Micki squealed. "What about dinner? Aren't you hungry?"

His eyebrows rose wolfishly. "Oh, like you wouldn't believe."

Thirty-five minutes later, still giggling like a couple of teenagers, they returned downstairs in their bathrobes and slippers to slake their other appetites. Michaela ladled up bowls of hearty beef stew from the pot on the stove.

"Hmm, not really warm enough," she decided with a contemplative frown. She licked the finger she'd stuck into her bowl to test the temperature. Opening the microwave, she placed them inside and set it to reheat.

"I bet it would've been fine half an hour ago," Gary teased. "But, no, you had to drag me off to the bedroom the minute I got home."

Grinning, Michaela threw a dishtowel at him. "I think your memory's failing, mister."

"Oh yeah? Now that I think of it, someone may have told me that recently," he parried back with a playful glint in his eyes, "but I'm kind of foggy on the details." Coming to her, Gary tossed the towel on the kitchen island, wrapped his arms around his wife and pulled her close.

When their food was ready, they sat at the kitchen table,

spooning up rich chunks of stew in its thick, beefy broth.

"Mmm," Gary said with an approving purr. "This is delicious. Exactly how I remember it."

"Glad you like it."

"Like it? I may just scrap the whole trophy wife idea and keep *you*."

"Very funny." Micki got up and carved two generous chunks from a loaf of crusty bread on the counter. She handed Gary one chunk and returned to her seat with the other for herself.

Gary tore off a bit of bread and sopped up some of the broth. "That was a lovely wedding."

She nodded. "It really was. Marie's dress was so pretty. That blue is a great color on her."

(12:45 a.m. Eastern Time, Wednesday, July 7)

Awaking from a snooze, Marc stretched. He realized he wasn't even close to hitting the seat in front of him. It felt good to have this much leg room on an airplane. *Marie was right. This is the way to travel.* Glancing around, he noticed several passengers wearing dark-blue sleep masks, taking advantage of the quiet within the cabin to sleep. He shifted position. Before reclining his seat, he glanced backward to be sure he wasn't intruding on the passenger behind him. No chance. These seats were so spacious, he could probably play the trombone and not hit the guy in the seat ahead of him.

With a suppressed chuckle at his absurd observation, Marc glanced at his dozing bride, her serene face framed by auburn curls. Now he looked down at the gold band on his left ring finger. It still didn't seem real… but there they were, legally married and on their way to spend two weeks in Portugal! *Portugal!* He smiled and gave another stretch, this time rolling his shoulders and stretching his neck side to side. He wasn't used to this much idleness.

A first-class flight attendant appeared at Marc's side. "Can I get you anything, sir?"

He looked up. Not wanting to awaken Marie, he replied quietly, "I'm fine. Thanks anyway."

"It'll be a long flight. Maybe a blanket and pillow?"

Now he reconsidered. "I'd like that," he said with an appreciative smile. "Thank you." But then again, her lilting Mediterranean accent could have made an offer of torture sound like a good idea.

The attendant returned a minute later with a second blanket, which she draped over Marie.

Marc gratefully accepted the pillow and blanket from the flight attendant, then settled back into his seat to rest. The steady rumble of the jet engines soon lulled him back to sleep.

When he awakened from his subsequent nap, Marc stretched, rubbed his eyes and glanced around the cabin. The lighting had been dimmed to facilitate sleep on the long overnight flight. He looked over at his bride, now awake and reading quietly beside him. After refolding his blanket, he reached for her hand. "Hi."

Marie smiled as his fingers entwined with hers. "Have a nice nap?"

Marc stifled a yawn. "Mm-hmm. You?"

"Delightful. What time is it?"

He looked at his watch. "Eastern Time? One seventeen a.m." He squinted his right eye shut as he calculated the time conversion. "So just after quarter past six in the morning Lisbon time."

"You missed Late-night Love Songs."

Marc grinned, shaking his head. "No, Dr. Lindemeyr, I'm afraid you're wrong. I didn't miss it one little bit." He leaned in to steal a kiss. "And not to change the subject or anything, but have I told you how happy I am that we're married?"

A sweet smile crossed Marie's face. "Not in the last couple of hours, no. Tell me again."

Before he could reply, a scream came from the rear of

the first-class section; the overhead lights flicked on inside the cabin. The passengers who were awake blinked in the sudden brightness; those who'd been asleep grumbled at having been jolted from their sleep.

"Just do as you're told and nobody dies."

The words themselves were more chilling than the tone in which they were delivered. The speaker's voice wavered, and his words came out sounding uncertain.

A man with a gun lurched into view, grasping a flight attendant by the hair. He had a wild, desperate look about him as he propelled the terrified woman toward the door of the cockpit.

"Get me in there – now – or I'll blow you away," he threatened as she trembled and cried.

All around Marc and Marie, passengers gasped. A few panicked and screamed. Marie gripped Marc's hand, her blue eyes wide with fear.

"The rest of you, shut up and no one gets hurt," the young man insisted, sweeping his gun back and forth across the aisle from one passenger to another.

Marc's insides tightened when he saw the gleaming black metal in the other man's hand; a moment later, he let out a gasp as his wife stood. "What are you doing?" he hissed, grabbing for her hand.

She waved him off. "Please," she said, advancing toward the gunman, her voice as calm as Marc had ever heard it. "You don't want to do anything drastic. Let her go. Please put the gun down and let's talk about this."

The gunman whipped around to face Marie. "Sit down and shut up," he ordered.

"Let's not do this," she continued, her voice as calm as if she were in session with a child. She gestured toward the captive flight attendant. "Let her go and we can talk. Just the two of us."

"What are you doing?" Marc repeated in a panicked whisper.

Turning toward her husband, she put back a hand to

stay him. "Trust me." Then she inched toward the gunman. "Whatever's going on," she began, "we can discuss it. You and me, okay? Just, please, let her go."

"No!" The young man locked his gaze on Marie. His jaw clenched. He tightened his grip on the flight attendant's dark hair and shoved the barrel of the gun into her back. The woman let out a muffled cry.

"Please," Marie repeated.

He didn't respond.

She took a different tack. "What's your name?" she asked conversationally.

Taken by surprise at the question, the man said, "Dan."

"Okay, Dan. My name's Marie. I just want to talk. Just us. Okay?"

He gave a stilted nod.

"She doesn't have the authority to get you inside the cockpit," Marie said, indicating the flight attendant. She made things up as she continued. "She doesn't have a key. Or the combination to the lock. Only the pilot can let you in – and he doesn't know you're out here. Listen to me, Dan. Let her go. This doesn't have to go any further. It can stop right here, before anyone gets hurt. And you and I can talk about what's going on with you. Okay?"

As if he were considering her words, the young man seemed to relax some of the tension in his shoulders. Suddenly, he shoved the flight attendant away, across the aisle. She bolted, sobbing, to the back of the first-class section.

As Marie let out a sigh of relief, Dan brought his now-free hand to rest around the handle of the pistol, steadying it. A moment later, he'd aimed the weapon at her.

Marc's breath caught in his throat as Marie raised her hands in surrender. The tremor in the gunman's hand shook the barrel badly. Noting the positioning of his hands, Marc guessed Dan had likely never held a pistol in his life – and there was a good chance he was nearly as petrified as his planeload of victims.

Marc thought back to all those times Patrick's dad had brought the two of them to the firing range during junior-high and high school. He recalled the cool metallic feel of the .45 Ruger pistol in his adolescent hands, and the rough texture as his fingers closed around its grip. He'd marveled at how heavy the weapon felt in his palm, given its size.

"Now remember," he heard Detective McNaughton's voice cautioning them, "never cross one thumb over the other when holding a semiautomatic weapon. It's a great way to rip your thumb clean off."

While youthful swagger made Marc fairly certain his best friend's dad was exaggerating, the image of having his thumb torn off had shaken him to his core.

Patrick's father had gone on to explain the workings of the pistol, describing how, when the weapon was fired, the round would be ejected as the slide flew backward – practically too fast to be seen – advancing the next round from the magazine into the chamber. "But don't worry, boys," he cautioned wryly, "you'll only make *that* mistake once."

Marc glanced again at Dan's quaking hands. His left thumb lay squarely over the right, as though trying to steady the weapon.

"Please." Marie's beseeching voice beside him sounded almost faraway. "You don't want to do this, Dan. Please. Put the gun down." She gestured slightly toward him. Her voice wavered. "Just put it down and let's talk about this."

"Shut up!" he shouted, his voice shaking almost as badly as the gun in his quaking hands. "I let her go, like you asked. Now *you're* my hostage, Marie."

The murky way he spoke his wife's name sent a shudder through Marc. It took every ounce of his control not to rush the guy, but he trusted that Marie knew what she was doing.

"And now you're gonna do what I tell you or *you* get blown away. Give me your cash and all your jewelry." Now he pointed the gun lower, at her heart.

"Okay." Her voice trembled just the slightest bit. "I'm

going back to my seat – that's where my purse is. And I'm getting my wallet." She kept her hands in the air as she made her way back to her seat.

Marie drew in her breath audibly and gave a wide-eyed, frantic glance at her husband, who was doing his best to retain his dispassionate exterior as the gunman followed her.

"When faced with an armed assailant," Patrick's dad's voice filtered through Marc's brain, shutting out everything else, "remember, the guy with the gun has the perceived power. That can lead to stupidity or, at the very least, over-confidence. Keep your wits about you, stay alert and look for a way – *any* way – to gain the upper hand."

He assessed the situation. Dan stood in the aisle, feet apart, arms rigid. What most troubled Marc was the position of his gun: pointed at Marie, aimed at center mass. His finger rested on the trigger, and his eyes were locked on hers. A little over two feet of space remained between Marc and the man with the perceived power.

Over the course of less than half a minute that felt more like five days, Marc leaned forward; he inched his arms in front of himself almost imperceptibly as the gunman repeated his demand for Marie to hand over all her valuables.

With a shuddering indrawn breath, Marie reached down to pick up her purse. The gunman's gaze followed her motion. He watched as her trembling fingers fumbled for her wallet.

This gave Marc the distraction he needed. In a single, fluid movement, he jerked both arms upward – imitating the beginnings of a butterfly stroke. Bringing them down again, he grasped the other man's forearms and tugged him toward the floor.

Having taken the gunman by surprise, Marc rose from his seat and, with a swift arcing motion upward and to his right, wrenched him further off balance. In doing so, Marc propelled the weapon's muzzle toward the aisle, away from Marie.

The pair struggled for the gun. During a scant minute that could have passed for two weeks, they engaged in a mighty battle for control of the weapon. He'd been in few physical fights in his life, but Marc understood this was one he could ill afford to lose. If he failed, he was certain he would be the first one Dan would kill, followed by who-knows-how-many others. *No way am I going to let Marie be widowed on our wedding day!*

Fueled by a combination of blinding panic and adrenaline, Marc hung tight to Dan's forearm and did his best to wrest the pistol from his grasp. No use. The guy had too firm a grip on it.

During the scuffle, it seemed for a moment as if Dan were wearying, giving Marc the upper hand. Digging deep, Marc summoned every shred of strength he had left. But before he could maneuver safely behind the gunman, bring him to the floor and subdue him, a deafening shot rang out.

Screams erupted in the cabin as panicking passengers who hadn't already taken refuge scrambled for cover behind seats.

Marc staggered backward, as the sound of the shot reverberated in his ears. Shaking his head to clear the noise, he reached for the armrest of the closest seat, to steady himself. Sudden and searing heat blazed through his right arm. Giving a yelp of pain and surprise, he looked down. Blood gushed from the hole torn through his shirt. Time and sound slowed to a near standstill.

Horror gripped him as a warm wetness flowed down his arm toward his wrist. An unexpected surge of heat overwhelmed him. His knees gave way beneath him and he stumbled against the man whose seat he had tried to use to support himself.

Secure the weapon! Marc's vision blurred as he attempted to crawl toward the gun, which now lay loose in the aisle. Pain shot through his arm, rendering him helpless, and he collapsed against the nearest seat. Tears sprang to his eyes.

Sweat beaded on his forehead and upper lip; he felt more sweat trickle through his hair and down his neck. His breathing grew erratic as blood pulsed through his veins, then poured, hot and wet, down the front and back of his arm. It pooled inside the cuff of his white dress shirt, then spilled out and puddled on the carpet.

A burly man a few seats up on the right kicked the weapon out of the reach of the screaming and writhing gunman, whom Marc knew had fallen victim to his semi-automatic's racking slide.

"*Existe um médico a bordo?*" shouted the man against whom Marc had slumped a few moments earlier as he lowered the swaying gunshot victim to the floor.

Despite the unfamiliar phrasing, Marie understood his meaning – particularly *médico*, the Portuguese word for doctor. "I'm a doctor." Jolted out of her dazed immobility, she leapt from her seat and raced to where her husband sat in the aisle, hunched forward and clutching at his arm.

"Let me see," she said, kneeling beside him and peeling his bloodied hand away.

He sucked in breath through clenched teeth. Staring at the blood pooled in his palm, he shook his head. "I'm fine," he insisted. He gestured toward the screaming man. "Go make sure he's okay. He's in worse shape than I am."

"You've been shot," she hissed, tears springing to her eyes. She swiped them away with both hands.

Marc nodded, panting and wincing through the pain, gesticulating toward the gunman. "And *he's* nearly torn his thumb off from not knowing how to hold that thing. Trust me, he's more in need of medical attention than me."

"Hush," Marie commanded, tearing away her husband's blood-sopped shirtsleeve to expose the wound. "Let me handle the triage, okay? I don't care if he bleeds to death." The grim look in her eyes mirrored her spoken sentiment. "*You're* my priority."

With the cotton cloth of his shirt now torn away, blood spurted freely from the gaping holes in Marc's arm.

Judging from the speed and volume of the blood flow, she surmised the bullet had at least nicked his brachial artery. She'd have to act fast to get it stopped.

Ignoring the warm rush of her husband's blood seeping into the front of her dress, Marie examined the entry and exit wounds, her expression somber. It was a certainty that fibers from his shirt had gotten pulled into the wound as the bullet passed through. It would have to be cleaned out and he'd need to be treated for possible infection.

"Looks like the bullet went straight through," she told him. "And since you can still move your arm, I'm guessing it didn't shatter the bone, but you'll definitely need medical attention once we land – and certainly IV antibiotics."

At the other side of the first-class section, Dan yelled frantically for help, holding his badly injured thumb.

His screams filled the cabin, distracting Marie, preventing her from thinking straight. From her position kneeling beside her injured husband, she looked up and turned back toward the howling man. She tucked a lock of hair back behind her ear. "Shut up!" she screamed, her voice carrying every bit as much fury as her glare.

All sound in the cabin ceased. Everyone – passengers and crew alike – turned to stare at her.

"This is all your fault," she continued, her anger boiling over. "So just shut the fuck up and let me do my job!"

Seemingly unaware she'd sworn at the gunman in front of a planeload of strangers, Marie turned back to Marc, her hands still shaking. After taking a moment to breathe deeply and compose herself, she undid his belt and slid it off.

"I hardly think this is the time to consider joining the mile-high club," he teased through his pain.

In spite of herself, Marie offered a half smile. "You wish." She cinched the black leather belt around his upper arm just below the shoulder in a makeshift tourniquet.

Marc's instinctive reaction was to pull away. "Ouch!"

She gave him a fierce look. "It's either this or bleed to

death. You choose."

The leather belt did little to stop the flow of blood. With a sudden stab of panic, she realized she couldn't tighten it adequately, and there was no way to secure it so it'd stay on until they landed and got him to a hospital. Frantic tears welling in her eyes again, Marie cursed under her breath.

One of the flight attendants hurried over with a large, soft-sided case that looked like someone's luggage. "This is our first-aid kit. There's a proper tourniquet in here." She unzipped and opened the case, then reached inside and handed Marie the device.

Fighting back a swell of overwhelm, she slid the bright-red fabric tourniquet up Marc's arm, still holding fast to the leather belt. Once she had the unit positioned, Marie released the belt.

Marc winced as Marie fastened the device and began tightening it around his bicep. When she was satisfied the tourniquet was tight enough, Marie secured the windlass. As if she had just shut off a faucet, the blood flow from both gunshot wounds eased almost immediately. Grabbing a pen from the first-aid kit, she glanced at her watch and scrawled the time on the label area of the tourniquet: 01:27 EDT.

Uttering a silent prayer, Marie turned away, hoping Marc wouldn't see the tears gathering in her eyes. She wiped them away, smearing his blood across her face like war paint.

She rummaged through the first-aid kit again. "We're going to need hemostatic gauze – and plenty of it," she informed nobody in particular. Somehow, though, the act of speaking aloud helped her regain a sense of control over the situation – and she needed that right now.

She dumped the contents of the kit onto the carpeted aisle and pawed through it. No hemostatic gauze. Cursing silently, Marie frowned at the packets of plain cotton gauze piled before her. "I guess these'll have to do. Here" – she scooped up several packs and dropped them into the green-uniformed young woman's cupped hands – "open these up and pack as much gauze as you can into both the entry and exit wounds. Cover them with more gauze and apply firm pressure to stop the bleeding. Keep applying pressure until the bleeding stops. If it seeps through, don't remove the gauze; just add more." She pointed to the man who'd shouted for a doctor. "You – do you understand English?"

He nodded.

"Good. Help her," Marie directed. "Be sure to apply constant pressure to both wounds until the bleeding stops."

Taking a steadying breath, she cradled Marc's cheek in her trembling palm, trying her best to hold eye contact with him. "I'm sorry, sweetheart. It's gonna hurt even more now, but this is the only way to control the bleed." Leaning down, she gave him a kiss on the forehead.

Marc and the flight attendant nodded in understanding.

Marie snatched up Marc's cast-aside belt. Folding it in half, she held it out in front of his face. "Here. Bite down on this."

He did as his bride instructed, a combination of fear and pain evident in his face.

"Prop his feet here," she directed, patting an armrest on the seat ahead of where Marc lay. "We're going to need to keep his legs and his arm elevated."

As two passengers and another flight attendant maneuvered Marc's legs to get his feet onto the armrest, Marie knelt over the first-aid kit and began rummaging through it.

Although biting down on the firm leather, Marc flailed and screamed as the flight attendant and the other passenger worked to stuff the gauze into his still-oozing wounds.

Cringing at the sound of her husband's agonized cries, Marie gave a panicked whimper; the array of syringes and bottles of painkillers included nothing she could safely administer to him now. Further inspection turned up an IV setup. Marie pulled out the items she needed. She'd begun to worry about the likelihood of Marc's going into hypovolemic shock from the blood loss, but now she felt a small measure of comfort, knowing the IV would help alleviate that... for now.

Sitting beside Marc, she rolled up his left shirtsleeve and tied a length of flexible rubber tubing she found in the kit around his bicep. "Make a fist," she instructed. "Now hold it tight for me."

"What about me?!" Dan screamed.

Marie turned around, glaring at him. "You shut up and wait your turn," she warned in a menacing tone, pointing a finger at him, amid gasps from the other passengers. "First I'm tending to the man you shot – who happens to be my husband – so you'd better count yourself lucky I'm going to see to your injury at all."

With that, she returned her attention to Marc. She took a few deep breaths to help settle herself before attempting to start the IV. The last thing she needed now was unsteady hands – especially when her husband most needed her to be at her professional best.

After prodding at the crook of his elbow, she located a vein. With a decided frown, she muttered, "This one could work... but it's not really that prominent. It might give us some trouble."

Marie tugged off the rubber tubing. "Relax your hand for a second."

She turned his hand over and flicked at it repeatedly with one finger, then slapped at the back of his hand rapidly to help raise a vein. Marie frowned for a moment, her brow furrowing, then drew in a sudden sharp breath. "I think I found one," she said to no one in particular. Ripping open a nearby packet, she swabbed the surface of his hand with an alcohol wipe.

"Marc, listen to me carefully. Look at me. Focus," she instructed as she reached for the needle. "Okay, I need you to make a fist again. Gently. Just a loose fist. Like that. Good. Hold it steady. Now you'll just feel a little pinch..."

Who are you kidding? He's not going to feel <u>anything</u> with that hole *through his arm!* She realized she'd spoken more for her own benefit than his. And, if she was being honest with herself, she needed something – anything – to feel almost normal amid this upheaval.

Holding her breath and biting down on her lower lip, Marie slid the needle into the back of Marc's hand and deftly found the vein, as if it hadn't been three years since she'd last started an IV.

As soon as she had the line in, she secured it in place with paper tape and attached the 0.9% saline bag. Next she rummaged through the first-aid kit and made a show of filling a syringe with a tiny amount of clear liquid – a harmless saline solution – from a small bottle. Then she injected that into the IV.

"There," she lied to Marc as soothingly as she could, "that should give you some relief in a few minutes." She turned away quickly so he couldn't read the deceit in her eyes. She had found nothing in that first-aid kit that could ease his pain. The bottles of lidocaine wouldn't help. And the aspirin would only thin his blood.

After checking on the gauze the others had packed into Marc's dual bullet wounds, Marie went over to Beatriz, the flight attendant Dan had held captive. She assessed the still-quaking woman's physical condition, checked her vital signs and spent several minutes talking with her, to evaluate her emotional status. Finally, Marie urged the terrified woman to seek professional counseling.

Then she went to attend to the gunman. She crouched over the man who'd not only caused Marc all that pain but had traumatized her, Beatriz and other passengers fifteen minutes earlier. She assessed the extent of the injury to his bloodied and flopping thumb. Over her shoulder – and above the sound of Dan's distressed wails – she called out to the pair applying pressure to Marc's wounds. "He'll probably tell you he's thirsty, but don't give him anything to drink. No water, no juice. Not even an ice cube. I don't care how thirsty he says he is. He can't have any liquids.

Understand?"

"Okay," the flight attendant replied. "Not even some of those little vodka shots? Wouldn't those help to ease the pain a bit?"

Icy panic surged through Marie as she recalled their frank discussion at her kitchen table that Saturday morning so many months ago. *I'm an alcoholic*, Marc had confided. He also admitted he had never divulged that bit of information to anyone – not even his best friend.

"No," she replied firmly. "That's the worst thing you could give him; it would thin his blood. The IV will keep him hydrated. Don't give him anything to drink."

Taking a moment to collect herself, she selected a roll of gauze, then turned toward her new patient. He looked like a kid – certainly no older than his early twenties.

As Dan screamed, Marie bit back the urge to remind him again it was his own fault he was in this predicament. Instead, she settled for, "Oh, shut up!" She stuck a small stack of tongue depressors between the gunman's jaws and instructed brusquely, "Bite down on this."

Once he was quiet, the frazzled doctor stabilized and wrapped Dan's flopping thumb in a few layers of cotton gauze. Then, as blood began to soak through the gauze, she snapped another tongue depressor in half and fashioned a rudimentary splint. Marie placed the two pieces of wood on either side of his still-bleeding digit, then secured them with more gauze. She continued wrapping it around his thumb until it looked like he had a half-pound ball of fresh mozzarella balanced there.

"He'll need a surgeon to stitch up that thumb once we land," she told the passenger who'd been restraining the still-howling gunman.

"Wait!" Dan screamed. "Marie! Don't I get anything for the pain?" he pleaded.

Marie leveled her gaze at him. Once she was sure she had his attention, she uttered a single word. "No."

She waited until the word registered in his brain and he

started to protest. A hint of a sadistic smile crossed her face as she delighted in his look of horror.

"Why does he get something for the pain and I don't?" he demanded of Marie, flailing an arm toward Marc.

"Why? Because he's the victim in all this, you pathetic asshole," she told the gunman in her most fearsome tone yet. "Ohh, you've got some colossal nerve, buddy, asking me for something to relieve your pain! This is all your fault. You're the one who caused all this ruckus. You wanted to be the 'big man' with the gun, so you get to deal with the consequences of your rotten decision. Suck it up and deal with your pain. I'm done with you." She turned away with a dismissive wave.

Upon returning to Marc, Marie avoided meeting the other passengers' gazes. She could feel her cheeks blazing. Mortified at her public eruption, she silently berated herself for not being able to maintain her professional demeanor while treating the gunman.

But the passengers in the first-class section didn't seem to mind. Several of them broke into spontaneous applause as she returned to their midst, in approval of her passionate outburst against the man who'd terrorized them. Some of them patted her on the back. Others reached out to shake her hand. One woman hugged her, weeping.

Meanwhile, after an exhaustive search by a few passengers and crew, a flight attendant found the bullet that had struck Marc – lodged in the headrest of a seat three rows back. One passenger wanted to dig it out with a penknife, but a flight attendant insisted they leave it there, as evidence.

For about fifteen minutes after the commotion died down and most of the other passengers returned to their seats, Marc remained on the floor of the plane, wincing in persistent agony, his legs propped on an armrest. Someone had slid a pillow beneath his head and covered him with several soft blankets to help keep him warm. But still he shivered.

Marie heard his teeth chattering and knew he was likely

going into shock, despite her swift application of the tourniquet and insertion of the IV. There was little more she could do for him now. Overwhelmed by helplessness, she drooped beside him on the floor in the aisle and clasped his hand, doing her best to keep him calm, yet alert. She checked his pulse; his heartrate was elevated. Extreme pain and shock would cause that. Feigning composure, she took over applying pressure to his wounds, to relieve the others who attended him earlier. In between times, she comforted Marc as best she could when the unabated pain made him hyperventilate.

And whenever the guilt overwhelmed her, Marie silently prayed for forgiveness, for having deceived Marc about having given him pain medication. Her well-intentioned lie stung as badly as a shot of lidocaine.

A steward approached. He looked to be about Marc's age, slightly taller and with a robust build. "Do you need anything, ma'am?"

Marie shook her head. Then, thinking better of it, she said, "Actually, yes. Can you help me get him to his feet? I want to move him back to his seat. He'll be more comfortable there than lying here on the floor."

The man nodded. "Of course. How do you want to do this?"

Her lips forming a grim line, Marie thought about the logistics. She got to her feet and stood in front of Marc. "I need you to stand behind him and get ready to support him if he needs help," she directed, motioning just beyond where Marc lay.

The steward nodded again and did what Marie said.

Marie braced her left foot sideways, abutting the toes of Marc's highly polished shoes, now spattered with blood. What remained of his white shirt was smeared with blood and soaked in sweat. She anchored her right foot about sixteen inches behind the left, facing forward, as if in a yoga stance. Leaning toward her husband, she murmured, "I need you to work with me here. We're going to get you back to your seat. You'll be more comfortable there."

Unable to form words, Marc panted in agony as tears filled his eyes. He shut his eyes tight against the throb in his arm. His jaw clenched and Marie knew the pain must have been excruciating.

"Don't try to talk," she instructed. "I know you're in a lot of pain, sweetheart. Just focus on what I'm saying, okay? I'm going to pull you onto your feet. Okay? I want you to squeeze my hand if you understood what I just said."

Marc managed a slight squeeze. As his eyes met hers, Marie saw fear in them.

"You're going to be fine, Marc. I promise." She hoped she wasn't lying to him again.

She grasped his left hand in hers and held his left elbow with her right hand. Despite his tan, his face looked pale, and his hand in hers felt cool and clammy.

On a count of three, she drew him to his feet. Swaying slightly, Marc gripped her hand as tight as he could while the steward steadied him from behind, ready to support him if he collapsed.

Gritting his teeth, he did his best to keep from crying out in the otherwise-quiet plane; he kept his utterance to an anguished whimper.

After getting him to his feet, Marie gave her husband a few moments to collect himself before moving him toward his seat.

"Easy now," she said, guiding him forward. She and the steward lowered him into the seat.

Marc winced as Marie helped him recline his seat and propped pillows beneath his injured arm. Before covering him again with blankets to keep him warm, she rechecked the wound, to ensure the bleeding had stopped.

Marie replaced the medical supplies in the first-aid kit still open in the center of the aisle. She closed the lid, zipped it back up and removed it from the walkway. Then she returned to her seat and settled beside her pain-wracked husband.

His overly fast breathing was still ragged and shallow, but at least it was beginning to slow somewhat. His teeth chattered from the hurt. But the pain etched across his face started to ebb a bit, as what he believed to be intravenous pain medication worked its deceitful magic on his system.

Around them, passengers appeared dazed, still running on adrenaline. A few exhausted ones slept, some snoring softly, others not so softly. Amid the hush of the cabin, Marie stroked Marc's hand and spoke quietly to him, so as not to disturb the others. She knew she needed to keep him awake until they could get him to a hospital.

From time to time Marie would nod off herself, both exhausted from the long day and drained from their frightening ordeal, only to jolt awake a few minutes later, afraid she might have allowed him to drift into unconsciousness.

At last, Marie glanced at her wristwatch – it was 3:47 a.m. Eastern Time. She couldn't recall how long it had been since this nightmare began. She checked the time she had scrawled on the tab at the front of Marc's tourniquet. Her weary shoulders sagged. A little over two hours. After ensuring the device was still holding, she lay her head back against the headrest, feeling as if it surely had been more like twelve hours.

"Excuse me," she addressed a passing steward a few minutes later. "Could you please tell me what time it is in Portugal now?"

"It's eight fifty-one a.m.," the dark-haired man replied quietly, having consulted his own watch. "We should land in about twenty minutes. Do you need anything?"

Marie nodded. "Yes. Could you please bring another pillow or two to prop under his arm?"

When he brought the pillows, the steward asked Marie which hotel they were staying at, so the airline could deliver their baggage for them.

By the time the jet approached terminal one at Lisbon Portela Airport, the runway was ablaze with red and blue flashing lights. As the airliner rolled to a stop, the hijacker was ushered off the plane in the custody of the *polícia de segurança pública*, the public-security police.

Before deplaning and being rushed to the hospital for evaluation, Beatriz hugged Marie and tearfully thanked her for her brave intervention. "I don't know what would have happened if you hadn't stepped in," the woman exclaimed as she headed for the exit. "Thank you, doctor!"

An emergency medical crew rolling a stretcher rushed in and whisked Marc from the plane to a waiting ambulance, with Marie at his side.

Neither of them was prepared for the crush of media that descended on them, despite the urgings of the medics attending to their gunshot patient.

Fading out of lucidity, Marc squinted at the bright lights in his face and waved off a cadre of reporters and cameramen. As someone jostled his arm, searing pain tore through him. He sucked in a breath through gritted teeth, his vision slipping out of focus. Marie held tight to his good hand as the crush of reporters packed in closer around them.

"No questions. Get back," the head medic insisted in Portuguese, loading the stretcher into the back of their blue and yellow ambulance. Shouldering away the most insistent of the reporters, he helped Marie up into the vehicle alongside her husband and secured the rear doors.

Sirens wailing, the ambulance streaked off toward the nearest trauma center.

As the medics assessed their patient's condition, they maintained an ongoing dialogue with Marie, practically having to shout over the siren's caustic scream. That Marc was still conscious and at least minimally alert was a good sign, they told her.

Marie knew this, but she felt reassured by the other medical professionals' assessment. Still, it was what they *hadn't* said that worried her. Marc's skin felt clammy. His lips had developed a faint blue tinge and, given his excessive blood loss despite swift application of the tourniquet, she knew they weren't necessarily leveling with her.

"Aren't you concerned about hemorrhagic shock?"

The technicians seemed startled at her familiarity with the medical terminology. As the medic in charge attempted to discuss Marc's condition in layman's terms, Marie shook her head.

"You don't need to break it down for me. I'm a doctor." She added, in as calm a voice as she could muster, "He lost several units of blood before I got that tourniquet in place. I checked about half an hour ago and it's still holding. But it's been in place about three hours. They'll need to restore normal blood flow as soon as possible."

While Marc drifted in and out of consciousness, the EMTs swapped out the depleted IV bag for a fresh one. They realized they didn't need to sugarcoat things for this wife.

Chapter 10

(4:27 a.m. EDT, Wednesday, July 7)
When the news director read the brief news alert from the AP wire, her breath caught in her throat. She printed the item out and ran into the jock-prep area, where the morning man was busy finalizing his show prep.

"Hey, Ken – give me two minutes."

Ken Coffey looked up from scanning the back page of the entertainment section of that morning's edition of the *Waterbury Republican*. "What's up?"

"Look at this." She handed over the news item and watched his expression turn grim.

> LISBON – Authorities in Portugal confirm at least three people aboard PortugAir Flight 720 bound for Lisbon Portela Airport were hospitalized early Wednesday morning after a shooting that occurred over international waters. The identities of those injured have not been released and details are sketchy at this time. Flight 720 originated from New York's John F. Kennedy International Airport Tuesday at 7:35 p.m. local time with 223 passengers and crew on board. The flight landed safely in Lisbon at 9:12 a.m. local time without further incident.

"Oh dear." Ken took off his glasses and rubbed the

bridge of his nose. "A midair shooting? Multiple injuries? That doesn't sound good. Is that what you're leading with?"

"That's not why I wanted you to see it. Where did Marc and Marie go on their honeymoon?"

He shrugged. "Somewhere in Europe, I think."

"Wasn't it Portugal?"

Now Ken nodded, his countenance somber. "I think you're right."

"They flew out of JFK, didn't they?"

His voice was flat. "I think so."

"How many flights do you think could leave JFK for Portugal on a Tuesday night?" A slight tremor quavered her voice.

Ken handed the sheet of paper back to his morning-show cohost. "I can't imagine it's more than one or two."

"That's what I was afraid of. This isn't good," Barb murmured as she left the room.

After her final newscast at nine, Barb phoned Gary at home. "I didn't want to wake anybody, so I waited to call you. Have you heard the news yet?"

"I didn't have a chance. I'm just getting ready to leave the house. What's up?"

"When did Marc and Marie's flight leave last night? Was it seven thirty-five?"

"I think that's what she said. Why?"

Barb gripped the receiver. "Gary, something happened on the plane. All we got from the AP was notification that at least three people were injured in an overnight shooting."

She heard his sharp intake of breath over the phone line.

"Their initial story didn't mention names, the extent of any injuries, or even what happened. I put in a call to the New York bureau chief early this morning, but we're still waiting on details."

Still, Gary said nothing.

"I'm so sorry to have to be the one to tell you this, Gar'. Still, I'd rather you heard the news from someone you know instead of from some generic news report."

"No, no. I agree. Thank you."

"Are you okay?"

"I think so." He let out a shaky breath and ran a hand through his hair. "Look, Barb, there's no sense in our worrying until we know whether there's something we need to worry about, right?" He tried to convince himself of that as much as her. "How soon do you think you'll hear back from that guy in New York?"

"Hard to say. Could be twenty minutes; could be six hours."

"Okay, look. Marie left me some information. I think it's got the number for their hotel. I'll try calling her there. Thanks for letting me know, Barb."

"Who was on the phone?" Michaela asked as Gary hung up the phone in the kitchen. Seeing his grave expression, she grew alarmed. "Gary? What's the matter?"

He pulled out a chair at the kitchen table and slumped into it. "That was Barb Dwyer. At the station. She called to say there was a shooting overnight. On the plane Marc and Marie were on. At least three people were hurt. That's all the report said. No one knows any more than that."

Sitting beside her husband, Michaela laid her hand over his. "That's terrible." Her face grew ashen. "Is there any way to find out what happened?"

He shook his head. "I don't know. Barb has a call in to the AP in New York, but she doesn't know when she'll hear back from them." He stood, letting his hand slide away from beneath Micki's. "I'm gonna call the hotel Marie said they'd be staying at, make sure they got in okay."

He headed to his study to find the paper Marie had written the flight information and hotel numbers on. It was atop a short stack of papers to the right of his computer monitor. Gary scanned the information on it and uttered a silent prayer to St. Christopher – the patron saint of travelers – before picking up the phone on his desk.

Fifteen minutes later, he returned to the kitchen, looking distressed.

"What did they say?"

"The lady I talked to at the hotel said she has no record of them checking in." He swallowed around the lump in his throat. Leaning down, Gary planted a kiss on his wife's worry-wrinkled brow. "I gotta go, honey. I promise, I'll call and let you know as soon as I hear anything."

Chapter 11

(9:15 a.m. Western European Time, Wednesday, July 7)
When the ambulance roared up to the emergency entrance of the *Hospital de Santa Maria*, a team of medical staff spilled from the building, ready to rush Marc in to surgery. The support crew ushered Marie into a surgical waiting area. She paced anxiously during the hour-long procedure to clean and irrigate the wound, repair his damaged artery and traumatized muscle tissue, assess the extent of possible neuromuscular damage, transfuse him with five pints of blood and finally stitch up the entry and exit wounds.

Fortunately, as Marie had determined, the bullet hadn't so much as nicked bone on its way through his bicep. While blood loss had been extensive, the resultant tissue damage turned out to be minimal.

It was another hour before Marc regained consciousness in the post-surgical recovery area. During that time, they started him on IV antibiotics; the nurses monitoring his vital signs kept Marie apprised of her husband's condition.

One of the nurses brought Marie to a small washroom, to fix her hair and wash off the now-dried smears and spatters of blood from her face. There was nothing she could do about her blood-soaked dress, but that didn't matter. All she cared about was returning to Marc's side. After cleaning up as best she could, Marie hurried back to the recovery room to wait for her husband to awaken.

When the effects of anesthesia wore off and Marc regained consciousness, the medical staff transferred him to a private room, where – jet lagged, drugged and exhausted – he glanced up to see his wife's worried face and immediately fell asleep.

Several hours later, Marc awakened and looked around.

All about him hung starkly sterile white curtains. A machine beside his bed whirred quietly. His heavily bandaged right arm throbbed. He seemed to be wearing one of those loose-fitting cotton hospital gowns. Marc struggled to recall where he might be – and how he had gotten here.

At the foot of his bed, he sensed a stirring. Blinking several times to help clear his vision, he raised his head a bit; it felt too heavy for his neck to lift and he let it fall back against the pillow with a groan.

"Oh, good, you're awake."

Marie's voice. His smile was automatic.

She laid aside her book and stood. At his bedside, she swept his hair back. Her lips felt cool against his forehead.

"How do you feel?" she asked, smiling tenderly.

"What happened?"

"You've had surgery. You were shot."

A foggy memory swirled in Marc's mind. "Oh, yeah… right." Then, "Where am I?"

"You're in the hospital. I think it's St. Mary's – in Lisbon."

"Lisbon," he echoed. A wan smile flickered across his lips. His brow furrowed. "Why is my throat so sore?"

"They intubated you." Marie reached for a cup on the bedside table and spoon fed him an ice chip. "What do you remember?"

Marc shook his head. "Not much. Lots of people screaming… and a burning pain in—" he grimaced and sucked in air through his teeth as he tried to shift position. "My arm," he finished. "*Oww.*" His breathing grew labored with the pain, bordering on panting.

"You're coming off the painkillers. Hang on. I'll ask the nurse to give you something."

"No – wait."

Marie's eyes reflected her concern. "What is it?"

He reached for her hand. "Thank you."

At Marc's words, a smile bloomed across her face and softened her gaze. She smiled and leaned down to kiss his forehead again. "I love you." Recalling something else, she added, "Before I forget how to say it: *Feliz aniversário*."

Marc smiled at her cautious Portuguese pronunciation. "Thank you."

"I know it's not the best way to spend your birthday…" Her thumb stroked the back of his hand; she was careful to avoid the area where she'd secured his IV. "But at least you get to celebrate it in Portugal."

"That I do. With my wife." His smile widened. "Whom I love more than I know how to put into words." He lifted her hand to his lips and kissed it. "Thank you. By the way, what time is it?"

Marie frowned at her watch. It was still on Connecticut time. "How many hours ahead are we now, five?" When he gave a drowsy nod, she said, "Then it's five seventeen."

Marc nodded. "Okay." After a pause, he added, "Now can I please have some drugs?"

As her husband drifted back into a drug-induced slumber, Marie settled into the bedside chair; she pulled a credit card from her wallet and initiated a call. She smiled at the sound of the familiar voice at the other side of the Atlantic Ocean, and suddenly realized how much she missed the cadence of English being spoken. "Hey, kiddo."

Gary peppered his sister with panicked questions. "Marie – my God! Are you guys okay? We heard what happened. It's been all over the national news all day. I called the hotel you're supposed to be staying at. They had no record of you. We've been worried sick! Where *are* you?"

"In the hospital."

"What?! Are you guys alright?"

Hearing the frantic warble in his voice, Marie knew

she'd better calm him down. "Gary, take it easy. Marc's okay. He tried to wrestle the gun away from the guy. It went off and he got shot."

Marie heard Gary's alarmed intake of breath.

Before he could speak, she went on. "Gary, he'll be fine. He took a bullet to the upper arm. It went straight through. Didn't hit the bone. We got the bleeding under control on the plane, and they rushed him into surgery as soon as we landed. He's resting. They'll probably release him tonight or tomorrow. And one of the flight attendants was taken to the hospital for evaluation – the guy had been holding her hostage and threatened to shoot her."

"What about the other person who was injured?"

Marie gave a little "pffft" of disgust. "The gunman. Serves him right. He didn't know how to hold the gun he was waving around and nearly tore his thumb off when it fired. I attended to him, too, an—"

"You treated the guy who shot your husband?"

"Only because your goofy brother-in-law insisted. *I* would have been perfectly content to watch him writhe in pain and bleed all over himself for three hours."

"Are you sure Marc's okay? You're not holding out on me...?"

Marie glanced at her sleeping husband and an involuntary smile crossed her face. "He's fine, Gary. We both are. A little unnerved, but okay. It's been a long-ass day and neither of us has gotten any real rest – at least he's had some great drugs."

"Can I talk to him?"

"He's asleep – or, more precisely, he's drugged. Come to think of it, even when he's alert, he's still pretty out of it. And despite how relatively minor the injury was, all in all, he's had a pretty rough go of it. I mean, the trauma itself – and he lost a lot of blood. A *whole* lot." She glanced down at the front of her dress and shuddered. Her voice got a slight tremor to it as she admitted, "I was really worried about him there for a while, Gar'. Not to mention the psychological ramifications."

"Everyone here's been worried sick about you two. And Barb – with her news-director cap secured on her head – wanted to talk one of you into an interview from a passenger's perspective. And after what you've told me, I'm guessing she'll *really* be interested to hear what Marc has to say."

Marie gave a weary sigh and ran a hand through her hair. "I suppose the news never sleeps, huh? I'll call you back when he's awake."

Nearly three hours later, Marc stirred again. His eyes fluttered and opened hesitantly. The room's brightness made him squint. He groaned and turned away from the fluorescent light fixture overhead.

Marie approached his bed. "How do you feel?"

He winced as he tried to move. "Hurtin'."

"I talked to Gary. He wanted me to ask if you feel up to giving Barb an exclusive."

"What a newshound." Marc managed a wan smile. "What did you tell him?"

Marie brushed his hair back with one hand. She leaned to kiss his forehead; he felt warm. But at least the color was returning to his face. "I said that's up to you, and we'd call him back once you were awake."

He struggled to sit up. "Not 'til after I've used the bathroom. I feel like I'm about to float away. Or burst." He rang for the nurse.

A young-sounding voice answered the buzz. "Can I help you?"

"I need the nurse," he replied, a note of urgency in his voice.

A few moments later, a dark-haired woman in blue surgical scrubs appeared. "Yes? How can I help you?" she asked in halting English.

When he told her in Portuguese what he needed, she nodded and disconnected his IV, then helped him out of bed.

His legs felt unsteady after nearly a day of nonuse. They'd put non-skid slipper socks on him in recovery to prevent his slipping on the linoleum when he did resume walking.

"*Você precisa de alguma ajuda?*"

Marc colored slightly and assured the nurse that, no, he didn't expect he'd need any help.

The young woman opened the door to the bathroom as Marc made his way unsteadily around the side of the bed. She said she'd be back to reconnect his IV when he was finished, then asked if he thought he'd need assistance getting back into bed.

"*Acho que não.*" He shook his head. Then he shrugged. "*Mas talvez?*" But maybe?

After Marc got settled back in bed, with an assist from Marie, the dark-haired nurse returned. "I see you got back in bed okay. Good for you," she said as she reattached his IV. "Before you know it, you'll be back to your regular activity." She gave him a smile and a pat on the shoulder.

A few minutes later, a food-service attendant came by with his supper. He thanked the slow-moving middle-aged lady who set the tray on his bedside table. He looked at it with a tired sigh.

Marie's gaze conveyed her worry. "What's wrong, sweetheart?"

"I'm not even hungry."

She gave a sympathetic nod. "The anesthesia and pain meds'll do that to you. But you need to eat something. You need protein to help you heal, and to regenerate the damaged muscle tissue." Lifting the cover from his meal, she assessed it. "The chicken is a terrific lean protein. The broccoli has plenty of iron, and this sweet potato is loaded with potassium. I'm impressed. They took your specific dietary needs into account."

"Please, can we dispense with the nutritional lectures right now? I just don't feel like eating."

"And look – chocolate cake for dessert... because healing burns a ton of calories. Either that or they must've known it was your birthday," she persisted, giving him a hopeful smile. "All that's missing now is a candle."

Marc shook his head. "Please stop." He picked up his watch from the table and fumbled to put it on. "I guess I can talk to Barb now."

Not wanting to argue, Marie reached for her credit card and placed the transatlantic call.

As the last pink and blue streaks of daylight slipped away outside his window, Marc accepted the phone Marie handed him.

"Marc! Are you okay?" Barb asked.

He managed a weary smile. "I guess so. They tell me I was really lucky."

***

That evening, instead of her usual six o'clock newscast, Lauren Fisher aired a five-minute interview Barb produced from the nearly twenty minutes she'd spent talking with Marc.

"Late last night, a hijacker terrorized the two hundred twenty-three passengers and crew on board PortugAir Flight Seven Twenty from New York's JFK Airport, bound for Lisbon. Luckily for the others, one courageous passenger stepped up in a daring attempt to disarm the gunman.

"We're pleased to bring you, by phone from a hospital in Portugal, an exclusive interview with the man whose heroic actions saved that planeload of people. If he sounds familiar, it's because that hero is Z97-3's nighttime announcer, Marc Lindsay. Marc, thanks for being on with us today."

"My pleasure, Barb. If I sound kinda loopy, it's just the drugs they've got me on."

"Understood. When did you first realize something was wrong?"

"We were several hours into the flight. It was quiet –

most people were trying to get some shuteye. All of a sudden, the lights came on in the cabin and a guy was holding a flight attendant at gunpoint, ordering her to let him into the cockpit. It was like something out of a bad movie.

"People were panicking. There was a lot of confusion. Then my wife – it sounds so strange to call her that; we'd just gotten married that morning – Marie's the real hero. She managed to gain his trust and got him to release the hostage. When she tried to reason with him, he turned the gun on her and demanded she hand over her valuables, so she came back to her seat to get her purse."

"That must have been terrifying, seeing a gun pointed at her. What else do you remember?"

"His hands were shaking. Really shaking. Badly. I remember seeing his finger on the trigger. I was afraid we'd hit turbulence or he'd flinch and end up shooting her."

"What did you do then?"

"I'd had firearms training when I was a kid; and I knew the right way – and the wrong way – to hold a semiautomatic. And I could tell the guy was definitely holding that gun the *wrong* way."

"How was he holding it?"

"With one thumb crossed over the other, like he was trying to steady it. You never hold a semi like that, 'cause when the slide racks, it tears off anything in its way. When she distracted him – it only took a second – I knocked him off balance and moved the barrel in a safe direction, toward the floor in the aisle. We struggled for the gun and it went off."

"What happened next?"

"All I was aware of was a burning feeling in my arm. And something warm and wet running down toward my wrist. All around, people were screaming and diving behind seats. I tried to get my balance, but when I reached out for something to hold, pain shot through my arm and I fell."

"What did you do then?"

"My objective was to get the gun. But I didn't make it.

I tried to crawl toward it, but the pain was too much. I couldn't move. Fortunately, another passenger was able to kick the gun away."

"What happened to the gunman?"

"He'd halfway torn his thumb off and was on the floor, up the aisle, screaming." He paused. "Then again, come to think of it, it mighta just been me I heard screaming. I'm sorry, I don't really remember much after that. I was… pretty well out of it by then."

"So who was other person injured?"

"I guess the flight attendant – she was pretty well shaken up. And who wouldn't be? Having a guy holding you at gunpoint…"

"You were bleeding profusely, Marc. How did they get it under control?"

"I had the good sense to marry a doctor, and she knew what to do. She applied a" – Marc paused, tapped at his forehead and then gestured awkwardly with his good hand as he fumbled for the word – "you know… that tight thing they put on, stops blood… what's it called?"

"A tourniquet?"

"Yeah. That's it. A tourniquet. She applied a tourniquet. Some other folks kept pressure on the wounds while she went to talk with the flight attendant and then took care of the guy's thumb."

"She gave medical assistance to the guy who shot you?"

His voice softened with his smile. "Yeah. She's pretty amazing, that wife of mine."

"So you're an honest-to-goodness hero."

"No. Not me. I was just in the right place at the exact wrong time. Marie's the real hero. She saved my life. And the life of that flight attendant. You should really be talking to her. I barely did anything. From what the doctors said, if she hadn't acted as fast as she did to stop the bleeding, I could have been in a real serious heap o' trouble."

"Where were you hit?"

He paused, tried to think. "I think it was row six in

first class."

Barb groaned. "Always the comedian. Let me rephrase that, Marc: Where did the bullet hit you?"

"Oh. I'm sorry. I'm a little foggy. Straight through my right bicep. Guess I won't be playing on the station softball team anytime soon." He gave a quiet chuckle.

"Do you have any idea why that particular flight was targeted?"

"Not a clue. I haven't heard anything. Then again, I've been in the hospital all day – and on some pretty powerful drugs... as you can tell. I'm surprised I've been lucid this long."

"In all honesty, Marc, you really haven't been all that lucid," Barb told him.

He gave another self-conscious chuckle. "Point taken. Sorry."

"We'll let it slide. Before we let you go, is there anything you'd like to say to your listeners?"

"Yeah, there is. If you're getting on an airplane, make sure there's a doctor sitting next to you. And if she's cute, even better. But seriously, the people who are important to you? Tell 'em you love them. Now. You never know when it'll be your last chance."

"Wise words. Thanks, Marc, for taking the time to talk with us. Get some rest and enjoy your honeymoon. And come back home safely. I'm Barb Dwyer, Z97-3 News."

After Gary finished reading the weather and pushed the remote button to start the first song for the final hour of his show, the afternoon newscaster entered the on-air studio.

Gary tugged off his headphones. "Hey, Lauren. What's up?"

"Hell of an interview, huh?"

He whistled. "Sounds like it was some ordeal. I can't even imagine what they must've been going through. Barb called this morning to tell me about it. I was going crazy, trying to find them."

"That's right – Marie's your sister! You must have been freaking out."

"Yeah. When I called the hotel where they were supposed to be staying, the desk clerk said they never checked in. I even talked to the manager, but he told me the same thing: no record of them checking in. So I called the airline to make sure all the passengers got off the flight safely. I didn't know what else to do. Marie finally called this noon. I swear, I've never been so glad to hear her voice!"

***

As they began to ease off on his IV pain medication, the nursing staff encouraged Marc to get out of bed and move around – as far and as often as he felt up to walking.

"You just can't leave the building," one of his nurses joked as she injected a final half dose of morphine into his IV Wednesday evening.

"That's unfortunate. I really wanted to go out for a pizza," he teased back before the drugs took effect.

Just outside Marc's hospital room late that night, reporters with cameras and microphones gathered like chummed sharks, peeking in through the door in hopes of catching a glimpse of the American hero.

"Out – all of you," a doctor insisted, waving them off before entering the room. "I'll not have you disturbing my patient."

All but the most tenacious broke away and headed for an exit.

The doctor rounded on those still gathered behind him. "I said go. This is a hospital, not a public street," he chided them. "Now clear off! And don't come back."

(8:30 a.m. Western European Time, Thursday, July 8)

Marc lay on the bed, his injured right arm loosely arced above his head. He breathed slowly, trying to adjust to the diminished level of pain medication. They'd taken him off morphine around six last night and started him on Percocet at bedtime. The nurses had discontinued his fluids late last night, but the IV cannula remained in his hand – in case they needed to administer meds, or if it became necessary to push additional fluids.

Marie climbed up beside him on the left side of his bed. He winced as he shifted position to accommodate her.

She rolled onto her right side and balanced there. "How're you feeling?"

"Pain med's wearing off."

Resting a hand on his chest, she leaned to kiss him. "I'm so proud of you, sweetheart."

The corners of his mouth hitched upward in a self-conscious smile.

"But when I think how close I came to losing you…" Her lower lip trembled. "I'm just so grateful everything turned out okay – all things considered."

Reaching up with his good arm, Marc pushed back the hair from her face and caressed her cheek. "Shh," he quieted her. "This is nothing. I nearly lost you; that would have been unthinkable." The twinkle returned to his eyes. "Now, if I'm not mistaken, Dr. Lindemeyr, we've got a marriage to consummate."

"How can you think about sex now?"

His right eyebrow dipped slightly. "In case you weren't aware, I'm a guy. And if there's one thing you should know about guys by now, it's this: We're always thinking about either food or sex. And the pain meds have basically killed my appetite."

Marie shook her head. "You're impossible."

"Maybe so. But I'm also a just-married, shot but otherwise healthy, red-blooded American male – which means I always want sex. But I think you're gonna have to do all the heavy lifting."

Marie looked doubtful. "You lost a lot of blood," she reminded him diplomatically.

Marc's expression changed; playful challenge danced in

his eyes. "Are you trying to imply the spirit is willing but the flesh is weak?"

She ruffled his hair. "I'm trying *not* to imply that, but yes. Maybe it'd be better if we waited another couple days; you know, give the uh... *flesh* a little chance to adequately recover."

"You do realize I got shot in the *arm*, right?"

"And you realize blood doesn't only circulate *through* your arm, right?" she mimicked.

Marc groaned and dropped his head back against the pillow. He stared up at the ceiling for a long moment. "You sure know how to kill a mood." Then he raised his head and looked at her. "Isn't there any chance I can persuade you otherwise...?" he kissed the tip of her nose. "C'mon, go see if that door locks. I bet it does. We could do with some privacy."

"While I'm at it, why don't I just ask them to infuse you with another unit of blood, to kind of help things along?"

His eyebrows rose roguishly. "Now you're thinkin'!"

Marie made a face. "You're incorrigible."

"No. We've been through this. I'm impossible. I also happen to be in bed with the beautiful, sexy woman who impulsively married me, dragged me away to Portugal – *and* made me scream at thirty-thousand feet," he said, a naughty glint in his eye. "Now if *that* doesn't warrant a bit of action, I don't know what does."

Marie shook her head and sighed in resignation.

"Besides," he reasoned, "you must have heard what they've been saying around here about me: I'm a hero. How many women get to sleep with a bona fide hero?"

(9:55 a.m.)

As Marc's next dose of Percocet took hold and he became sleepy and incoherent, Marie ventured out to the nurses station.

The head nurse nodded in understanding of her faltering request. "Let me get one of the doctors for you."

When the young physician came to talk to her, the new bride explained her concern.

"I see," Dr. Cabrera said, his brow furrowing. "When was the incident?"

"Early yesterday morning."

"And there was no neuromuscular damage?"

Marie shook her head. "None that they could determine."

After a moment's consideration, the doctor gave a pensive nod. "As long as you're careful not to further injure his arm, I see no problem."

"And there's no issue, considering the hemorrhagic shock?"

The doctor's dark brows dipped and moved dangerously close together. He rested a hand on Marie's shoulder. "Let me check his file. I'll be right back."

The doctor strode to the nurses station and asked for Mr. Lindemeyr's file. After reviewing it, he came back to speak to Marie. "Looks like he was down a couple quarts," he told her, "but I see we took care of that while he was in surgery. He should be good to go."

"Thank you, doctor."

Having given her appropriate reassurance, Dr. Cabrera excused himself and returned to the nurses station. After a brief conversation with the head nurse, he continued on his rounds.

After the doctor left, one of the nurses motioned Marie over. With a conspiratorial grin, she pulled a sign from a file cabinet and held it up to show her. It cautioned, in both Portuguese and English, *"Testes médicos em andamento. Não entre.* Medical Testing in Progress. Do Not Enter." Assuring Marie it should ensure the couple's privacy for an hour or so, she took it and a roll of tape down the hall to affix it to Marc's door.

Closing herself in the tiny bathroom in Marc's room, Marie frowned at her disheveled image in the mirror. Swiftly shedding her bloodstained clothes, she rummaged through a tall cabinet until she found a facecloth and towel, then gave herself a quick wash. After digging in her purse for a pouch of travel-size toiletries, Marie brushed her teeth and combed her hair. She applied deodorant, then stuffed the toiletries – along with her rolled-up panties and bra – back in the purse, then pulled her sullied dress back on.

Exiting the bathroom, she retrieved a worn paperback novel from her purse and settled into a bedside chair to pass the time.

When Marc began at last to stir, Marie made sure the sign was still securely taped to his door. She shut the door, praying the staff would heed it and steer clear. She slipped out of the dress she'd been wearing since Tuesday morning, draped it on the bedside chair and climbed into bed beside Marc. After giving him a little nudge to rouse him from his sleep, she kissed him awake, pressing her body against his. Shoving his hospital gown aside, she shifted position until she was straddling him, and kissed him again.

When his eyes fluttered open, Marc found himself gazing into his wife's eyes. He managed a sleepy, drug-induced smile. "Well, hello," he murmured. Raising his left hand, he ran it along Marie's back; startled at feeling bare skin, Marc's eyes widened. His smile broadened as he drew her near for a kiss.

"How are you feeling?" she asked, nuzzling the side of his throat. "Think you can manage a little consummating?"

Marc groaned and let out a tremulous sigh as she maneuvered around beneath the sheet and slid him inside her.

"Was that a yes?" she asked, her breath hot against his ear.

His good arm tightened around her. He twined his fingers in the thick softness of her hair and pulled her close. "Oh, woman, you're lucky I can only lie here."

Bracing her hands against the bed, Marie gave a throaty laugh and pushed herself upright so she knelt astride him again. She watched his expression change from surprise to deepening pleasure to frustrated torture as she rocked tantalizingly slowly atop him.

She felt him start to move against her and met his thrusts with slow, measured motions of her own.

Marc's breathing grew erratic and his upward thrusts turned to bucking movements beneath her as his passion mounted.

"Slow down there, pal," Marie cautioned, brushing her breasts over his chest. "You don't want it to be over too soon." Now she raised herself just enough to dangle her breasts in his face.

Marc stretched up to capture one of them. He swirled his tongue around the nipple and, when it hardened at his ministrations, he drew it into his mouth and sucked at it fiercely.

Marie shuddered. Steadying herself again with both hands against the bed, she dropped her head backward and let out a moan as Marc's tongue sent her body into little spasms of desire. She bucked hard against him, causing him to cry out in tormented pleasure. She was certain the noises he was making would have brought nurses running, had his mouth not been muffled against her breast.

Incongruously, she thought how fortunate it was the nurse had disconnected him earlier this morning from the monitors tracking his blood pressure and heart rate. Otherwise, she'd be rushing in, thinking he was having a stroke.

Marc moaned aloud, collapsing against the bed amid a shuddering climax that erupted deep inside Marie.

Marie sagged against her husband, her heart clattering. She felt Marc's body heave as she lay atop him. When she slid off and lay beside him, her head against his chest, she felt more than heard his heart racing. She draped an arm across his torso.

Marc lifted a weary arm and stroked her hair until they drifted off to sleep.

Later that afternoon, Marc was discharged from the hospital, with orders from the doctor not to overdo it with his injured arm, which hung in a sling.

"See that? 'Arm.' *Braço*. They didn't say anything about not overdoing it with any other body parts," he teased his wife as they exited the sliding glass doors to step out to the sunny circular portico out front.

She suppressed a grin as the taxi she'd called for pulled up. "We'll see."

"Buzzkill," he grumbled, repressing a grin of his own.

Bedraggled and unkempt, and still in the same blood-stained clothes they'd worn since Tuesday, they clambered into the taxi's back seat for the ride to the hotel. Upon learning Marc was the man who'd thwarted the hijacker on Flight 720, the driver refused to let them pay for the cab ride.

In the hotel, Marc apologized to the desk clerk for their late check-in, explaining he'd had an unscheduled hospitalization upon arrival. The attendant recognized him from the news and assured him she would waive company policy so there would be no fee for the missed night's stay.

"No, no, no. I don't want you to do that," he insisted in a jumbled mashup of Portuguese and English, his fluency flagging as his fatigue and pain increased. "I only wanted to explain why we didn't arrive on schedule."

"No. Please, sir. It will be our pleasure to do this," the earnest young woman assured him, her dark eyes wide and expressive. Then, smiling, she leaned in and added, in English, "Frankly, if we could comp your entire stay, I'd do it in a heartbeat."

"Oh, no, please don't do that," interjected Marie, who'd been standing quietly at Marc's side. "There's no need for that. Please."

The clerk retrieved the couple's stored luggage and smiled as she handed over their room keys, then wished them a good stay – and thanked Marc for his heroic actions.

Uniformed porters jockeyed for position to carry their bags to their fourth-floor suite.

Once inside the suite, Marc thanked the eager young bellhops, who quickly retreated to the lobby.

"Why didn't you tip them?" Marie asked, horrified.

"In Portugal, it's an insult to offer someone a tip," he explained, giving a solemn headshake. "It may feel counter-intuitive – and kind of rude – but trust me, it's rude if you *do* tip."

Now Marc tugged back the drapes to get his first eager glimpse at the city he hadn't seen in nearly two decades. "Isn't this great?" He looked at Marie, who looked discouraged.

She slumped onto the king-size bed, a slight pout forming on her lips. "This is *not* how I envisioned our honeymoon, that's for sure."

"C'mere." He motioned for her to join him. When she did, he draped his good arm around her and drew her close. He kissed her on the temple. "That's okay. Now we've got a great story to tell our grandkids."

Marie sighed and slid her arm around his waist. "I suppose." Her brow wrinkled in concern.

"It'll be fine, *querida*," he assured her, giving her another kiss. "Look at it this way: It can only get better from here."

She still didn't look convinced.

"We're alive, we're together, we're married. And we're in Portugal. What more do we need?"

Marie gazed down at her once-lovely dress, now hopelessly wrinkled, filthy and smeared with her husband's blood. Her mouth twisted into a wry smirk. "I don't know about you, but I could use a shower – and some fresh underwear."

Chapter 12

(Friday, July 9)
After enjoying their room-service breakfast of cheese, toast and jam, espresso and fresh fruit – sweet, ripe *melão* and *melancia*, two types of melons, and juicy *cerejas* and *pessegos*, cherries and peaches – the newlyweds reviewed brochures for various tourist attractions around Lisbon.

"What do you want to do today?" Marie asked, spreading an array of glossy pamphlets across the coffee table in their suite. She sank into the couch.

Slouched beside her, Marc cast a sidelong glance at his wife. "I'll give you three guesses."

"I meant out in public," she replied, elbowing him in the midsection.

"Ohh, I don't think they encourage that kind of thing in public."

"Very funny. I meant sightseeing."

"Oh. That. Why didn't you say so?" He grinned back. "I guess we can go check out some of the art museums. And I hear the zoo and botanical gardens are nice." He picked up the brochure for the *Aquario Vasco da Gama*. "Look, there's an aquarium, too."

Marie glanced at it. "Ooh, that's a different one." She reached for the one marked *Oceanario de Lisboa*. "I was looking at this one before – it looked really interesting."

"We can go to both. We've got plenty of time."

"What do you want to see?" she asked.

"I'd love to walk around Lisbon for a day. Early on, I

was doing some reading on the plane; did you know Lisbon is Europe's second-oldest capital?"

"Really? After what – Athens?"

He leaned over and gave her a kiss. "Ding, ding, ding. Correct answer! Johnny, tell the lady what she's won," he said, mimicking a seventies TV game-show host.

Marie giggled and mussed Marc's hair. "I'm kind of surprised it's not Rome," she commented. "But I'm sure the architecture's amazing."

"That's what I'm counting on."

"Did you see this? The Carmo Archaeological Museum. I thought you might like seeing it."

Marc reviewed the brochure. "Looks great. But we don't have to be on the go every second. I'd also like some down time – to meander through shops and maybe just hang out at the beach."

"Did you want to visit family while we're here?"

He gave the question some thought. "We can if you want. Just know that if we go see one, the others will get bent out of shape if we don't spend a day with them, too. And then there goes our entire honeymoon."

Marie wrinkled her nose. "Good point. How about we just stop in to see your grandmother, then?"

Her mention of Avó Madalena brought a smile to his face. "We could get away with that. 'Course, we show up there, we might just give her a heart attack."

Just after eleven, the phone rang. Answering it, Marc spoke little, but entirely in Portuguese.

Upon hanging up, he informed Marie – as if it were the most natural thing in the world to say – a limo would be waiting outside their hotel to pick them up precisely at 12:30.

"A limo! Whatever for?"

"Ar-are you kidding me?" she stammered when he related what the caller had told him.

Marc shook his head. He checked his watch. "Doesn't

give us much time, does it?"

"Not really. What do you even wear to something like that?"

"My guess is you should wear a pretty dress, my love. You think my grey suit is okay?"

She shrugged. "How should I know? It's not like we can really ask anyone…"

Marc's right eyebrow arched. "Maybe we can. Hang on a sec." He picked up the phone and dialed a short series of numbers. In apologetic and somewhat-rusty Portuguese, he explained their situation to the concierge and inquired what style of dress would be suitable.

When he got off the phone, he looked more confident. "My guess was right. You should wear a dress appropriate for business; and my grey suit will be fine."

"Only problem is, your belt has teeth marks and your white shirt is destroyed."

He frowned. "So it is. I guess a pale-blue shirt will have to do. Think I can get away with the dark-blue tie? Or should I stick with grey?"

(12:28 p.m.)

The swift-moving elevator had scarcely deposited Marc and Marie in the lobby when the limousine pulled up. The chauffeur tucked his cap beneath his elbow as he entered the hotel's grand foyer. He approached the concierge desk, explaining he was there to collect the American couple.

When the concierge motioned discreetly across the lobby, the driver came over and greeted Marc and Marie with a slight bow. "*Senhor, senhora, se você vir comigo, sua limusine espera.*"

Marc nodded. "*Obrigado, senhor,*" he replied. Escorting Marie, he followed the man outside.

Donning his cap once more, the chauffeur opened the rear door for his passengers, shut it after them and slid back into his seat to embark upon the twenty-minute ride through town.

"This is one way to go sightseeing," Marie remarked.

Smiling at her observation, Marc gave her hand a gentle squeeze. "Sure is. Not one I might have considered, though – or ever imagined we'd be doing."

While they rode toward their destination, he indicated points of interest along the way. As he did, Marie made a mental note of several places she wanted to follow up on in their explorations of the city. Mostly, though, she simply enjoyed the luxury of riding in the back of a chauffeur-driven limousine in a foreign country at her husband's side.

Marie's breath caught in her throat and her jaw slackened as the sleek grey vehicle drew to a stop. When they exited, her gaze automatically swept upward. She and Marc stood before the imposing multi-tiered pink stucco façade of the *Palácio Nacional de Belém*.

"This is... magnificent," she breathed barely aloud.

Marc squeezed her right hand. "I think the word you're looking for is palatial," he teased.

Her heels clicked delicately as the couple strolled, arm in good arm, along the brick walkway; the flowing hem of her blue floral chiffon dress grazed her calves. "When are we expected?"

"One fifteen." He glanced at his watch. "That gives us a bit of time to wander the grounds."

"Without an escort? Won't we get shot or something?" Turning toward him, she brushed a loose strand of her auburn hair from the lapel of Marc's dark-grey suit.

"I've already been shot," he deadpanned. "I don't recommend it, but it's really no big deal."

His fanciful nonchalance made Marie laugh, despite her nervousness. "What do you think they want?"

He drew his fretful bride close and kissed her. "How should I know? All they said was to be ready to leave at twelve thirty. You look fantastic, by the way." After kissing her again, Marc flagged down a uniformed palace guard.

Imposing in his blue military-style jacket, white trousers

with knee-high boots and gleaming gold-trimmed blue helmet, the dark-haired guard stood at attention before Marc, his sword resting across his right shoulder. "Yes, sir?"

"We've got a one-fifteen appointment," Marc told the other man in flawless Portuguese. "Is it okay if we walk the grounds while we wait?"

"Certainly, Mr. Lindemeyr. I'll come and collect you at the appointed time."

As they meandered away, Marc wondered how the guard knew his name.

At the designated time, it was not the palace guard but President Paolo Madeira Pinho himself, accompanied by his lovely wife, Isabella, who came to find the newlyweds in the sprawling palace gardens.

"Ah, Mr. and Mrs. Lindemeyr," he hailed them in warm, near-fluent English, his arms outstretched in greeting. "It's such a pleasure to meet you both. Welcome! Welcome to our fair country – and our home."

The president, who looked to be in his mid 40s, wore a dark-blue suit with a grey tie that almost perfectly matched his close-cropped hair. His deep brown eyes assessed Marc, noting the sling cradling the younger man's right arm.

"Mr. President," Marc greeted him, accepting the president's diplomatically extended left hand. "Thank you for the warm welcome. Please, call me Marc – and this is my wife, Marie."

The president kissed Marie's hand. "*Senhora* Lindemeyr. Welcome. May I present *minha esposa*, Isabella." With a benevolent sweep of his hand, he directed them toward a small seating area overlooking the formal gardens.

"Our people are most grateful to you, sir, for your heroic actions the other morning," the president said, once they were seated. "And to recognize your courage in the face of death, we wish to present you with a token of our esteem at a brief outdoor ceremony this afternoon."

Seeing the look of combined dread and dismay on

Marc's face at his words, the president gave a dismissive wave. "Oh, it's nothing to be alarmed about, I assure you," he added with a gentle laugh. "Just a simple ceremony."

Before Marc could say Marie was the real hero – and the one they should be honoring, the president gave another hand signal and two uniformed guards escorted the American couple inside for a private tour of the palace.

***

"*Senhor* Lindemeyr, on behalf of a truly grateful nation," President Madeira Pinho declared in his native language during a nationally televised mid-afternoon ceremony on the palace lawn, "it is my honor to award you this medal for heroism in the face of gravest danger." He seamlessly switched to English. "The motto of the order is 'Talent to do well.' You have done that. And, as Grand Master of the Order, I hereby decree you are henceforth a *Grã-Cruz* – Grand Cross – member of the *Ordem do Infante Dom Henrique* – the National Order of Prince Henry."

Amid applause from the audience, the president lifted the medallion by its blue-, white- and black-striped ribbon and placed the ruby-enameled cross around Marc's neck. Then he pinned the accompanying gold medal to his lapel.

Standing off to one side, next to the first lady, Marie looked on with pride as the president addressed her husband again.

He continued in English for Marc and Marie's benefit. "*Senhor* Lindemeyr – or should I say Good Sir Knight – you may not believe so, but you are a national hero to our people. *O Herói do Vôo Sete Vinte.*" At those few words in Portuguese, a cheer erupted from the audience.

Marie noticed Marc looked downward and colored slightly. She wondered what the words meant. It must have been something good, to yield that kind of reaction from the people. She knew it would be terribly impolite to ask the first lady for a translation during his speech, so she decided she would ask Marc later what the president had said.

"The Portuguese people thank you most appreciatively for your valiant actions in defense of our fellow countrymen," the president continued.

Following the public ceremony, Marc was spirited away indoors for a press conference and photo op with the president; then all the Portuguese news networks and the U.S. networks' foreign correspondents awaited their turns to interview the Hero of Flight 720, as the president had dubbed him, garnering such a favorable reaction from those in attendance.

Marc bristled as one of them referred to him as a hero during the press conference.

"*No*," he insisted with an emphatic headshake. "I'm no hero. I was just in a lousy place at the right time. My wife is the one who talked the guy down and got him to release his hostage."

"But you could have been killed," someone countered.

"So could we all have," Marc replied, the twinge in his arm beginning to make him testy. He did his best to ignore the reality that his pain meds were wearing off. "I just did what anyone would have done."

Meanwhile, Marie enjoyed her private visit in the east conservatory with first lady Isabella Josefina Raposa da Costa, who – much to Marie's relief – was nearly fluent in English.

The two women spoke at length about a range of topics, from the beautiful array of colorful and fragrant flowers in bloom throughout the sprawling gardens outside the palace, to the first lady's interest in protecting the country's fragile aquatic life, to Marie's work as a pediatric psychiatrist and the honeymooners' plans for their stay in Europe.

Doing his best to ignore the increasing twinges of pain flicking through his injured arm while on camera, Marc gamely endured the same questions over and over from

Portuguese and American television reporters – just with different intros and interviewers.

So as not to show preference, President Madeira Pinho's press secretary alternated between the two countries' reporters when it came time for the individual interviews. And he determined the order of the reporters' interviews by random drawing.

Toward the end, the combination of meds wearing off and the stress of switching back and forth from speaking English to Portuguese began to make Marc edgy. And there was no opportunity for him to request a glass of water so he could take another pain pill. By the time he got to the final interview, all he wanted was to go back to the hotel and lie down. Still, aware he was under heightened scrutiny, he maintained his pleasant humor and polite façade throughout all twelve TV interviews.

"Police say PortugAir Flight Seven Twenty, originating from JFK in New York on Tuesday evening, was over international waters early Wednesday when a hijacker attempted to take over the flight," the last of the seven American reporters informed a nearby camera when his turn arrived. "That's when he encountered an American couple headed to Portugal on their honeymoon. While the bride convinced the hijacker to release the stewardess he'd taken hostage, the groom, a radio announcer from Danbury, Connecticut, took matters – quite literally – into his own hands.

"When Marc Lindsay, as he's known on air, tried to disarm the gunman, a struggle ensued. During the scuffle, he was shot in the upper arm at close range, but managed to wrest the gun away from the attacker. We're speaking now with Marc Lindsay, the Hero of Flight Seven Twenty. Marc, can you tell us what happened?"

"I need to start with a correction, Alex. After I got shot, the gun fell loose. I never actually got possession of it. Another passenger kicked it away. I just kind of sat there and bled."

"What was going through your head while all this was

happening?"

"Honestly? 'Dear God – don't let him shoot Marie.' We'd gotten married that morning and I was *not* ready to lose her. Not so soon. And certainly not like that."

"How did you know what to do?"

"Growing up, my best friend's dad was a cop. He made darn sure we knew how to properly behave around firearms. I hadn't held a weapon in I don't know how long, but I'm grateful for that training all those years ago."

"If it hadn't been for that training, and your bravery in the face of danger, who knows what might have happened – to all of you? You're a true hero."

Marc shook his head. "You wanna talk about heroes? The real hero in all of this was my wife. Marie's a therapist. She kept her cool and talked the guy into releasing his hostage. Plus, I'm alive right now because of her. She got my bleeding under control, took care of the flight attendant and *then* tended to the hijacker, who'd almost torn his thumb off 'cause he didn't know how to safely handle a gun."

The reporter looked startled. "Your wife helped the gunman?"

"I'm sure she probably had words with him, but yeah. She's the real hero, Alex. You should be interviewing her. I was just in the wrong place at the right time. And that really is the truth."

"What are your plans for the rest of your stay in Portugal?"

Despite his pain, Marc aimed a dazzling smile at the camera. "For starters, I'm going to try my best not to get shot again. Other than that, we'll likely go sightseeing, visit family and enjoy some quiet time together."

Once the camera stopped, Alex Farmer thanked Marc for granting him the interview, adding, "After all this publicity, you might have to resort to wearing a disguise out in public – especially with that telltale sling."

"I'm afraid you may be right."

"I hope not, but, hey, I'm so glad I got a chance to meet

you, Mr. Lindemeyr," he replied earnestly, shaking Marc's extended left hand.

"Please, it's just Marc."

"Okay. Marc. Enjoy the rest of your honeymoon. It was an honor meeting you. Thank you again... for your heroism – and for granting me the interview."

As Marc left the briefing room, he got the feeling his awkward off-camera exchange with the young reporter just then might be only the tip of the iceberg.

After the last of the media departed, the newlyweds were shown to the presidential quarters, for a more-relaxed private audience with the president and first lady.

"I understand you are here on your honeymoon," the president intoned in careful, precise English as they settled into what had to be the most comfortable couch Marc had ever sat on. The president loosened his tie, and motioned for Marc to do likewise.

"That's right, yes," Marie replied as one of the culinary staff carried in an ornate silver coffee service and set it on the gleaming rosewood sideboard, alongside delicate china cups and saucers. Lifting the coffeepot, the uniformed older woman began to pour refreshments for the guests.

"When were you married?"

"Tuesday morning – in the U.S.," Marc told him.

"Oh my!" the first lady exclaimed, her long, delicate fingers flying to her mouth. "So you really are freshly married."

Marc's fingers curled around his bride's. The lilt of her accent brought a smile of familiarity to his lips. "You could say that."

"So Lisbon was your first stop," she deduced. "Where are you headed next?"

"I have no clue," he replied candidly, remembering not to shrug. He'd read somewhere it was impolite to do so when being addressed by a head of state. Marc inclined his head toward Marie. "This was all her idea – we weren't even supposed to be married 'til September."

"No?" Isabella asked, tilting her head on her graceful neck. "What happened to your plans? Why did they change?"

"Marc is going back to school this fall, so we couldn't have gone on a honeymoon then. And because his birthday was this week, and he hadn't been back here since he was a teenager, I figured I'd plan something extravagant while he had time," Marie explained. "The elopement kind of came together this past week. We had a civil ceremony, but we still plan to have a proper church wedding in September."

"I think that's beautiful," the first lady commented with a brilliant smile. "How long are you planning to stay in our county?"

"Two more weeks," Marie said. "Sixteen days in all."

"Well then," the president said, clapping his hands together, "seeing as we have newlyweds, Marc's knighthood and a birthday to celebrate, it will be our good pleasure to cover the cost of your honeymoon. It's the least we can do for our national hero."

Marc couldn't be sure he'd heard correctly. He leaned forward slightly, his gaze intense. "I'm sorry, sir – what was that?"

"Bella and I would like you, Marc and Marie, to be our guests. It would be our honor and great pleasure to personally pay all the expenses associated with your stay in our beloved country – including the costs of your hospital stay and all your attendant medical care."

Marie felt her mouth drop open indelicately. "Oh my goodness – you don't need to do that!"

"It would be our pleasure," Isabella reiterated her husband's sentiments with a gracious nod.

"I – I don't know what to say," Marie stammered, still gaping at them.

Beyond knowing better than to shrug, Marc also realized it would be monumentally impolite to turn down the couple's offer. He gave his wife's hand one long, slow squeeze – their previously established signal for yes.

Her gaze still fixed on the presidential couple, Marie gave Marc's hand a return squeeze to convey understanding. "Thank you! That's such a generous offer," she replied graciously.

"We considered offering to serve as your hosts," Isabella admitted, toying with her hands in her lap, "but I imagine you've got an itinerary drawn up – or at least some things in mind – and we didn't want to be an imposition on your time... that is, any more than we already have been."

The president's gaze flicked almost imperceptibly to the mantel clock. It was almost half past five.

Attentive to her husband's discreet glance, Isabella stood. "Speaking of imposing on your time, we mustn't keep you any longer. After all" – she flashed a winning smile at Marie – "you have dinner reservations for this evening."

(6:35 p.m.)
Marc looked across the table at Marie. "This is unreal," he murmured, shaking his head.

When Marie had mentioned earlier they were looking for a romantic spot to enjoy their first dinner out in Lisbon, the first lady suggested her longtime favorite restaurant, *A Pérola Ibérica* – The Iberian Pearl – and insisted on personally calling to reserve a table for them.

"Your table will be ready at half past six," she said with a kind smile, replacing the phone in its cradle. "They were delighted to reserve a quiet spot for two – at my request."

The Lindemeyrs had thanked the first lady profusely; but now, Marc wondered whether their heartfelt expressions of appreciation had been a gross underestimation of the gratitude due her.

As the *maître d* showed the couple to a table in a private alcove overlooking the burgeoning Tagus River, Marc gave a discreet glance around the rest of the dining area. It was Friday evening and the restaurant was packed. Tuxedoed waiters glided elegantly from table to candlelit table. Decorated in complementary shades of azure and pearl, with gilt-framed seascapes on the walls and lavish brocade drapery in blue and sea green, the restaurant's décor evoked sweeping images of the Atlantic Ocean. Around the luxurious dining room, a dozen other couples in shimmering finery dined on sumptuous culinary creations while engaging in muted conversations in lilting Portuguese.

Marie closed her fingers around Marc's, startling him from his musing. "What's unreal?"

"All of it. Eloping. Being in Portugal. Your saving that hostage. Getting shot. Meeting the president, for goodness' sake!" Looking around, he gestured subtly. "This. You pick. Any of it."

A gentle smile lit her countenance. "You forgot getting knighted."

A momentary flash of frustration – or warning – crossed his face. *I did not forget it.* His shoulders sagged. "Can we just let that drop? Please?"

Marie squeezed his hand. "Of course."

"Good. Because I'd like to enjoy a romantic evening with my wife." He managed a smile and drew his hand away. He fumbled in his pants pocket for the painkillers they prescribed before he left the hospital. Grateful for the non-childproof cap, he unlidded it and shook a small white tablet onto the table. He recapped the bottle and slid it back into his pocket, then put the pill into his mouth and reached for his water glass.

"This really is an amazing place," she said, glancing about as Marc set the goblet back on the table, within the condensation ring on the light-blue linen tablecloth. "Looks like we're in the middle of the ocean."

"Well, you did say you wanted something reminiscent of the sea, didn't you?"

"Yeah, but I didn't expect Isabella to come through like this!"

"Isabella? So now you're on a first-name basis with the

first lady of Portugal, eh? You don't waste a moment, do you, my love?"

Marie looked like she didn't know what to make of his comment. Her smile eroded.

Marc offered her a kind smile and squeezed her hand. "I'm teasing. You two seemed to hit it off right famously. And you obviously made quite an impression on her."

"I guess. After all, we did have some private time to chat while you were busy getting grilled by all those reporters."

"You definitely got the better end of the deal."

"How so?"

"You got to sit and talk to the first lady while I was, as you put it, getting grilled. In fact, you can probably see the char marks," he kidded, inspecting the front of his suit jacket. "You know how I hate that kind of attention – hell, I don't even like birthday parties. All I wanted to do was crawl away from those cameras and hide under a rock."

"It couldn't have been that bad," Marie said. "Seriously, Marc, what was it like?"

He gave a low groan. "Grueling. Especially since the pain meds were wearing off." Now he let out a quiet sigh. "Okay, to be honest, it wasn't exactly *agony*, but I couldn't wait for it to be over!"

She gave him an adoring smile. "Well, it's over now and you can relax and enjoy your meal. That is, after you translate everything on the menu for me."

When they'd finished their dinner and savored warm, cinnamon-dusted *pastéis de Belém* and coffee, their waiter returned to clear away their dishes; he informed the couple their bill had already been seen to by the first lady at the time she called to make the reservation.

After leaving the restaurant, the newlyweds took a stroll along the shore of the Tagus River by the light of the waning gibbous moon. They walked hand in hand in amicable near-silence while a light breeze off the water played with their hair and ruffled the hem of Marie's dress. Every now and then, they'd stop to share an observation, a kiss or a snuggle.

Marie periodically asked if Marc wanted to head back. "You're recovering from surgery," she reminded him. "You need rest. You shouldn't overdo it."

But he insisted he was fine.

As the evening grew late and the temperature began to drop, Marie shivered slightly in the chilly air. Before long, her teeth were starting to chatter.

Marc slid his arm out of its sling, wriggled free of his suit jacket and draped the jacket over his wife's barely covered shoulders. "There. That better?"

"Mmm, yes." She slipped her bare arms into the jacket's Bemberg silk-lined sleeves, then stretched upward to kiss him. "Thank you."

After repositioning his injured arm in the sling, he started to walk again, but she hadn't resumed moving and he felt himself being tugged backward by her arm linked through his.

"Everything okay?" he asked, turning to look at her.

Marie nodded. "Mm-hmm." She gazed up into his face. "How did I ever get so lucky?"

Marc's eyes twinkled in the moonlight. "What a short memory you've got, *querida*. As I recall, luck had nothing to do with it. It was all a result of your bad decisions – one after another. First, you made the fatal error of saying yes when I asked you out. Then you said yes again when I asked if I could kiss you goodnight. And you foolishly said yes a third time when I asked you out on a second date." He shrugged. "By then, I'm afraid you were pretty much a goner."

I guess I'm just a girl who can't say no – especially to a guy like you. Marie hooked both index fingers through the belt loops on Marc's pleated-front trousers and pulled him nearer. She reached up and planted a searing kiss on his mouth. "Is that how it happened?"

Giving an "aw-shucks" grin, he nuzzled her throat. "I

admit I may have left out a few minor details – and likely a whole lot more of your yeses – but that's pretty much all there was to it."

It was nearly eleven by the time the taxi deposited them at their hotel. As they rode up in the elevator, Marc's right arm ached, but it wasn't yet time for another pain pill; more than pain relief, though, he was aching to take Marie to bed.

Back in their suite, he emptied his pockets, placing his wallet and the bottle of pain meds on the coffee table.

Marie set her purse on the table and slid out of his suit jacket, which she laid across a chair.

Marc put his arm around her and kissed the side of her throat. She turned toward him and began kissing him hungrily. As they kissed, she ran one hand up along the side of his throat and up through his hair. With her other hand, she loosened, then undid, his tie and started to undo his shirt.

"This damn gunshot wound is really pissing me off," he murmured into her hair, his voice thick with passion. "Without it, I'd have been picking you up right now and carrying you over to the bed."

"I know," Marie responded, her breath hot against his throat. "And I'd be letting you."

She sought his mouth again and kissed him, long and hot. As they kissed, she steered him over to the bed, where she finished unbuttoning his shirt. Grappling next with his cufflinks, she left them on the nightstand while he removed his sling. Marie guided his injured arm out of its sleeve, then tugged the shirt off and cast it aside. She did the same with his undershirt.

That accomplished, she unfastened his belt and trousers, but stopped when he began to laugh.

"What's so funny?"

"I know we're both in kind of a rush to undress here, hon, but don't you think I should take off my shoes first?"

he asked. "It'll be so much easier to get my pants off that way."

"Oh, I suppose so," Marie assented, blushing. "If you insist on doing things the easy way. Although, truth be told, I was gonna just yank 'em partway down so you'd be hobbled and couldn't get away." Her eyes twinkled.

"You are a cruel woman."

"And you're wasting time, mister," she chided playfully.

Prancing a few steps away, just out of reach, she made a grand show of slipping off her airy dress. With a sultry smile in his direction, she tossed the cast-off garment over the chair. She kicked off her heels and swiftly shed her bra and panties. By the time Marie finished removing her jewelry, Marc had managed to untie and remove his shoes and socks. She returned to within his reach and wasted no time in relieving him of the rest of his clothing. Wrapping her arms around him, she pressed her naked body fully against his, reached up on her tiptoes and planted a smoldering kiss on his mouth. As she drew back, she ran her tongue across her upper lip, offering Marc an alluring, open-mouthed smile.

The newlyweds climbed up onto the bed and scrambled toward the middle of it. Giving Marc another fiery kiss, Marie maneuvered him onto his back and crawled on top of him, careful not to jostle his bandaged arm.

"Mmm... I kinda like this arrangement," he commented with a coy wink. "I get all the fun and none of the work."

"Don't get too used to it." The corners of her mouth turned upward in a seductive smile. "Remember, this is only temporary. I fully expect to be flung onto the bed and taken advantage of – repeatedly – once that arm of yours is healed. Because, despite what it may seem like, I'm not a real big fan of being the aggressor."

"You coulda fooled me. Anyway, you can call it what you want. I'm just gonna lie here and enjoy the view." With a languid smile, he reached out with his good hand and caressed her creamy white breast. "And what a view it is."

Minutes later, swept up in the midst of their lovemaking,

Marc momentarily forgot his injury as he tried to take a more active role. As soon as he wrapped his arms around Marie in an attempt to roll her onto her back, he let out a yelp.

White-hot pain shot through his bicep. An instant later, his erection withered.

Alarmed at his outcry, Marie jerked back from him, worry in her eyes. "Are you okay?" She peered down at his face, now contorted in agony.

Clenching his teeth, he took a shuddering breath. "I... I'm fine," he replied, panting. "I just... forgot." His cheeks blazed in embarrassment at his sudden loss of arousal.

Marie pushed herself upright, so she was kneeling with one leg on either side of his body. "Ohh, honey..." She reached out to caress his cheek.

Marc pushed her hand away.

Without another word, she climbed off and settled beside him. He averted his gaze, refusing to even look in her direction. When she tried to snuggle next to him, he sat upright.

"Don't," he cautioned with a terse headshake. Scuttling away, he got up and went to sit at the edge of the bed, frustrated by his physical limitations. With a tremulous sigh, Marc sank his head into his one good hand – the one that just a few minutes earlier had been caressing his bride's ripe, voluptuous breast. He clenched his teeth and cursed the pain radiating through his arm.

Marie went to the sink. She filled a glass with water and brought it to him, along with a pain pill from the bottle he'd left on the coffee table. She sat close to him and silently held out the water and the pill.

Not looking up at her, Marc plucked the small white tablet from her outstretched palm, then accepted the glass of water. He drank it down in three big gulps. It felt refreshing, soothing. And the glass felt cool against his palm. The simple act of drinking the water calmed him; his sense of anxiety begin to ease. But the embarrassment lingered.

Marie reclaimed the empty glass.

"Thank you," he murmured, still staring at the carpet. *Please don't ask if I want to talk about it. Please...*

She rested a hand on his arm. As he tensed, she leaned in and kissed him on the cheek.

His head drooped. He drew in another shuddering breath; it wavered almost as much on its way out.

Marie leaned her head against his shoulder in what Marc could only guess was a gesture intended to convey comfort. It just made him feel worse. Now, on top of everything else, he felt pitied.

He swallowed hard. "Please don't." The words came out as a whisper. He looked over at her, feeling trampled.

When Marie gazed at him, it was difficult for Marc to identify the look in her eyes. Was it sympathy? Disappointment? Perhaps disdain? No, he decided. It probably wasn't any of those. *Then what?* "I'm sorry," he mumbled with a diffident shrug.

She caressed his face. "For what?"

Was that a note of surprise in her voice? Marc gave a defeated sigh. "For ruining everything."

Her hand stopped. "No..." Now her tone held a worried edge.

The movement of her hand through his hair and along his scalp felt nice; some of his unease dissipated.

"You didn't ruin anything, Marc," she cooed, her voice as soothing as the touch of her hand. "I know none of this has been easy for you. And I hate that it's making you feel so... distraught."

Needy and distressed, he leaned slightly in to her caress, craving her touch, and grateful for the sense of security and relief it provided.

"I wish there was a way I could make it all better," she went on after a pause, still stroking his hair, "some way to rewind these last three days and undo everything so it never would have happened... but I can't." Her voice faltered the slightest bit.

His shoulders sagged.

Leaning in toward him again, she kissed him tenderly on the cheek. "C'mon, honey, why don't you come back to bed? You've been under a lot of stress… especially today, with the president, all those interviews – all that attention focused on you. I know it was a lot to take. I bet you could really use a good night's sleep. I'm sure things will seem better in the morning. Alright?"

With a reluctant nod, Marc stood and let Marie gather him into her arms. Her embrace felt safe and comforting, her kiss reassuring. Unable to express himself in words, he allowed her to lead him by the hand back to bed.

Once they were settled again, Marie turned off the bedside lamp, slid back over to join Marc on his side of the bed and kissed him on the cheek. "Goodnight, sweetheart. Sleep well. I love you."

In the dark, Marc reached for his wife's hand and gave it a gentle squeeze. In his vulnerable state, it was the only means of communication he could manage – and he hoped Marie understood.

She gave him a little kiss on the shoulder; then lay her head against him with a sleepy sigh.

Marc slid his arm behind her shoulder and drew her closer.

Chapter 13

(Saturday, July 10)
Marc awoke a little before six to find Marie curled in a ball, her back to him, still asleep. When he returned to bed after using the bathroom, he marveled at how much easier it was starting to get, accomplishing routine tasks without using his injured arm. He slid beneath the sheet, settled himself again and turned onto his side; his bandaged right arm felt stiff and achy. He raised it a few inches, wincing at the twinge that shot through it. He brought his arm forward and draped it around Marie's waist, testing his ability to withstand the pain for the sake of some small measure of normalcy. Finding the physical discomfort not too awful, he scooched a bit closer to her and settled back to sleep, his face nestled close enough to her hair to smell the comforting aroma of her ginger-peach shampoo.

When Marie awoke just after eight, she felt Marc's arm around her. She let out a little sigh of perfect ease, knowing she was safe in the arms of the man she loved. Doing her best not to disturb him, she rolled onto her back. With the sun streaming through the windows, she had plenty of light and a front-row seat to assess the bandage covering the entry wound at the front of his arm.

The outer bandage still looked okay, but her concern turned to the dressing that lay beneath it; the hospital staff had applied a fresh dressing before they released Marc, so it needed to be changed today. The staff had provided her with everything she'd need for dressing changes until he went to the outpatient clinic to have the wounds evaluated next week – and the stitches removed the week after.

Stowing that thought away, Marie resumed turning until she was facing Marc; his arm remained in place across her body. A prickling sensation skittered along her spine as she imagined the degree of pain he must have endured to give her this sense of comfort.

She studied his face. It looked so tranquil in sleep. *As if he hasn't a worry or care in the world.* She smiled at the notion, although she knew good and well that wasn't even close to being true. A kernel of sadness for him built in her insides, gnawing at her early-morning peace.

A few minutes later, almost as though he could sense her watching him, Marc's eyes opened. He blinked a few times until he could focus. When he saw Marie's blue eyes gazing back, his smile was reflexive. "Good morning," he murmured.

She leaned in to kiss his upturned lips. "Hi." She cuddled close, loving the nearness of him. "It was so nice to wake up with your arm around me."

Slowly bending his arm, and wincing a bit, he smoothed her hair back, away from her face. "It was nice to fall back to sleep that way, too."

As Marc kissed her, Marie felt his erection nudging at her thigh. Despite her admission last night of how much she disliked being the aggressor, she took full advantage of this opportunity. She rolled him onto his back and lay atop him, their bodies practically in full contact from shoulders to feet. Raking her hands through Marc's hair, she kissed his mouth with renewed passion – almost as if their lovemaking hadn't been interrupted the night before. Pressing her palms against the bed for leverage, Marie raised her torso. She let her legs slide off his so she was straddling him, and inched backward just enough that she was able to slip him inside her.

As she moved atop him, she established a tantalizingly

slow tempo. Marc uttered a low groan and met her motions with deliberate upward thrusts of his own.

Marie lowered herself to her elbows and felt the crazy beating of Marc's heart as she kissed him. His mouth felt hot against hers and his building passion fueled her own.

Gradually, she increased her speed, until she found a pace to suit them both. It wasn't long before she raised herself to an upright position again. Marie realized being on top had its advantages; she could easily control the pace, the angle and the depth of penetration... plus it gave Marc ample opportunity to watch her delighting in the stimulation she herself craved – all the while driving him into a frenzy.

Little by little, his breathing grew more erratic and, not long after Marie ground her pelvis against his one final time – sending herself into a wildly vocal, pulsating orgasm before drooping against his body – he let out a shuddering breath as he climaxed.

Panting hard, as much from passion as from exertion, Marie rolled off him and collapsed in a crumpled heap at his side.

His heart still pounding, Marc stroked his wife's sweat-soaked hair as they snuggled together. "That was amazing," he murmured. "As for your not liking to be the aggressor, I call bullshit. You looked like you were enjoying that way too much."

She raised her head from his heaving chest and regarded him with a devilish grin. "Okay, so maybe I changed my mind."

After they showered, Marie cleaned and re-dressed Marc's wounds.

"How's that feel?" she asked, securing a new covering to the exit wound. She ran the pads of her fingers along all four edges of the bandage, securing it to his skin.

"Doesn't hurt as much today," he reported. "But it's beginning to feel a bit itchy."

"That's a good sign."

"Are you sure?"

"As long as it's not red or swollen, itching can be an indicator of healing. Look at this area, over here." She pointed to the entry wound's upper edge. "See that?"

Marc glanced over, then just as quickly turned away with a squeamish shudder. "That's okay. I don't need to look at it. I'll take your word for it."

Marie smiled, endeared by his reaction. "Fair enough. It looks like it's starting to heal. There doesn't seem to be any sign of infection – certainly no excessive drainage, no funky smell or pus oozing from anywhere. So it's coming along nicely."

He made a face. "Yeesh! Do we *have* to talk about funky smells and pus before breakfast?"

"Well, no. But it's important to know to look for these things."

"I'll leave that to you," he insisted. "In the meantime, what do I do about the itching?"

"Try to ignore it."

"That's easy enough to say. But how would you propose I do that?" he challenged.

Marie leaned in and kissed him. "You're on your honeymoon. I'm fairly confident you can think of *something* to keep your mind off the itching." She ruffled his still-damp hair.

Marc wrapped his good arm around her and pulled her first to himself, then down into his lap to kiss her. "Marrying you was the best thing I've ever done."

Slipping her arms around him, she kissed back. "I'm glad you think so. I tend to agree." She drew away and got to her feet again. "But for now, I've got to get this other wound dressed – and then we've got to go eat and get on with sightseeing, because I don't know about you, but I'm ready to see something besides the inside of this suite."

***

After seeking recommendations from the concierge on where to enjoy a leisurely breakfast on a beautiful Saturday, the newlyweds set out on foot to find one of the several local *pastelarias* he suggested. They were delighted to find the café they chose had plenty of outdoor seating, so they ventured inside to order their food and then sat at one of the small tables out front.

Although the *pastelaria* served everything from coffee, juice and a variety of pastries to full meals, Marc and Marie wanted lighter breakfast fare; they both opted for the *bolos de arroz* and *garoto*.

As they enjoyed their savory muffins and tall mugs of espresso with milk in the warmth of the mid-July morning, the honeymooners reviewed the full-color pamphlets for the attractions they wanted to explore.

After breakfast, Marc and Marie ordered *garotos* in paper cups to go, then ventured out to the *jardim zoológico*, for what they hoped would be a peaceful stroll through the combined zoo and botanical gardens.

Marie grew concerned when Marc flinched at an unexpected twinge. "If you're in pain, we can go back to the hotel," she said. "We don't have to be on the go every minute. I love sightseeing, but I love you more, Marc. And your well-being means more to me than all this touristy stuff."

Marc leaned in and kissed her. "I'm fine," he assured her, trying to mask his discomfort. He slid his good arm around her. "C'mon, let's go see some animals."

Several fellow patrons approached them to say they recognized Marc from the news reports as the Hero of Flight 720, and thanked him for his heroism. Most just wanted to shake his hand and express their thanks. Other patrons, not wanting to intrude on his private time, simply waved or nodded in recognition. Still other folks, upon recognizing him, motioned discreetly toward him from a distance and whispered to one another.

From his first visit years earlier, Marc knew it was considered monumentally rude in Portugal to point at another person, and he appreciated their restraint and respect for his privacy.

One little girl not quite Erin's age ran up to him, with her paper zoo map in hand, and asked for his autograph, which he graciously, albeit reluctantly, gave her.

When they caught up to their daughter, her parents explained an elderly neighbor, to whom their daughter was especially close, was on the flight. The mother asked if Marc would consent to having his picture taken with the little girl, Fátima.

"*Claro. Seria um prazer,*" he told the girl's mother with a reticent smile. "It would be my pleasure," he translated for Marie, who gamely moved aside. Marc crouched to pose beside the dark-haired child, who wrapped a slender arm around his shoulder.

After her mother had taken the picture, Fátima gingerly patted Marc's injured arm, her tiny brow furrowing in concern. "*Isso doi?*"

"*Um pouco.*"

"*Eu beijo e deixo melhor?*" Leaning in, the girl planted a tender kiss on his arm, just above the sling.

Marc smiled. "*Isso é melhor. Obrigado.*"

With an enormous smile, Fátima gave him a big hug and a kiss on the cheek. "*Muito obrigado, Senhor Herói. Você salvou a vida do meu amigo!*" She skipped away, holding her autograph and waving goodbye to the Hero of Flight 720.

Marc waved back, smiling at his diminutive admirer through a sudden haze of tears.

"What did she say?" Marie asked, rejoining him.

He wiped at his eyes. It took him a moment to compose himself enough to reply. "When I said it hurt a little, she asked, 'I kiss it and make it better?' And just now she told me, 'Thank you so much, Mr. Hero. You saved my friend's life.'"

As they strolled along through the botanical gardens, an American couple, who looked to be in their 60s, stopped them to say their son, Portuguese daughter-in-law and two grandchildren had been on Flight 720.

"Thank you so much for saving their lives," the wife gushed, hugging Marc.

"Our daughter-in-law is expecting a son this fall. She said she plans to name him Marc," the husband added.

"That's certainly not necessary," Marc replied, deeply uncomfortable at the couple's words – especially the news about their grandchild's being named after him. His palms grew clammy and his chest began to feel like it was constricting.

"I don't know how much more of this I can take," he confided to Marie as the older couple continued along the cobbled path.

"You're doing fine," she assured him, linking her arm through his and patting his hand.

He shook his head. "I'm really not. I'm not used to this – all this being recognized. People just walk up to me and act all familiar. It's unnerving."

"I can understand that. And when you're not used to being singled out, something like this can seem overwhelming."

Marc smiled in spite of himself. "You realize you're slipping into doctor mode."

"I know." Marie's nose wrinkled. "Sorry. You may want to consider calling Dr. Merino."

He gave a jittery nod as they resumed walking. "I've thought about it." He shrugged. "Maybe that'll help."

Paola Merino and Marie had solidified their friendship long before Marc began dating Marie. By then, Paola had already been treating Marc for several years. While they'd concluded their therapy for the most part, Marc still saw Dr. Merino a few times a year for what he termed "emotional tune-ups." She also maintained her availability, in person or via phone, on an as-needed basis.

Marie made a vague backward gesture over her shoulder. "Let's go back to the hotel so you can call her."

"I don't need to do that. We were going to stop for lunch, and you said you wanted to check out some of those little shops we saw last night along the waterfront."

Marie stopped walking. She looked Marc in the eye. "Listen to me. Your well being is more important than lunch – and yes, even shopping." She glanced at her watch. "Why don't you call her now, before it gets too late. We can check out the shops another time."

Marc nodded numbly. "Okay." His brow wrinkled. "Wait. It's too *early* back home. We're five hours ahead. It's six in the morning there. I doubt she would appreciate my waking her up for this. Besides, it's Saturday."

"If I know Paola – and I do – she'll make time to talk, weekend or otherwise. Besides, it'll take time to get back to the hotel, so it won't be that early by the time you call. And anyway, you can leave a message at her office," Marie suggested. "That way, she can carve out some time to talk and call you back when it's not the crack of dawn."

Chapter 14

(7:23 a.m. Eastern Time, Saturday, July 10)
Despite Marc's repeated insistence his actions had been anything but heroic, foreign correspondents in Lisbon saw things far differently. Several major U.S. newspapers' headlines boldly proclaimed, "Honeymoon Hero! American Newlywed Thwarts Airline Hijacker" and "First Class Hero!"

Others said, " 'Hero of Flight 720' Honored by Portuguese President"; "American Citizen Knighted by Portuguese Leader Following Midair Heroism"; and "American Hero Honored with Knighthood!"

Not surprisingly, given the local tie-in, many papers in Connecticut picked up on the story. When Gary retrieved the morning newspaper from the sidewalk, the color photo above the fold was an image of his best friend having a beribboned medal placed around his neck by a man in a dark suit. The headline and accompanying page-one editorial leapt out at him.

Knight-time DJ!

Local radio announcer Marc Lindsay, who does the 7-to-midnight shift at Z97-3 (97.3 WZBX-FM in Middlebury), made history yesterday when he became the first American in recent memory to be knighted by the president of Portugal.

President Paolo Madeira Pinho conferred the honor on Lindsay, a Danbury native and resident, in a public ceremony outside the presidential palace in Belém, a section of Lisbon. Lindsay was awarded the Grand Cross of the Order of Prince Henry for his heroism in thwarting a midair hijacking early Wednesday morning.

During a transatlantic flight originating Tuesday evening from New York's John F. Kennedy International Airport, a gunman aboard PortugAir Flight 720 took a flight attendant hostage and demanded access to the cockpit. But the hijacker wasn't expecting to encounter any pushback. According to Lindsay, his wife, Marie, a licensed psychiatrist, was the real hero. She talked the hijacker into releasing his hostage, bravely offering herself in the other woman's stead.

The would-be hijacker turned the gun on the psychiatrist and demanded she hand over her valuables. As his wife reached for her purse, Lindsay took matters into his own hands.

Lindsay, who told reporters he had just gotten married that morning and had no intention of losing his bride so soon, knocked the other man off balance, pointing the barrel of the .45-caliber pistol in what he termed "a safe direction," away from his wife and other passengers. While the two men struggled for control of the weapon, it discharged.

Lindsay was shot in the right bicep at close range. His wife, who was not injured in the altercation, had the presence of mind to use her medical training to attend to his gunshot wound, using supplies from the airliner's first-aid kit.

The hijacker, described as a white male in his early 20s, was also wounded in the fracas. His thumb was badly injured by the racking action of the semiautomatic pistol as it fired.

In addition to assessing the previously captive flight attendant's physical and emotional condition, Lindsay's wife reportedly also performed an emergency medical procedure on board the plane that helped save the gunman's thumb.

Upon landing at Lisbon Portela Airport shortly after 9 local time Wednesday morning, Lindsay was rushed by ambulance to the Hospital of St. Mary in the country's capital, where he underwent emergency surgery to repair damage to his arm. Luckily, the bullet's trajectory took it straight through Lindsay's arm. It exited without striking bone.

The unidentified flight attendant was taken to a trauma center for evaluation.

The would-be skyjacker, detained by passengers during the flight, was placed in the custody of the country's public-security police and taken away for questioning. His motive is still undetermined.

Lindsay was released from the hospital Thursday afternoon and is recovering in an undisclosed location, where he is honeymooning with his wife.

Lindsay has been described by coworkers as "a regular guy," "a nice guy who pretty much keeps to himself" and "not the sort of fellow you'd expect to be caught up in any sort of scuffle."

Pete Donovan, the program director at

Z97-3, for whom Lindsay has worked for nearly 14 years, said while news of the hijacking came as a shock to him, word of his employee's intervention didn't.

"Marc's a pretty amazing guy. I've known him a long time, and he's one of the most loyal people I know. I'm not a bit surprised he took the action he did," Donovan said of his nighttime announcer, "especially given that someone he loves so much had willingly placed herself in harm's way."

Then again, it seems that saving lives is nothing new for Lindsay. Until six months ago, he spent several years working part time as a lifeguard for the Danbury YMCA. And a year ago, he was credited with saving the life of another man who was involved in a swimming accident during a party at a friend's home.

Donovan said he was thankful Lindsay's injury didn't end up being more serious.

"Of course, we're especially relieved – and grateful – the whole situation ended on a positive note. The Z97-3 crew is like a big family; and not only has Marc been a major part of this family for years, but Marie is also family around here; she's our afternoon guy's sister," he added.

Lindsay is expected to return to his regular shift in two weeks.

As for his immediate plans, Lindsay lightheartedly informed reporters he was "going to try my best not to get shot again." He and his new bride plan to do some sightseeing and enjoy some quiet time together.

And after what the couple has been

through this week, they deserve nothing less than that.

On the front porch, Gary scanned the story, then brought the paper inside and showed it to Micki. "You're not gonna believe this. Marc's been knighted!"

"What?" Michaela glanced at the headline, then at her husband's astonished expression. "No way! Let me see that." She took the paper and read the editorial for herself. "That's so cool!"

Gary leaned against the countertop. "Now that this is out, we're gonna have to do one of two things."

Michaela gave him a puzzled look.

"We either have to hide the paper or tell Erin about Uncle Marc getting shot."

"I say we level with her. She'll find out sooner or later; and I'd rather she hear about it from us – in a comfortable environment, where we can control the discussion and answer any questions she has."

"I agree. Looks like we had this conversation just in the nick of time." Gary shoved off from the counter and straightened up, then motioned toward the living room.

Erin sailed into the kitchen, still in her jammies, and hugged her dad. "Hi Daddy! Hi Micki!"

"Good morning, punkin!" he greeted her with a noisy kiss. "You're up early."

"How'd you sleep, sweetie?" Michaela asked.

"I slept pretty well. And I had a fantastic dream!" she said, going to hug her stepmother. "I dreamed I was flying. I wasn't going much of anywhere; I was just hovering over the back yard and I watched Mandy playing on the swings. But it was so awesome!"

"That sounds like fun," Michaela enthused. "Come to think of it, I used to have flying dreams, too, when I was your age."

"Really?"

"Yeah. I understand they're pretty common among

girls; I don't know about boys, though. Gary, did you ever have dreams about flying when you were a kid?"

He shook his head. "Not that I can remember."

Micki turned back to Erin. "Do you want pancakes for breakfast?"

The little girl thought about it for a moment, then shook her head. "Nah." Her eyes gleamed as she looked from one of them to the other. "Can I have a peanut butter and banana sandwich?"

"I don't see why not," Gary replied with a shrug. "In fact, that sounds good to me, too. How about you, Mick?"

Micki was already reaching for the peanut butter from the cupboard. "Better make that three," she said. "But you know what? We should probably have them before Mandy gets up. The doctor wants her to get more protein – and we won't be able to get her to eat a plate of scrambled eggs if the rest of us are devouring peanut-butter sandwiches."

Gary was about to say he didn't know anything about that decree from the doctor – and anyway, didn't peanut butter have plenty of protein? But a look from Michaela stopped him. "Good idea, honey. Always thinking."

As the three of them sat at the kitchen table, eating their sandwiches, Erin asked whether Uncle Marc and Auntie Marie would be coming by to pick up Oscar that weekend.

Gary and Michaela exchanged a glance. Michaela raised an eyebrow, indicating that was her husband's ready-made opening to begin the conversation.

"Not this weekend, hon," Gary said. "Oscar's going to be with us a while longer. But ya know what? There's something we wanted to talk to you about. It's about Uncle Marc and Auntie Marie."

She looked up at her father, her expression turning fearful. "They didn't break up, did they?" Her lower lip trembled. A bit of banana quivered there.

Michaela reached over and dabbed at it with a napkin. "No, sweetie. Nothing like that."

"Just the opposite, actually," Gary continued. "You know how they're planning to get married in September?" He waited for her nod. "Well, they decided they didn't want to wait. So they got married earlier this week – just a small ceremony with the two of th—"

Her eyes widened. "They eloped?"

Gary looked startled. "How do you know about elopement?"

She sighed. "Daddy, I'm almost eleven," she said in a matter-of-fact tone. "And I read. Give me some credit, huh?"

Michaela bit back a giggle.

Erin clasped her hands to her heart. "Ohh! That's so romantical! When did they elope?"

"Tuesday."

Her dreamy expression morphed to disbelief. "So you waited 'til now to tell me?"

"Well, there's more," Michaela added.

Erin's eyes bulged and her mouth dropped open. "Is Auntie Marie pregnant?"

"No!" they blurted in unison.

"Then what?"

"There was..." Gary wasn't sure how to word it. "Let me start by saying everything turned out okay. You with me so far?"

The little girl nodded, beginning to look worried.

"Auntie Marie and Uncle Marc are fine," he reiterated. "Remember that. Everyone's fine."

She sighed again. "Daddy! I get it. Auntie Marie's fine. Uncle Marc's fine. Oscar's fine. I'm fine. You're fine. Micki's fine. Everybody's terrific. Would you get on with it? I'm growing old here."

This time, Michaela couldn't suppress her mirth.

Erin looked at her. "Well, I *am*. For someone who makes a living communicating, he's sure having a hard time getting a sentence out." She looked at her dad with a beleaguered expression on her face. "Would you *pleeeease* just tell me already?"

Micki shrugged in agreement. "She's got a point, hon. Spit it out."

"You're both gonna gang up on me?" Gary gave an exaggerated sigh. "Alright... Uncle Marc has family in Portugal, so Auntie Marie figured it'd be a nice surprise to go there for their honeymoon."

Erin beamed. "That Auntie Marie! She's so sweet!" She took another bite of her sandwich, grinning as she chewed.

He smiled. "She sure is. But here's where it gets a little dicey."

Erin's look of delight shifted back to one of worry. She forced herself to swallow a half-chewed lump of sandwich. "Daddy, you're starting to frighten me. What happened to 'everybody's fine'?" Her lower lip quivered. She looked to Michaela for reassurance.

Micki stroked the little girl's hair. "It's okay. Everything really did turn out okay. Uncle Marc and Auntie Marie are both fine."

"So what happened?" Erin gripped her napkin in one fist and tried her best to be brave.

"There was a bad man on the plane with a gun."

The sandwich fell from Erin's hand. Tears sprang to her eyes. "Did they get shot?"

"Don't get ahead of me," Gary said. "When Uncle Marc was your age, his best friend's dad taught him how to handle firearms, in case he was ever in a situation where there was a gun around."

Erin's tears threatened to spill over. "Did he get shot?"

"I'm getting to that."

She thumped a fist on the table. "Did he get shot?" she asked again, fiercely.

"Yes," Micki replied. "But he wasn't hurt too seriously."

Erin turned her fearful gaze from Micki to her dad. One tear after another slid down her cheek. She braced herself for the news. "What happened?"

"Uncle Marc tried to get the gun away from the bad guy. But in the struggle, it went off. The bullet went through Uncle Marc's arm – right about here." Gary indicated on Erin's arm the place where the bullet struck. "It took half a second. In and out. Uncle Marc told me if you're going to get shot, that's about the best way it can happen."

"What happened then?" Erin blinked away tears. Her face looked like it was crumpling.

Gary gave his daughter a hug. "Auntie Marie used a tourniquet – do you know what that is?"

Wiping at her tears, she sniffled and shook her head. "I don't think so."

"It's a tight band they put on an arm or leg to stop a wound from bleeding," he explained. "Auntie Marie put one on Uncle Marc's arm 'til they were able to get him to a hospital."

"Where'd she get it?"

"It was in the first-aid kit they had on the airplane."

She blinked slowly as she absorbed this information. "Was there a first-aid kit on the plane Grandma, Grandpa and I took to Ohio?"

Gary nodded, his expression serious. "I'm sure there was."

"Are you sure Uncle Marc is okay?" Erin's tears spilled over again. "Absolutely for-real *sure?*"

He wiped them away. "I'm positive, honey. He told me so himself. And he asked me to tell you not to worry. As soon as the plane landed, they took him to the hospital. Auntie Marie was there with him. The only time she wasn't right beside Uncle Marc was when they took him in for surgery to fix his arm."

Her little brow furrowed. "Why did he have to have surgery?"

"They had to stop the bleeding and fix the artery that got hit, then close up the bullet holes."

"Bullet holes? There was more than one?"

Micki stroked Erin's hair. "The bullet went in the front

of his arm and out the back, so there were two wounds. But the surgeons took good care of him and he'll be fine."

"Is Auntie Marie okay?"

"Daddy talked to her, too. She was scared – and worried for Uncle Marc – but she's fine."

"So what happened to the bad guy with the gun? Did Uncle Marc beat him up?" Erin asked, a hopeful glint in her eyes.

"Not exactly."

"Auntie Marie beat him up?"

Gary tweaked her nose. "No, silly. No one beat him up. But he didn't get away – and he didn't get out of it unhurt, either."

"Good!" A sudden smile brightened her face. "What happened to him?"

"He wasn't holding the gun right. So when it went off, he ended up hurting his thumb."

"That's all? He hurt his thumb?" Erin spat out with disgust. "Uncle Marc gets shot and the bad guy just hurt his *thumb?!* How is that even fair?" she wailed.

"From what Auntie Marie said, it was a pretty bad injury. He was bleeding a lot from that little wound, and he was in a whole lot of pain."

Erin folded her arms and made the fiercest expression she could. "Good!"

Because now was not the time for a discussion about enjoying others' misfortune, Gary let his daughter's exclamation stand.

"But that's not the end of the story." Michaela reached for the folded newspaper.

Erin turned worried eyes toward her stepmother. "Oh, no! What else?" she moaned.

"This is where it gets good," Dad assured her, patting her arm. "You'll want to hear this."

The enthusiasm in his voice piqued Erin's interest. Her expression brightened. "What is it?"

"Uncle Marc" – Michaela unfolded the newspaper and

handed it to her – "is a hero."

The girl's eyes widened. "For real?"

"Yup. For real. They even met the president of Portugal. And he honored Uncle Marc with a really big award. He knighted him."

"You mean like in chess? He gets to ride a horse now? And carry a sword? How cool!"

Gary couldn't repress his grin. "He's not that kind of knight, punkin. But they had an official ceremony yesterday and he was given a medal." He paused. "You know how the Cowardly Lion in *The Wizard of Oz* was awarded a medal for courage?"

Erin nodded. "Uh huh."

"Sort of like that. Uncle Marc was awarded a medal for bravery, and they made him a knight. I don't know how to explain that, exactly. We don't have knights here in the U.S."

"Oh!" Erin's eyes lit up with comprehension. "Like the knights in *Bedknobs and Broomsticks*?"

"Yes… well, except he doesn't have a suit of armor."

"That's okay," she said with a confident nod. "He's Auntie Marie's knight in shining armor."

A broad smile overtook Gary's face. "You could say that."

Erin sighed with pleasure. "That's so romantical!" She scrambled to her feet, clutching the paper to herself. "Can I keep this?"

"Of course you can."

"Thanks, Daddy!" Erin hugged him, then scampered upstairs to savor her new treasure.

Chapter 15

(12:02 p.m. Western European Time, Saturday)
"Hi, Doc. It's Marc Lindemeyr," he said at the beep. "I've run into a situation here and I was hoping I could talk with you." He gave her the phone number for the hotel and included both the country code and their suite number, then added, "Of course, I'll reimburse you for the phone bill."

To his surprise, Dr. Merino called back twenty minutes later.

"Hi, Marc." The therapist's lilting Mediterranean voice was a soothing balm. "I wasn't expecting to hear from you. How can I help?"

"Well, I didn't expect to have to bother you from halfway around the world," he admitted sheepishly, "especially on a weekend – so I guess that kinda makes us even."

When she realized who was on the phone, Marie made a discreet exit, saying she was going to go read in the lobby for awhile because the lighting was better down there.

Marc nodded. She could have said she was going out to hunt water buffalo; he understood she was leaving so he could speak freely with his therapist.

"Before we start," Dr. Merino said, "I understand congratulations are in order."

His shoulders drooped. "Please," he implored, sounding defeated. "Not you, too."

"I meant on your nuptials," she clarified. "I nearly let something slip at our last session."

"You knew about it then?"

"Just about the trip to Portugal. She told me about that in April. Why else do you suppose I would have renewed your prescription in June?"

"She was planning it back then?"

"Oh yeah. Devious little wife you got there, Marc."

He scratched the side of his nose and sighed. "You got that right."

After a brief pause, the therapist asked, "What's going on?"

"I'm guessing you probably heard what happened on our flight."

"I did. It seems you've managed to make quite a name for yourself."

"That's an understatement. So much for running off to a foreign country for some peace and quiet," he said, sinking into the chair by the phone. "I can't go anywhere now without someone recognizing me – and wanting to thank me for saving the life of someone they know. I can't even be anonymous in our hotel. When we got here, the bellhops argued over who got to carry our bags to our suite. Folks have even started calling me the Hero of Flight Seven Twenty over here."

"They're calling you that around here, too."

Marc groaned. "It's starting to get unnerving, and I don't know how to deal with it."

"Sounds like you can't avoid it – unless you want to spend the next two weeks holed up in your suite. Or wearing a wig and dark glasses. How've you been handling the sudden fame thus far?"

"Mostly I've been dreading it."

"Okay, but when it happens, Marc, what do you do?"

"Usually I smile and say, 'thank you.' What else can I say?"

"What, indeed?"

Marc hated it when she asked that. "Don't start that again."

"I'm serious, Marc. How else might you respond that wouldn't seem off-putting?"

"I've tried downplaying it – but that hasn't worked. Now I just sort of let them gush. I even got asked for an autograph this morning."

"You did?" Dr. Merino gave a little laugh. "Well, that *is* unusual. I hope you obliged."

"It was a little kid. How could I not? Apparently an elderly neighbor she's really close to was on the flight. Then her mom asked if she could take a picture of me with her daughter – Fátima was her name. What, was I gonna refuse? Afterward, she gave me a hug and a kiss and said, 'Thank you, Mister Hero, for saving my friend's life.' " His voice trembled a bit toward the end.

"That had to be something."

"It almost made me cry," he admitted, blinking away a mist of tears. "In fact, I'm kinda getting all teary now, just thinking about it."

He could practically hear the smile in his therapist's voice. "You're a tender soul, Marc. I'd be concerned if you didn't get emotional over that."

"I suppose. But, you see, Fátima was the exception. She was just a little girl. Saying yes to her was easy. And in her eyes, I guess I did seem like a hero. And I didn't mind posing for the picture – I honestly didn't. Or signing an autograph. But what I really need is some kind of coping mechanism to help me deal with the rest of them – with the grownups who approach me and fawn all over me."

"I see. Let me ask you something. For the picture, how did you pose with Fátima?"

Marc paused to think. "I crouched down next to her and she had her arm around me."

"So you got down to meet her on her level."

"Yeah." He wondered where this was going.

"Marc, you're doing fine."

He didn't understand – and said as much.

"Don't you see? You're being realistic about this. You're,

literally, down to earth with regard to your response. You met Fátima on her level, and she was comfortable enough relating to you that she put an arm around you. That's huge, Marc! That made you so real, so approachable, to her."

"I didn't want to be towering over her. That's just not good photography. I'm not a giant or anything, but she was just a little kid. It's how I would've posed for a picture with one of my nieces."

"Exactly. You were welcoming and human to her. You did exactly the right thing, Marc. You were someone she felt comfortable relating to," the therapist praised him. Then she shifted gears. "You said something else that's important. You said you want to develop a 'coping mechanism' for when you get approached by adults. That's so proactive, Marc. And I think your response to Fátima this morning holds the answer you're looking for: Just be human. Relate to people as they are."

Marc thought about that. "That makes sense."

"Let me ask you this: How do you envision someone you admire might respond to a set of awkward circumstances such as this, like the situations you've been finding yourself in?"

"I… I don't really know," he replied truthfully.

"Take a minute to think about it. Think about someone you admire. How would that person have handled being in the kind of spotlight you've found yourself thrust into?"

Marc pondered her question. His eyes narrowed as he thought. "I don't know who I could think of who might even fit that description," he admitted.

Dr. Merino tapped a fingernail against the receiver. "What about Edward Sheldon? You told me when you met him, you felt more or less star struck, and you were particularly effusive with your admiration. How did he respond to that?"

Marc thought back eighteen-plus years to a November morning, after the career-day assembly at Danbury High, when he'd shown his drawings to the noted New Haven architect. The man had been kind to the high-school sophomore, and even invited the teen to come in to spend a day at his design office, shadowing him, during Christmas break.

He smiled at the fond recollection. "He was... gracious. That distinguished, well-respected, prominent architect was perfectly gracious to a gawky teenage kid who was nothing less than captivated by his work."

Marc was sure he could hear the therapist's smile. "Excellent," she praised him. "Good job, Marc. Now, would it be fair to say you would strive to emulate him?"

The question caught him off guard. "I suppose."

"Might it not be too much to ask that you summon your inner Edward Sheldon next time someone approaches you in public, and thanks you for your heroism?"

Marc took a deep breath. He looked down at Edward Sheldon's gold wedding band on his left hand. Its presence imbued him with a sense of calm. He smiled. "I guess not."

"See that, Marc? When you look at things from a different perspective, you gain new insights on them. Less than half an hour ago, you had no concept of how to handle the sudden – and, to a degree, unwelcome – honor of being Portugal's newest hero. And now, given a bit of distance, and somewhat of a different outlook, you have a viable coping mechanism in your toolbox."

"Yeah, but you did that."

"I disagree. All I did was ask you the right questions, to lead you to where you needed to be. You did all the work. That was all you."

Although he knew she couldn't see him, he nodded.

"So when someone you don't know approaches you in a public market, a restaurant or even at the beach, and says, 'Thank you for saving my sister-in-law's cousin's veterinarian's older brother's neighbor's best friend,' you can look them in the eye and graciously accept their thanks. And then perhaps even say... what?"

Marc struggled for words. "Umm..." He shot a hand

through his hair. "I... I don't have the slightest idea. I honestly don't know what to say. That's part of what's so awful – I mean, it'd be one thing if I could respond with something – *anything* – even halfway articulate. But I can't even think of something that would come close to being appropriate in a situation like this."

"Why's that, do you think?" she prompted.

An awkward silence stretched across the phone line.

"Because I don't feel like the hero everyone's making me out to be," he confessed. "I feel like a fraud. An imposter, even." Having made that admission, he felt like he could breathe again.

"Okay, this is good. Why do you say you feel like a fraud or an imposter?"

"I didn't do anything for that planeload of people. Not a damn thing. I didn't care about them. I wasn't thinking about two hundred twenty other people at the time. All I did was try to stop some guy pointing a gun at my wife. Hell, anyone would've done that. I did nothing heroic. If anything, it was purely selfish on my part – I didn't want to lose her. Period. End of discussion."

"Hmm. Okay. Thank you for sharing that. Let me see if I understand what you're feeling here. The way I understood what you said just now, because you had one set of motivations, that should necessarily discount or negate the outcome entirely?"

"I... I don't know," he replied a little too quickly.

"Marc," she chided. "You know that's not an acceptable response. So I'm going to pose the question again: Are you saying because you envisioned a particular outcome – of not wanting to lose your bride – that, in itself, dismisses any greater good that might have resulted from your actions?"

Taking a shaky breath, he gripped the phone. "Yeah."

"What if I said you were wrong?"

He felt his spine stiffen as his frustration mounted. "Then I can choose not to believe you."

"Why? Are you that bent on punishing yourself for

what you think you did?"

"What do you mean?"

"Because you admit your intent was to protect your wife, does that mean you shouldn't have been honored or recognized for your actions' also having saved two hundred twenty other people?"

He crumbled a bit inside. "I – I guess not."

"Why?"

Marc let out a sigh of frustration. "Why what?"

"Why do you guess not?"

He got up and began to pace. "Look, I'm agreeing with you. Isn't that enough? Can't we just leave it at that?"

"Do you want to leave it at that?"

"Yes." He raked a hand through his hair. "As a matter of fact, I do."

"You seem pretty sure of that."

His words were clipped. "I am."

"Fair enough. In that case, we can leave it at this: You acknowledge that knighthood – being honored for saving the lives of two hundred twenty people – is something you'll publicly accept, although you admit you intended only to protect the life of one of those people?"

He stopped pacing. "What's wrong with that?"

"Don't get defensive," she soothed. "I was only trying to clarify things."

Silence hummed across the phone line for several seconds.

"Sounds kind of selfish, huh?" Marc reflected.

"Little bit. What do you want to do about that?"

"Maybe give it some more thought?"

"Are you asking me or telling me?"

"Telling you."

"Good. Let's hear some of that thought process. Walk me through it."

"Okay. Just because my attention was focused on saving Marie, it doesn't negate the fact I thwarted a gunman who could also have potentially harmed everyone else on board."

"And?" she prompted.

"And it's normal for people to want to express gratitude for that."

"And?"

"Eventually the novelty will wear off, folks will return to their lives and I can fade into the background and go back to being plain old ordinary Marc Lindemeyr."

"And in the meantime, when someone thanks you for your heroism, then what?"

"I look them in the eye and say, 'I'm glad I was in a position to help.'"

"There you go! I knew you'd come up with something appropriate."

During a long silence, Marc pondered another niggling issue. "There's something else," he admitted at last.

"What's that?" Dr. Merino asked.

"Marie refuses to acknowledge her role in all this."

"What role is that?"

"The part where she offered herself up in place of the original hostage."

"What?" Marc could almost see her eyes bugging out in alarm.

"The guy had a stewardess at gunpoint and demanded entry to the cockpit. Marie talked him into letting her go, and she took her place. But no one's talking about that. Especially her. I tried to tell the president, but he didn't listen. What I told you before is true: I just wanted to save my wife."

Dr. Merino was silent for a long moment, probably absorbing this new information. "I see. Does that change things?"

"You bet it does!"

"How?"

"Now I really feel like a fraud — like I'm taking credit for something I didn't do."

"Have you considered that maybe she doesn't want the accolades? That she's deliberately sidestepping the attention?"

The question took Marc aback. "N-no. I hadn't thought about it that way."

"Perhaps she's content to let you be in the limelight, because you're already a public figure. Maybe she's uncomfortable with being in the spotlight, or she feels she was just doing what she was trained to do. But you, on the other hand, stepped up to do something well outside your realm. You might want to talk with her about that."

"Yeah. Maybe I'll do that. If she seems open to it."

"Good. Now... how are you dealing with the psychological effects of being shot?"

Marc played dumb. "What psychological effects?"

"The underlying issues. If they aren't surfacing yet, they will. And when they do, it won't be pretty. Or easy. There's likely to be paralyzing fear, anger – perhaps rage. Possibly even flashbacks... and for sure, nightmares. I don't want you to be blindsided by them."

"I'm fine," he assured her. He swallowed hard. There had been that one nightmare...

"Really, Marc? I've worked with plenty of gunshot victims over the years. I'm familiar with what to expect. You can deny it all you want, but you can't ignore the reality for long. Just know that."

He sighed aloud. "Fine. Can we talk about something else now?"

"I understand you don't want to talk about this, but it's critical for your mental health and your emotional stability. As your therapist, I would be remiss if I didn't bring it up."

His fist clenched around the receiver. "I appreciate that. But I told you, I'm fine."

"I know what you told me. All I'm saying is be aware of your feelings. You've been through a tremendous trauma – from seeing a man holding a gun on your wife to trying to get it away from him and getting shot yourself. That's a lot to deal with, emotionally. I want you to realize you don't need to go through that alone. There's no need for heroics here."

He smirked at her last sentence. "Interesting choice of words."

"You know what I meant. There's no reason for you to carry the emotional load by yourself. It's not going to do you any good to try. You'll be far better off to leave the strong silent guy stuff by the wayside and admit you may need help dealing with your emotions. There's no shame in that. Okay?"

"I suppose."

"When things start to come apart, give me a call. I promise I won't even say 'I told you so.' "

Although he knew she couldn't see him, he nodded. "Okay. I appreciate that. Thanks, doc."

"It's what I'm here for. In fact, why don't we schedule you now for ten a.m. on Monday, August second."

Marc jotted the date down on the notepad supplied by the hotel and stuck the sheet into his wallet. "Ten a.m. Sounds good."

"And if something should crop up in the meantime, give me a call and I'll clear some time for you."

He knew she meant the nightmares. "I promise, if something happens, you'll be the first one I call."

"Good. Now go enjoy the rest of your honeymoon — tell that wife of yours I said hi, and be sure to have some *pastéis de Belém* for me."

Marc grinned. "Will do. And you don't have to tell me twice. Those things are amazing!"

(3:27 a.m. Western European Time, Tuesday, July 13)

Marie's screams awakened Marc.

Adrenaline pulsed through him. "*Querida!*" He snapped on the bedside lamp, then shook his sleeping wife's shoulder. "Wake up!"

With a gasp, she opened her eyes. She looked about the suddenly bright but still-unfamiliar room.

"It's okay," he comforted her, instinctively draping his arm around her. He winced as she clung to his injured bicep. "It was a bad dream. You're okay."

As Marie listened to her husband's soothing voice, her terror ebbed. She sat up in bed and clasped her arms around her knees.

Recognizing her self-comforting gesture, he sat up and rubbed her shoulder. "Do you want to tell me about it?"

She rocked back and forth, and for a moment Marc thought she hadn't heard his question. "I don't know," she replied at last, in a tiny voice.

He didn't have to ask to know she'd seen the hijacker again; he'd haunted her dreams the past three nights. The fear in her eyes told Marc what she couldn't bring herself to articulate.

He almost wished he'd admitted to Dr. Merino he'd begun having nightmares, so he'd have had a frame of reference, some way to approach helping Marie through her nightmares. Dr. Merino could have helped to walk him through them – and he could have helped Marie. For now, he'd have to rely on his instincts to comfort her.

Disregarding his own pain, he wrapped both arms around his trembling wife and gathered her close, in what was becoming a familiar routine. He laid her head against his chest and smoothed her sleep-mussed curls. "Shh," he comforted her. "You're safe, sweetheart. Everything's fine now."

Marie cuddled close to him. "I keep seeing him," she whimpered.

He snugged his arms around his wife, trying to ignore the pain shooting from the still-tender bullet wounds. "I know."

"And it scares me."

"Of course it does. It was a terrifying experience. But you stayed calm and you did everything you were supposed to do – and you're safe now. He can't hurt you."

"But it seemed so real," she insisted, a little warble in her voice.

"It's okay, honey. It's over. It was a bad dream. That's

all."

"I know. And I know I shouldn't let it bother me," she said, still clinging to Marc, "but I saw his eyes... and they felt so real, staring through me."

Little by little, the tension left her, and gradually her breathing returned to normal. Her heart stopped clattering so terribly and she drooped wearily against her husband.

"You must be exhausted," he murmured into her hair. "You haven't had a decent night's sleep since we left home."

Marie looked up at him, her eyes glistening with tears. "I'm so sorry I keep waking you up."

"Hey..." Marc stroked her cheek. "Don't you worry about that. Alright?"

She nodded.

"Think you can go back to sleep now?"

Another nod. "Mm-hmm."

Marc planted a kiss on Marie's forehead. "Let's keep those bad dreams to a minimum, huh?"

Marie rewarded him with a brave smile. "I'll try."

A grin crinkled the lines around his eyes. "Do or do not. There is no try," he intoned, in a dreadful imitation of Yoda.

She balled up a fist and gave him a playful punch in the chest. "Oh, you and that darn Star Trek creature!"

"Star Wars," he corrected.

"Whatever," she grumbled.

"Well? Am I wrong?"

"No," she replied grudgingly.

He shrugged. "So what's the problem?"

Marie smiled and shook her head. "No problem," she said with a sigh, resting against him.

"Hey," he said after a minute had passed and she still showed no signs of attempting to go back to sleep. He poked her in the shoulder. "Get back on your side of the bed, woman."

She looked up at him in mock surprise. "What?"

"You heard me, woman. Quit encroaching." Now he

gave her a playful nudge. "Move it!"

"Excuse me? I'll have you know, bub, I was not encroaching."

Feigning pique, he put on a stern expression. "You most certainly are, madam. You're encroaching on my side of the bed, you... you damn interloper."

Marie suppressed a giggle. Teasing indignation surfaced in her voice. "Interloper, am I? Well, we'll just see about that next time you come nosing around here, wanting sex."

"Oh yeah? Is that how it's going to be?"

She tousled his hair. "Yeah. That's how it's going to be. And what do you say to that?"

He leaned in and kissed her – a slow, sensuous kiss that left her breathless. "I say, don't start something you don't intend to finish."

"That's mighty big talk for a guy who needs help cutting his food," Marie replied saucily. She bit her lower lip and fixed him with a smoldering gaze.

Marc turned toward her. "Ohh... Now you've gone too far, woman." He pushed her back against the pillows. "We'll just see about that." Paying no heed to the pain in his arm, he clambered atop her and nudged her legs apart. He grimaced as he put weight on his right hand.

"Wait – wait!" Marie cried out as she saw him flinch. "Don't hurt yourself." She struggled to a sitting position, then pushed Marc onto his back, where he lay like an upended turtle. She climbed on top of him and took control.

After they were both sated and Marie rolled off him, panting, Marc gazed at his wife with a drowsy smile. "You're an animal."

A languid smile crossed her face, as though he'd just given her the best compliment ever. "I know," she replied with a purr.

His voice wavered. "Are you disappointed?"

"About what?"

Marc gestured feebly with his good hand. "That I

couldn't..." he broke off, uneasy.

She rested her chin atop her folded hands on his chest. "Do I look disappointed to you?"

"Now that you put it that way... not exactly."

"Then what's the problem?"

"I dunno. I just thought by now I'd be able to – you know..."

"Give it the ol' college try?" Marie finished for him.

He shrugged. "Well, yeah. I guess."

She grinned in triumph. "What happened to 'Do or do not. There is no "try" '?"

Marc's throaty chuckle acknowledged his defeat. "Guess you got me there."

"You hate it when I turn your words around on you, don't you?"

He shook his head. "Ahh, go to sleep, ya damn interloper," he muttered. "And get back on your side of the bed."

Marie scooted away in compliance with his wishes. She straightened the covers and lay down again. "Hey," she warned in her fiercest voice, "don't make me come back over there and screw the daylights out of you again."

Marc turned out the light with a quiet, "Hmmph!" and grumbled, "Promises, promises."

Chapter 16

(8:45 a.m., Tuesday, July 13)

Hunger nudged Marie from her sleep. She yawned and stretched hugely, then rolled over and draped an arm across Marc's bare torso as he slept. She crept closer and nuzzled his throat, kissing him awake.

He opened his eyes and smiled. "Hi."

She met his gaze and smiled back. "Good morning."

Marc reached up with one hand to caress her cheek. "How'd you sleep?"

Marie's smile grew as she recalled the remedy for her bad dream. "I slept fine. How about you?"

"I had the strangest dream. I was accosted in the middle of the night by a verbally abusive shrew who threw me on the bed and had her way with me."

"Ohh..." She stretched forward and kissed his mouth, long and slow. She ran her hands through his hair. "You poor thing. How you must have suffered."

"It was pretty terrible," he agreed. "Then she had the nerve to threaten me with 'more where that came from.' Can you believe the nerve of that woman?"

"I don't know how you tolerate such abuse." Marie kissed him again. "My poor darling."

"With any luck, I'll have that dream again so I can build up my resistance. Or a tolerance for it." A corner of his mouth twitched upward in a playful grin.

"I see." Marie sat up abruptly and planted a quick kiss on his lips. "Well, while you drift back off to dreamland to do battle with your evil wench, I'm in dreadful need of a shower."

"I couldn't agree more."

"Hey!" She shot him a caustic look. "You're startin' to get a little aromatic yourself, pal."

"I know. I can hardly stand myself. But it's hard to shower without getting all this bandaging wet."

"I guess you'll have to rely on that horrible woman, then – and hope she doesn't decide to take advantage of you while you're all soapy and totally at her mercy."

"That would make for quite an ordeal."

Marie grinned wickedly. "It sure would."

Marc threw back the covers and bolted from the bed. "Race you to the shower."

After they showered and made love again, Marie changed the dressings on Marc's wounds.

"Looks like it's healing well," she said as she inspected and cleaned the exit wound, applied a fresh dressing and affixed a new bandage. "How's it feel?"

"Like it's tightening at the edges."

She nodded. "That means it's healing."

"I thought itching meant healing."

"It does."

"Make up your mind. Which is it? Itching or tightening?"

She gave him a smile tolerant of his playful questioning. "They're both part of the healing process." Now she set about changing the dressing on the other wound.

"So, is that normal?"

"Yes. They're just different signs of healing. You'll get used to it."

"Wow, no sympathy from you at all, huh?"

Marie grinned. "I'm afraid not."

"How much longer, do you think, before I'll be able to resume… shall we say, 'customary honeymoon activities'?"

"I had a feeling you were gonna ask that. You don't

want to risk doing anything that would cause pain or further injury – like last night," she said with a hint of chiding in her voice, "but then again, you also don't want to let the muscle atrophy, so it's a good idea to give it some exercise."

"What would you recommend?"

Marie winked. "Sex. Plenty of it. And as often as possible."

After breakfast at the *pastelaria*, Marc called his grandmother.

"*Bom dia, Avó Madalena. É seu neto, Marcos.*"

Marie listened to the rhythm of his voice as he spoke his grandmother's native language.

They talked for a few minutes, gentle laughter sporadically punctuating his words. From time to time Marc would look up and meet Marie's gaze. At those moments, he'd break into a smile.

Through his hesitant cadence as he faltered with his less-than-fluent command of the foreign language, Marie managed to pick up translations of a few of Marc's words as they spoke. From the gist of his half of the conversation, she gathered they'd be going to visit her tomorrow afternoon.

Just before two the following day, Avó Madalena welcomed her grandson and his bride into her home. She kissed the two of them on both cheeks and pulled them into her cozy little home, chattering excitedly.

Marc did his best to translate the old woman's rapid-fire Portuguese for his bewildered wife, but only managed to interpret every other sentence or so.

The aroma of strong espresso permeated the house. Avó Madalena ushered her guests into the kitchen to sit and have refreshments. "*Marcos, Marie, sente-se! Conte-me tudo,*" she commanded.

Marc turned to Marie. "She said, 'Sit! Tell me everything,' " he translated.

He explained how they'd eloped a week ago, at which

the woman gave a brief expression of displeasure – until Marc assured her they were still planning to have the big church wedding in eight weeks' time.

Now she smiled, a broad gap-toothed grin that brightened her entire countenance. She patted their hands and nodded her approval.

As Marc explained about the drive to New York to catch their flight, Avó laughed and laughed at his retelling of Marie's ruse about going away for a business trip.

"*Menina inteligente*," she remarked, nodding and tapping an arthritic forefinger to her temple.

"She says you're a clever girl," he translated, although Marie had already surmised what it meant.

His grandmother's eyes filled with tears and her hand flew to her mouth as he explained the basics of their ordeal with the gunman.

"*Estou bem, Avó.*" 'I'm fine, Grandma,' he told her. "*Estou bem.*"

When he got to the part about being summoned to the presidential palace, his grandmother's eyes grew big and round in amazement. Her proud smile widened, pushing her rosy cheeks upward, almost to the point where they forced her deep brown eyes into narrow slits.

She asked him what meeting the president was like and what he'd thought of the palace.

Marc assured her the president and the first lady were lovely, gracious people, and he and Marie had been treated quite well. He reached into his pocket and pulled forth the blue leather box with his medals inside. Opening it, he removed the enameled cross on its broad ribbon and handed it to his grandmother for inspection.

Her smile grew even wider than it was when she greeted them at her doorstep. Now, instead of being an expression of delight, it was a reflection of utmost pride. She beamed at her grandson and patted his cheek. Then she turned to Marie. "*Estou tão orgulhosa dele.*"

Marie shook her head. "I'm sorry. What?" She looked at

Marc, seeking interpretation.

A slight pink hue tinged his cheeks. "She said she's proud of me."

Marie smiled. "Well, I should hope so!"

The old woman smiled as Marc translated his wife's reply.

When Avó Madalena asked how long the two would be staying in the country, and Marc said they'd be leaving the middle of next week, she insisted they come back Sunday for a celebration with the whole family.

"*Toda a família?*" he asked. "*Quantas são?*"

The old woman shrugged. "*Vinte e dois.*"

"Twenty-two?!" Marc squawked. He wiped his good hand down his face. "*Algum deles fala inglês?*" He turned to Marie. "She wants us to come back Sunday for a 'little party' with twenty-two of my relatives. I just asked her if any of them speak English."

The old woman gave a slight shrug and an indefinite hand gesture. "*Alguns deles.*"

"Some of them. Great." Wearing an expression of hopelessness, he turned to Marie. "I don't want you trapped for a whole afternoon with two dozen people whose only English is 'Can you tell me when the bus is due?' 'Where's the bathroom?' and 'Sylvia is at the pool.' That's not fair to do to you."

Marie laid a reassuring hand on his arm. "It's okay. They're your family, and it's only for one afternoon. It'll be fine – especially since a lot of them can't get to the States for the wedding... right?"

Marc's expression eased. "You've got a point." He squeezed her hand. "Thank you. This is going to mean so much to them."

Sunday morning, the concierge summoned a taxi for the Americans, so they could attend early Mass at *Igreja de Santo António de Lisboa*. St Anthony of Lisbon was the church closest to Marc's grandmother's house. After Mass, they walked to a neighborhood café, for a light breakfast.

"We're not going to want more than coffee and maybe a pastry," Marc cautioned, glancing at his watch. It was just after 9:30. "If I know my grandmother, she's preparing a feast – so we'd better show up there plenty hungry."

"What time are we due?"

"She said around one, so we can enjoy some quiet before the familial onslaught."

Marie laughed. "Oh, Marc – it won't be that bad!"

"You just wait."

After breakfast, they strolled along the Tagus River, watching the waterfowl fishing, diving and squabbling along the shoreline.

"What kind of bird is that?" Marie asked, pointing toward the river.

Reaching out, Marc lowered her pointing finger to her side. "Don't," he cautioned. "You're not supposed to point in Portugal. Not even at birds. It's really rude."

Marie's mouth rounded into a silent O. Blanching, she put a hand to her mouth. "I'm sorry. I didn't know."

"I figured," he replied gently. "That's why I told you."

He turned to face the direction toward which she'd pointed. "Now, which bird is it you were asking about?"

She motioned with her head toward the river. "That white one, on that flat rock over there."

Marc squinted. "Hmm... if I had to guess, I'd say it's some sort of water bird."

Marie pursed her lips. "Gee, that was helpful. Thanks."

"Any time. Glad to be of service, ma'am."

As they turned to continue walking, Marc slid his arm around her. "Actually, I think it's some species of egret."

"An egret?"

"They're a common water bird. C'mon, you must know about egrets. Frank Sinatra even sang about them. I think he might have even had some."

"Sinatra? Had egrets?" She poised a hand on her hip. "You're making that up."

His expression was serious and Marie couldn't quite tell whether he was pulling her leg. He shook his head. "I am not making that up. I swear. He really did – in the song 'My Way.' Listen." He began to sing, "Egrets, I've had a few, but then agai—"

Groaning aloud, Marie elbowed him in the ribs. "Why do I listen to you?"

"Because apparently you've mistaken me for some kind of authority on Portuguese waterfowl." A grin overtook his face. "C'mon, woman, give a guy a break, huh?"

"Ohh... you're lucky I like you," she grumbled, linking her arm in his.

"You gotta admit, though, it was pretty funny."

"I don't have to do anything of the sort."

"Fine. Be an old poop, then." Marc stuck his tongue out at her. "I thought it was funny."

"Oh, so pointing is rude but it's fine to stick out your tongue at someone? Good to know."

"It's not, actually. It's the height of rudeness. Even worse than pointing. And I fully expect to be drawn and quartered in the public square at noon on Tuesday."

"Why wait 'til Tuesday? Why not do it tomorrow?"

"They can't. There's a municipal regulation against drawing and quartering on Mondays."

"Seriously?"

"Really? *Really?* You're gonna fall for that? What happened to not listening to me anymore?"

"I didn't expect you to lie to me again – at least not so soon. Besides, it sounded like it could have been plausible."

"Like they'd permit drawing and quartering in the public square any other day but Monday! You crack me up."

Giving a loud squawk of alarm at the sound of Marc's sudden laughter, the egret took off from its perch on the rock, with a pounding thump of its massive wings as it took to the air.

***

When the taxi dropped them at Avó Madalena's little

stone house just after one, Marc and Marie found the road out in front of her home was already jammed with cars. More autos filled the driveway; and still more littered the front and side lawns. Music, conversation and laughter spilled from the open windows, along with faint aromas of roasting pork.

As they made their way, hand in hand, up the walk to the front door, Marie gave Marc a hesitant glance. "Tell me again why I shouldn't be nervous?"

He squeezed her hand. "Don't worry, *querida*. They'll love you."

His smile melted her fears and she gave his hand a return squeeze in acknowledgment. She shifted the bouquet of roses, tulips and angelica they'd bought at the open-air market to her other arm and held tight to Marc's arm as they mounted the stone stairs.

"Do you think she'll like the flowers?" she fretted.

He kissed her on the temple. "Are you kidding? They're from you. She's going to love them. Then again, you could have brought her a handful of dandelions and she'd love them," he reassured her as he gave a firm knock at the door. He barely needed to do that, as their approach had already been noticed from inside.

The door swung open and half a dozen loud relatives surged onto the porch. They engulfed the couple, hugging them and dragging them inside. Marc tried to shield his arm from the jostling of the swelling crowd, but quickly realized he'd have to endure the pain because the jarring wasn't about to let up. He silently thanked the patron saint of pain meds that he'd thought to take a Percocet before they left the hotel.

Marie protected the bouquet of flowers from being squashed as best she could amid all the manhandling and hugging.

Rich aromas filled the little house, aromas every bit as enticing as anything Marie could recall from Carpaccio or *A Pérola Ibérica*.

She recognized Marc's Tio Roberto and Tio Mauricio right away; she'd met them and Avó Madalena at Marc's parents' home last Christmas Eve. They broke into broad grins and rushed her, each of them in turn folding her in a mighty embrace. The only reason any of the others looked the slightest bit familiar was they all rather looked alike, with dark hair, mocha-hued complexions and mahogany eyes. And that became its own problem. Everywhere she looked, it was virtually the same face. Everyone wore different clothing and some of the women sported varied hair lengths and styles, but the faces all looked so similar! There was no way she'd ever keep them all straight.

Marc didn't recognize many of them, either. He had to introduce himself to most of his cousins and other assorted kinfolk before he could properly introduce them to Marie.

At last, amid a great deal of murmuring, the sea of relatives parted to let the matriarch, Avó Madalena, through. The old woman in her simple dark-blue dress with the polka-dotted apron over it tottered over to her American grandson and his bride and hugged them both.

Marie held out the bouquet to Marc's diminutive grandmother. "*Essas flores são para você*," she carefully enunciated the Portuguese words Marc taught her on the way over. These flowers are for you.

Avó Madalena's face erupted into a wide grin and she pulled Marie into a firm embrace.

When she released Marie at last, the old woman tucked the bouquet gently under one arm, then took the newlyweds by the hands and tugged them toward the kitchen, where more family members waited to greet them. The crowd even spilled out onto the back *varanda*.

Marc looked around in a mix of amazement and distress. *Oh my goodness! There's <u>way</u> more than twenty-two people here – there's got to be at least forty!* He introduced each of them in turn to Marie. Even those he was meeting for the second time he hadn't seen in two decades, so he had to explain who he was. Lucky for him, a fair number of these relatives spoke English, so he didn't need to rely quite as heavily as he'd feared on his shabby Portuguese skills.

"Grandma, what did you do?" he asked the old woman in Portuguese.

Smiling, she reached up and patted his cheek. "*Acabei de convidar a família.*" I just invited the family.

"But you said twenty-two," he reminded her in her native language.

She laughed. "*Você teria vindo se eu dissesse cinquenta?*"

Caught off guard, Marc let out a hearty laugh and shook a playfully chiding finger at his wily grandmother, then pinched her pillowy cheek. "*Você não joga limpo, seu patife!*"

The old woman's laughter rang through the kitchen.

"What did she say?" Marie asked, looking startled at both their reactions.

"She asked if I would have come if she'd said there would be fifty."

And what did you say to her?"

"I called her a rascal and told her she didn't play fair."

Avó Madalena delighted in feeding her family. As soon as one baking dish piled with roast pork, stuffed squid or cod emerged from the oven, someone carried it out to the picnic table out back, while another dish took its place in the oven. The pattern repeated itself with assorted crocks of fresh vegetables. Steaming bowls of green beans, roasted peppers and cauliflower emerged from the oven racks to be brought outside.

Throughout the afternoon, Marie enjoyed chatting with several of Marc's cousins while Marc bonded with his uncles and some of the male cousins. Marie found her husband's family captivating, and delighted in the easy conversation they shared. She was grateful when his cousins happily spoke English to work around the language barrier. Even when they slipped occasionally into Portuguese, she still found she was able to pick up a few words here and there.

Whenever Marie caught sight of Marc, he was engaged in animated conversation with one or another of his dozens of relatives, listening intently as someone spoke, or had his head thrown back in laughter. Watching him enjoying the easy camaraderie of his extended family filled her with a kind of warmth she hadn't expected to feel, surrounded by so many foreign language-speaking people she didn't know.

When they returned to their hotel suite late that night, Marie marveled at how much she had enjoyed the day. "I was afraid I'd be the odd man out. But they were so welcoming! They made me feel right at home – like part of the family!"

Her words bubbled with enthusiasm as they undressed for bed. "Your cousin Lorena is fascinating! I could have listened to her talk for hours. What a go-getter! She owns a flower shop in Amadora, and she teaches private painting and flower-arranging classes in her workroom at night."

Marc's smile was warm. "I'm glad you had a good time, *querida*. I was worried you'd hate it. Every time I looked over at you, I half expected to see you glancing at your watch, eyeballing me or giving me the 'let's get out of here' signal."

"That'd be kind of hard to do, especially since we don't have one," she reminded him.

Marc's eyebrows dipped. "That explains a lot. Do we at least have a 'let's go to bed' signal?"

"We do indeed. And this is it. So watch carefully." Grinning, Marie took him by the hand, led him to the bed and turned out the light.

Chapter 17

(8:23 a.m. Western European Time, Tuesday, July 20)
Marie leaned back in her seat and smiled across the table at her beloved before sweeping her gaze beyond the outdoor seating area at their favorite *pastelaria*. "Hard to believe this is our last full day here."

Marc rested his chin in his hand. "I know what you mean," he replied, a smile overtaking his bronzed face. "It still doesn't quite seem real." Despite his half-Nordic heritage, he had been graced with his Portuguese mother's rich olive complexion – and great capacity for tanning.

Marie adjusted her wide-brimmed hat. Although she was half Italian, she had inherited a skin tone far lighter than either of her brothers. "That's for sure. These past two weeks have been like living a dream. It'll be so hard to go back to our normal lives once we get home."

"We could always just stay here," Marc suggested. "You'd pick up the language in no time."

"Somehow, I don't see that going over too well."

He reached for her hand. "Alright. We'll go home. As long as we come back someday. But for now, how would you like to spend the day?"

Marie nibbled at her ham-and-cheese sandwich. "I'd love a nice long walk on the beach with my husband. Then we should pick up souvenirs for the girls – and Christmas gifts for everyone."

"There's some cute shops down that way," Marc said, remembering at the last second not to point. He jerked his head in the direction he meant. "What do you think we should get them?"

As they munched at their sandwiches and sipped their *garotos*, Marc and Marie discussed the sorts of gifts they might like to bring back for various relatives and friends.

Marie reached into her purse and retrieved a pen and a miniature notepad. She made a list of names, then filled in the spaces beside them, once they settled on what to get for each person.

"And we *definitely* have to get you those shoes," Marc said, recalling the alluring contour of her calves in the handmade pumps she'd tried on in that leather shop. His nose twitched; he could almost smell the captivating aroma of fine leather that permeated the tiny boutique.

"Ahh... those shoes. They were glorious!"

He tried to keep his smile merely appreciative, but desire glinted in his eyes. "That's one way to describe them."

"I just don't know which color I want: the peacock or the red. What do you think?"

"Get 'em in every color they have. And never wear any other shoes than those. Ever again."

Marie gave her husband a coy smile. "Oh, you liked 'em, huh?"

Marc's gaze darted away guiltily. "You could say that."

She tilted her head back a bit, exposing the delicate curve of her throat. Her lips parted in a bewitching smile. "Perhaps I should think about getting a leather miniskirt to go with 'em?"

Marc shifted awkwardly in his seat and adjusted the napkin in his lap; a deep flush rose in his cheeks at her suggestion. He looked down at his plate, then up at her again as soon as he recovered a bit of his composure. "You're enjoying this, aren't you?"

Marie bit her lower lip and gave a slow, enticing wink. "Oh yeah." Then she nodded toward the street. "You ready to go?"

Marc paled. He stared at her in horror. No way was he

about to stand up now! "No!" Trying to conjure up a logical excuse to linger at the table until his predicament resolved itself, he said, "I – I'm not done with my coffee." Glancing into her cup, he added accusingly, "And neither are you."

Her laughter sounded musical as she reached over to touch his hand. "I was kidding. You have plenty of time to, um... recover."

"You are evil, you know that?"

Marie offered him a contrite smile. "I'm sorry. I just couldn't help myself."

"Hmm," Marc grumbled in response, trying to look fierce.

They drank their coffee in companionable silence for a time.

"And don't forget: We've got to stop back at the palace tomorrow," Marc reminded her, "to bring Izzy and Paul our receipts."

Marie's eyebrows shot upward. " 'Izzy and Paul'? Now who's getting familiar?" she kidded, an expansive smile brightening her countenance. "Seriously, you don't think they really meant that about paying for our honeymoon!"

"I do," he replied with a solemn nod. "As we were leaving, he pulled me aside and insisted we keep track of every receipt, then go back before we went home, so they could 'settle up' with us."

Marie sat back in her seat with a concerned sigh. "I don't know about that." She shook her head, looking about as uncomfortable as she sounded. "It just seems so... over the top. Besides, it's not like we can't afford this trip."

"I'm not comfortable with it, either, but I think we'd better do it. At least bring a few token receipts. They made a really generous offer and I don't want to insult them – or piss him off. After all, he might rescind my knighthood and make me give back the fancy medal." Marc gave her a slow smile. "And then I'll just be that boring guy you married. And what fun would that be for you?"

Marie shook her head in amusement. "None at all, I'm afraid." She reached over and patted his hand. "None at all."

"At the very least, they'll be expecting the hotel receipt and some of the restaurants. And the hospital bills. He specifically mentioned those."

Marie nodded. "Alright, but we shouldn't hand over receipts for everything. I mean, I don't want them paying for gifts for our families or anything we buy for ourselves."

"You mean like your dozen pairs of shoes and those matching miniskirts?"

"Exactly. Now are you finished with your coffee yet? Or has the mention of those shoes left you compromised again?"

After a leisurely morning of ambling barefoot along the sandy shoreline – inhaling the salt air and reveling in the warmth of the summer sun on their tanned faces – the honeymooners stopped at one of the little street vendors' carts for lunch.

Having reviewed their options – and Marie surprised Marc by correctly translating the names of most of the menu items – they ordered grilled-sardine sandwiches topped with fire-roasted red peppers on big soft rolls. She vacillated when she got a look at the fishes' shiny, grill-charred silver bodies, almost ordering a chorizo sandwich, but Marc convinced her to try the sardines, which he explained were classic Portuguese street fare.

The vendor corroborated Marc's story, explaining in English he'd sold out of them most days during the St. Anthony street festival the previous month.

Marie's eyes brightened at the street vendor's mention of the St. Anthony festival. Finally, something she could relate to! Despite what Marc had said about how the festival was celebrated in Lisbon, she couldn't help envisioning it being similar to the one he'd brought her to back home.

"Wait. You said you sold out of sardines *many* days?"

she asked, her eyebrows rising. "How long does the festival go on here?"

"The whole month of June," the street vendor said.

"Really?"

"Yes." He nodded as he tended to the fish lining his grill. As he spoke, he split two rolls and opened them on sheets of foil, piled each one with sardines and topped them with roasted peppers. "It goes all month long, but starting on the afternoon of June twelfth and continuing throughout the thirteenth, the streets are packed. It's a big street party. Much revelry and dancing."

"The feast of St. Anthony is a big deal in Lisbon. Far bigger than in Bridgeport," Marc said.

"Why's it go on for so long?"

"St. Anthony is seen as the city's patron. The festival incorporates both religious and secular activities. And June thirteenth, the actual feast day, is a holiday in Lisbon. It's quite an experience," Marc said. Marie held his sandwich as he counted out escudos to pay the vendor.

Marc watched with delight as Marie took her first bite of her sandwich. The combination of the soft yeasty roll, the rich flavor of the sardines and the sweetness of the roasted peppers left her with a look of enchantment Marc understood well. He'd had a similar reaction when he tried his first grilled-sardine sandwich here nearly two decades earlier.

"What do you think?" he asked as she chewed her first mouthful of the heady grilled fish.

"This is amazing! The fish is flaky and perfect. I taste the salt, but it's not overpowering."

"That's a common misconception, that sardines are salty. They are when they're canned, but fresh, it's all a matter of preparation."

"Same with the oily taste. It's pleasant – almost like mackerel," Marie enthused. "Oh, I'm so glad you talked me into getting this!"

"I thought you'd like it. And the bones are so soft, you can just eat them. It saves time on deboning them, and it's a great way to up your calcium intake."

"Now I understand why he sold out of them so often," she exclaimed. "This is delicious!"

As they ate, they strolled up the narrow cobblestone road to the seaside marketplace.

"Tell me more about the St. Anthony festival," Marie prompted.

"The streets are packed! You can see how constricted they are now, on an ordinary day. Just imagine them jammed with thousands of people, drinking and eating – even jumping over bonfires."

"You're making that up!"

Marc shook his head. "True story. Remember my Tio Roberto?"

Marie nodded.

"He kind of set himself on fire when he tripped while jumping one."

"No!" Her jaw dropped. "What happened?"

"I should preface it by saying he'd had a little too much wine earlier in the day and his depth perception was compromised. He misjudged the distance and face planted at the edge of a bonfire."

"Did he get burned?"

"Some of his friends who were nearby put him out right away, dusted him off. I doubt he was any the wiser. He was pretty out of it. I think he could have been hit by a bus and not known the difference."

"You saw it happen?"

"Oh yeah, the whole family did. And most of the neighbors. Plus, about two hundred other folks. My mother was mortified – and she read me the riot act afterward about not getting any ideas of following in my 'foolish uncle's footsteps.'" He paused, gave an embarrassed shrug. "I guess you can figure out how well that all turned out."

Marie laid a hand on his arm in a gesture of support.

Months ago, when their relationship had turned serious, they'd discussed what Marc had gone through in his efforts to get — and stay — sober. He admittedly had moments of weakness, and still attended AA meetings; but his thirty-fifth birthday two weeks earlier had marked fourteen years of sobriety.

By the time they finished their sandwiches, they had nearly arrived at the leather boutique where Marie had found those shoes Marc liked so much.

Eager to get on with their shopping excursion, she licked the last of the oil from the sardine sandwich off her fingers, wiped her hands on her napkin and gave Marc a huge smile. "I had no idea sardines could taste that incredible!"

"Just be thankful they cut the heads off."

Marie made a face. "Did you have to spoil it for me? Did you?!"

He laughed and hugged her. "Oh, don't be such a baby. C'mon, isn't that the leather shop up ahead?" He wiped his hands on his napkin, located a trash receptacle a little way up the road and got rid of the detritus from their lunch.

Hours later, when they headed back to the hotel, Marc and Marie were laden with shopping bags from several small shops in the marketplace. They chattered with glee about the exquisite finds for their family members and other loved ones.

They sank gratefully into the back seat of the cab Marc hailed. Before he could tell the *taxista* where to drop them, Marie spoke up. "*Você poderia nos levar, por favor, ao Grand Hotel?*"

"*Certamente, madame,*" he replied, and set out in the direction of their hotel.

Marc looked at his wife with an expression of surprise.

Marie's smile spanned her entire face. "What? You think you're the only one who can speak the language?"

She shrugged. "I've managed to pick up a phrase or two these past couple of weeks."

He nodded in approval. "Nicely done. I take it you'll order dinner for us tonight, then?"

"Only if you don't mind having to eat an umbrella and a can of red paint," she teased, recalling his anecdote on their first date, about when Emily took him to Carpaccio for his birthday and urged him to order for them in Portuguese.

"Ah, but you forgot the two lightbulbs," he reminded her, chuckling.

"How careless of me," Marie exclaimed. "I hear they're the best part!"

"Yes, but only if they're properly grilled."

"And have the heads cut off," they said in unison, laughing aloud.

Chapter 18

(10:35 a.m. Western European Time, Wednesday, July 21) As the taxi deposited them outside the presidential palace in Belém, Marie's insides felt as if someone had decided to take up knitting in there.

"What if they tell us to go away?" she fretted.

Marc took her hand. "Don't worry. Izzy and Paul are expecting us. Besides, they're the ones who told us to come back today, remember?"

"I know. But it still feels so awkward."

He gave her hand a reassuring squeeze. "It'll be fine, sweetie. Trust me."

As they approached the palace gate, one of the guards greeted him by name, adding, "How can I help you, sir?"

Marc explained the reason for their visit.

The guard nodded. "Yes, sir. You're expected. Come this way."

He directed them inside and escorted them to a large anteroom. "Please, make yourselves comfortable. The staff will announce you."

"We really appreciate your generosity," Marc said, in English so Marie would understand, once the two couples were seated in the same parlor they'd sat in during their first visit.

The president nodded and gave Marc a benevolent smile. "It is our pleasure. Are these the receipts from your stay?" he asked jovially as Marc handed him the brown kraft envelope.

"Most of them," he admitted after a brief hesitation.

"Why not all?" Isabella asked.

Marie spoke up, gesturing toward her husband. "As Marc said, we really appreciate your generosity – but we didn't want to take advantage of your kindness. What's in there are receipts for the hotel, the hospital and a few restaurant meals. Mr. President, we couldn't ask you to pay for the gifts and souvenirs we bought."

President Madeira Pinho nodded. "Fair enough. Our intent was never to make either of you feel uncomfortable. And please, call us Paolo and Isabella."

She gave a gracious nod. "Certainly. Thank you, Paolo and Isabella."

With a discreet hand motion, the president summoned a uniformed attendant, who stood at attention before him.

He handed the envelope to the man and instructed him in Portuguese, "Please take care of this right away."

"*Sim, senhor,*" the man replied. He nodded and departed immediately, the heels of his highly polished shoes clicking against the marble floor.

He returned less than five minutes later with a business-size envelope. Bending at the waist, he leaned forward and spoke quietly into the president's ear.

The president accepted the envelope with a slight nod. "*Muito bom. Obrigado, João,*" he told his attendant as the man straightened again, turned and departed.

"When must you go back to the United States?" Isabella asked in careful, precise English.

"We leave this afternoon," Marc replied. "We just have to go back to the hotel to get our luggage and then we're off to the airport."

"You must at least stay and join us for lunch," the first lady insisted.

Marc and Marie exchanged a glance.

Marie smiled at the other woman. "We'd love to."

"Wonderful!" Isabella sprang to her feet and dashed out of the room.

Paolo smiled as he handed the envelope to Marc. "It has only been a few months. She is still not accustomed to being served. No doubt she's off to alert the chef we'll have guests for lunch."

After their farewell lunch, Paolo instructed his personal chauffeur to take the Lindemeyrs back to their hotel to get their bags and then transport them directly to the airport.

Before the newlyweds left the palace in the president's limousine, Paolo took Marc aside and spoke with him for a few minutes in Portuguese.

Marc nodded several times during their conversation. "*Sim,*" he said at last. "*Sim, eu entendo.*" Yes. I understand.

He pocketed the card the president handed him. Then the men rejoined their wives.

When Marc and Marie were ready to leave, the two men shook hands; the women hugged. Then Paolo kissed Marie's hand and Isabella hugged Marc.

A moment later, the Lindemeyrs climbed into the limo and waved goodbye.

An hour later, they were back at the airport, ready to head home.

While Marc checked their luggage, Marie went to the ticket counter to see about changing their seats. They'd been booked into the same seats as on the trip over – and she didn't want to trigger any unnecessary anxiety; Marc was bound to feel enough stress just getting on a plane again. And she wasn't crazy about the idea of sitting there, either.

When Marie explained the situation, the airline attendant gladly accommodated her request; she switched their seats to the other side of the aisle, farther back in the first-class section.

As they boarded the plane, Marc drew a shaky breath.

The Unintended Hero

He hadn't expected to feel this kind of anxiety. Because he was holding his carry-on, he couldn't reach for the comfort of Marie's hand. His breathing grew rapid and shallow, his chest tightened and his heart rate quickened.

Hearing the change in his breathing, Marie turned, concern in her blue eyes. "Are you okay?"

He gave a slight headshake. "No."

She nodded. "That's perfectly natural." She put a hand on Marc's shoulder and shepherded him ahead of her to his seat. She hoisted his bag into the overhead compartment, then did the same with her own. She had him take the window seat and settled beside him on the aisle.

"Look at me," she murmured. It was evident to both of them that Marie the therapist had taken over.

As he met her gaze, she kept her voice deliberately low, so it came across as calming, and so he would have to listen closely. "The anxiety you're feeling is normal, Marc. I'd be concerned if you weren't anxious. You're returning to an environment that was traumatic. But it's a different situation today. The man" – she avoided saying 'gunman' – "who caused trouble last time isn't here. There's no reason to believe there'll be any sort of unpleasantness."

Marc opened his mouth to speak. No words came out. He looked away, unsettled.

Marie squeezed his hand. "I realize it's hard to bank on reason when fear's right there, but it's going to be okay, Marc. Trust me."

He took a deep breath, released it slowly. He focused on the sound of Marie's voice.

"You're going to be fine," she assured him. "Just keep breathing nice and slow. And if you start to feel anxious at any time, take my hand. I want you to concentrate on the feel of your hand holding mine and your slow, steady breath. Block out everything else. Okay?"

Marc gave a hesitant nod and intertwined his fingers with hers.

Marie patted his arm. It was going to be a long flight.

Chapter 19

(5:50 p.m. Thursday, July 22)

"Hi Val." Marie heaved her large suitcase onto the bed, unzipped it and began to unpack. "I just got your messages. We were away for a couple weeks. What's up?"

"The apartment's ready, so you can start bringing things over whenever you want."

"Great! We're so excited about the move. Marc's already got his place half packed. But I've barely started," she admitted, glancing around her bedroom.

"That's fine. I just wanted to give you the option of moving in early. We also want to invite you two over for dinner one night this week or next."

"How sweet! Only thing is, Marc works nights. It'd have to be a weekend, if that's okay."

"That's fine. Is this Saturday too soon?"

"I don't think we have anything scheduled – at least, not that I'm aware of."

"We'd love to get to know you two better. We enjoyed having lunch with you that day we met. You seem like such a nice couple."

"We're really not," Marie kidded. "Marc runs a counterfeit-printing operation in the back room of his apartment; and I do experiments on small animals."

Val laughed – a throaty, conspiring laugh. "You realize if that were true, I'd find it out. And Tim would help me disappear you."

As Marie joined in the devious laughter, Marc entered

the bedroom. He nodded toward the phone in his wife's hand, as if to ask who it was.

"Marc just came in; let me ask him," Marie said. She covered the mouthpiece. "Val and Tim want us to come for dinner Saturday night. Are we free?"

"Sure. Ask her if we can bring dessert."

"This Saturday's perfect for us. Can we bring dessert?"

"That'd be great. And what kind of wine do you folks like?"

Marie hesitated. "Uh" – she glanced up to see Marc leaving the room – "we... don't drink."

"Oh – I'm sorry!"

"No need to apologize," Marie assured her. "It's nothing you'd have had reason to know."

***

Because Marc had started packing just after they signed the lease, Marie suggested they pack his apartment first, and live at her place. "I mean, we're married now. It just makes sense we'd live together, right? Besides, my place is bigger. And we can have a cat."

Marc spent much of Friday packing. Marie went grocery shopping, collected their mail from the post office and then retrieved Oscar from her brother's house.

Erin threw her arms around her. "Auntie Marie! Welcome home! I'm so glad to see you!"

Marie hugged her. "Thank you, sweetheart! It's good to be back. I missed you so much."

"Is Uncle Marc with you?" the girl asked, craning her neck to look beyond her aunt.

"No, he's at his apartment, packing, getting ready to move."

Erin's smile broadened in complicity. "I heard you two ran off and got married. That's so romantic! I also read that Uncle Marc's a hero. I can't wait to give him a big hug and tell him how proud I am of him!"

Marie hedged. "Ya know what, honey? Uncle Marc's

kind of private about things. He hates when people make a fuss over him. I know you want him to know how proud you are of him. I'm proud of him, too! But I think he'd appreciate it a whole lot more if you didn't say anything."

Erin's expression drooped. "Not at all?"

Marie shook her head. "He's been having a rough time, and I don't want to cause him any more stress. I figured you were grown up enough to understand." She squeezed her niece's hand. "Okay?"

Erin frowned. "I don't want to make Uncle Marc sad. But someday, when he's feeling better about it, will you tell him I'm really proud of him?"

Marie hugged her. "I sure will."

Michaela poked her head into the living room. "Marie! I thought I heard voices in here." She came over to hug her sister-in-law. "Welcome home! Are you here to pick up Oscar?"

"I am. Did he enjoy his stay here?"

"Maybe not as much as Amanda did… but he was a good sport."

After bringing her little tuxedo cat home, Marie filled Oscar's food and water bowls and put away the groceries. Then she made sandwiches, sliced carrots and celery sticks, shook two portions of chips into a zip-top bag and grabbed sodas to bring to Marc's apartment.

When she arrived, the living-room bookcases stood empty. Marc's audio components and music collection were ready to go; photos and paintings were carefully wrapped. The only item in its original spot on the wall was his prized possession: his sister's painting of the Portuguese fishing village, created from a handful of photos he'd shot during their summer trip in 1975.

Clearly labeled cartons containing all his belongings from the emptied rooms lined the back wall of the living room; the wall of boxes stood ten across and four high.

His long-unused surfboard lay atop the backmost row. Each carton bore the name of the room it came from, numbered for inventory purposes. On the coffee table lay a handwritten manifest detailing every item contained in each box.

"Wow. You've been busy. How'd you move all those boxes with your injured arm?"

"Some of 'em were light enough to pick up and carry with just one arm."

"And the others?"

"Those I moved first. I slid them across the floor and into place, then piled the other boxes on top," he replied. "I loaded books a few at a time into boxes I'd built on top of other cartons, so I wouldn't have to move them full. I'm no fan of pain. I'm not going to do anything that hurts."

Despite Marc's insistence he was capable of helping to carry cartons down to the car, Marie remained dogged in her refusal to let him do so.

"What if you lose your balance on the stairs?"

"I fall. And some of my stuff breaks," he said with a curt shrug. "Your argument's a non sequitur."

Hands on her hips, she glared at her husband and huffed out an irritated sigh. "It's perfectly germane and you know it."

"Marie." Her name was a warning. "One has nothing to do with the other. And please stop treating me like a six-year-old."

"I'm not," she insisted, her frenzied voice beginning to spiral upward. "I just don't want you to risk losing your balance, falling down the stairs and getting hurt."

In the midst of his annoyance, Marc glanced at the simple gold band on his left ring finger. *How would Edward have handled this?* He took a deep, calming breath and approached his cross wife.

"Hey..." His tone softened as he ran his hands along Marie's tanned forearms. The motion didn't hurt his arm nearly as much as he expected it would. "I'm sorry. I know your heart's in the right place. I realize you've got concerns about my balance issues just now. I do, too. I don't want us to fight over this, because it's not worth getting you upset. How about we sit down and have lunch? Then I can continue packing while you carry some stuff down to the car. Okay?"

Marie snuggled close. Her smile returned as she nestled against her husband's chest. "That's a wonderful idea. Thank you, sweetheart." She stretched up and kissed him on the cheek.

(5:30 p.m., Saturday, July 24)
"Welcome!" Val greeted the couple at the front door. "Come in. I'm so glad you could make it." She gave Marie an impulsive hug, but stopped herself just short of embracing Marc.

"What happened?" she exclaimed, indicating the sling on his arm. "You broke your wing!"

"Long story," he said with a dismissive wave. "It's really nothing."

"Ooh, it smells great in here," Marie offered as they followed Val toward the kitchen.

"Here, let me take that," Tim said, reaching to relieve Marc of the still-warm blueberry pie balanced on his one good hand. "That is elegant!" he exclaimed, noticing the intricate cut-out pattern in the top crust. "Marie, this is beautiful!"

Marie let out a little laugh. "I'm afraid I'm not that talented. Marc's the culinary artist."

"No kidding?" Tim turned. "Looks like structural design isn't the only interest we share."

"Don't let one pie fool you," Marc countered with a headshake. "I'm a rudimentary cook at best. I can whip up a decent sautéed chicken in mushroom gravy, steamed green beans and barely passable buttermilk biscuits, but that's about it. Beyond that, I'm a boxed-mac-and-cheese kind of guy. Or if I need protein, the occasional grocery-store rotisserie bird."

Val and Marie laughed at his candid response.

Tim looked disheartened. "That's too bad. I was hoping to get some good recipes out of you."

"Oh, recipes I've got," Marc assured him. "I just can't do anything with 'em. What've you got up your sleeve for tonight?"

"Nothing special," Tim deadpanned. "Just some chicken in mushroom gravy with steamed green beans and barely passable buttermilk biscuits."

"At least dessert will be edible," Marc muttered.

When Marie stared at him, appalled, he broke into a grin.

The two women looked at each other in resignation as the guys laughed their heads off.

"They're two of a kind," Val said with a groan, looking a little worried. "I shudder to think what's going to happen next month, once you two are moved in upstairs."

"They'll be inseparable," Marie ventured, "like best friends in kindergarten. Playing in the sandbox, giggling, pulling pranks, shooting spitballs. We'll have to keep them separated."

Val laughed and nodded in agreement. "You're probably right."

Over dinner, the newlyweds told Val and Tim about their elopement.

"What? After all that wedding talk the day you two came to look at the apartment? Dresses and cakes, caterers, flowers and all that garbage?" Tim looked over at Marc. "It got so bad we had to leave, remember?"

Marc held up his hands, palm forward. "Don't look at me – this was all her idea."

Tim turned toward Marie for an explanation.

"We'll still have the wedding Mass in September," she said. "I hope you'll be able to join us."

"We'd love to," Val chirped, patting her husband's

hand.

"It won't be an actual wedding," Marc clarified, "because we're already legally married. They call it a convalidation. It's like putting an official stamp of approval on the marriage."

"So it was a civil ceremony? At city hall?" Val asked.

Marie shook her head. "A justice of the peace married us at a little restaurant in Redding."

"How nice!"

"Hah! She lured me out there under false pretenses," Marc said, trying to sound put upon. "Told me she wanted to take me to lunch for my birthday because she was gonna be away at a psych conference all week. Little liar. She wore a pretty dress, even talked me into putting on a suit. Then she sabotaged my car so it wouldn't start. Got me out there and it was all hogwash."

"You could have said no," Marie teased.

"Yeah, right. In front of the J.P., your brother and my sister? I don't think so."

"So it was a coerced marriage. That'll work in your favor if you want to get it annulled."

Val shot Tim a dirty look. "Oh, hush!" she admonished, then asked, "Where'd you go for your honeymoon? I take it that's where you've been these past couple of weeks."

"Fibber McGee here told me she was headed to Houston for a week," Marc said, thumbing toward his bride. "I thought I was just going to dump her at the airport to catch her flight and then try to get to work on time. But when we got to JFK, she sprang it on me that I wouldn't be late for work because I wasn't going to work. We were going to Portugal."

"Oh, you poor thing," Val said, the level of snark in her voice rising. "How you must have suffered! It must have been awful for you."

"Why Portugal?" Tim asked, starting the coffee maker.

"Marc has family there," Marie said. "He'd gone almost

twenty years ago and always talked about wanting to go back. So I figured, why not?"

"Did you have a good time?" Val asked, clearing away dishes.

The newlyweds exchanged an awkward look. "Once we got there, yeah," Marie replied.

Val tilted her head. "Why? What happened before you got there?"

Marie cast a glance at Marc, who gave a reticent nod.

"We heard about that!" Tim gasped after Marie's bare-bones summary of their ordeal. "But we didn't really pay attention to the name. That was you?"

Marc looked weary. "Yeah." He gave an awkward glance from Tim to Val and then back. "But if you don't mind, I'd really rather not talk about it."

"I don't blame you a bit. That must have been frightening," Val commiserated as she set the pie and dessert plates on the table. "I've been shot in the line of duty, so I totally get how scary and unnerving it can be. But good on you, Marc, for stepping up to do something."

"Thanks," he murmured, glancing away, embarrassed.

Before he could mention her role in the ordeal, Marie diverted the conversation. "Gunman notwithstanding, Portugal was lovely. We spent two weeks touring historic sites, parks, zoos... we even went to the beach. Plus shopping – and chowing our way through Lisbon. I swear I must have packed on about fifteen pounds!"

Val shook her head as she sliced wedges of Marc's freshly baked blueberry pie. "You don't look like you've gained an ounce. But I guess now's a bad time to ask if you want ice cream."

The guys looked at each other and laughed.

"Timing really is everything," Marc commented, the laugh lines around his eyes crinkling.

"I feel like a regular porker," Marie replied patting her middle. "Then again, I may just have redistributed the fat. After all, we did do a lot of walking. So, yeah, ice cream sounds great."

"I always wanted to tour Western Europe. I spent six months stationed in Germany back in the eighties, but I never got to do any sightseeing," Tim said as he poured the coffee. "And once I got back here and reconnected with Val, it no longer seemed that important. What did you like best about Portugal?"

"The food," Marc kidded. "Without a doubt. That was the best part."

Marie punched him. "You goofball! We spent two weeks steeped in all that architecture and history, and you say the food was the best part?"

"What? I can like the food best if I want. And you can't tell me you didn't scarf down your fair share of *pastéis de Belém*."

"What about getting to see your family?" Marie chided. She turned toward Val, her smile blooming. "That was my favorite part. I loved getting to meet all his relatives and hear their stories."

"Yeah. I must have blocked that out." Setting down his fork, Marc turned to Tim and Val. "Picture this: Cram just short of a thousand sweaty people into an eight-hundred square-foot house on a summer afternoon, after my grandmother spent all morning cooking and heating the place to about ninety-five degrees. Oh, and did I mention there was no air conditioning? That was real fun."

"Don't believe a word he says," Marie countered, amused at his histrionic description. "It wasn't a thousand people – it was fifty. And they weren't all inside. They had plenty of picnic tables set up in the back yard. It was a perfectly wonderful afternoon – with a beautiful breeze – and he's just being a pouty little ingrate."

Tim and Val laughed at the other couple's playful bantering.

"Then again, looking around and seeing practically the same face on every single one of his relatives took some getting used to," Marie continued. "But it was still my favorite part of the trip."

Before the Lindemeyrs left late that evening, Tim and Val gave them the keys to their new apartment. Tim assured them the place had been aired out, "so the kitchen doesn't smell like paint anymore."

"I've cleaned it top to bottom," Val added. "You can go ahead and start moving in any time you like."

"And remember, if you want someone to help you lug heavy boxes up the stairs," Tim put in, "ask someone else."

Laughing, Val elbowed him. "Would you behave, please?"

But Tim and Marc were already snickering.

"Are you sure you wouldn't rather rent to a nice ax murderer or something?" Marie asked. "This arrangement looks like it could end up being real trouble."

***

By the end of the weekend, Marc had all his essentials – clothes, toiletries, favorite coffee mug, other personal items and his cherished fishing-village painting – moved to Marie's place. He was now officially moved in. And he'd nearly finished packing his apartment.

"That was fast," Marie said as they relaxed on the couch early Sunday evening. "Pretty much all that's left now is to call the moving company."

"Well, it's easy when you're a minimalist." Marc put his arm around her and drew her close. "I expect I'll have it finished before I leave for work tomorrow."

She looked up at him with a languid smile. "That's right. Tomorrow we go back to 'real life.' It's gonna seem strange, being back at work after being away three whole weeks – and a new name."

He stifled a yawn and stretched. "It sure is. I'm beat! We should go to bed, get a nice long night's sleep. I predict tomorrow's gonna be a beast of a day."

Marie snuggled close and nuzzled his throat. "I was

hoping you wouldn't be too tired," she murmured. "I was kind of thinking we could celebrate our official first night in our first-ever marital apartment." She planted a series of warm, wet kisses along his throat.

Marc groaned. "Oh, woman, I swear you're going to be the death of me." He turned toward her and his slightly open mouth met hers.

His kisses were soft, tentative at first, then they increased in intensity.

Marie changed position to accommodate him on the couch; they lay side by side, kissing and touching, their legs intertwined.

Marie's hands instinctively moved to the sides of Marc's face, caressing him and pulling him close as they kissed. With a low purr of contentment, she raked her fingers through his hair, delighting in its softness.

Over the next several minutes, she reveled in the fine art of kissing Marc. His lips felt warm and gentle, unhurried, as they explored her skin. And although only able to use one hand, his slow, sensual caress left her quivering with the promise of more.

Before long, Marie upped the ante. She shifted position so she lay beneath him, relishing the feel of his lean body atop hers. He was already hard and he groaned as he ground his jean-clad pelvis against hers. His breathing grew more and more erratic. He drew back for a moment, breathless with desire.

Marie pulled Marc close again and kissed the side of his throat, then breathed hot and wet against it. As he shuddered with building passion, she nipped at his earlobe and whispered dirty things to him.

That did it.

He took possession of her mouth and kissed her long and fervently. His hands were in her hair, holding her fast as they kissed. Marie wrapped her legs around his narrow hips; then, moaning aloud, she tipped her pelvis up and thrust against his groin. At the same time, she drew her nails across the back of his neck, desire coursing through her.

"Race you to the bedroom," he breathed hotly in her ear.

Chapter 20

(7:15 a.m., Monday, July 26)
By the time Marie came into the kitchen in search of breakfast, Marc was already up, showered and dressed. A large travel mug of coffee – extra light, just how she liked it – awaited her on the counter, along with her purse and keys.

"I know it's not a *garoto*, but it'll have to do," Marc told her, indicating the mug, as she came over to kiss him good morning.

Marie caressed his cheek. "Thank you, sweetheart. It smells wonderful… and it'll do fine."

"I made your lunch. It's in the fridge."

She gave him another kiss. "You're way too good to me."

"Well, don't get used to it, lady," he warned, drawing her close. "This is all gonna come to a screeching halt once classes start up again."

"I know. I'm just going to enjoy it while it lasts."

She broke from him and stuck her head into the refrigerator in search of yogurt and a peach. While she was in there, she took out the lunch bag and set it beside the coffee mug on the counter. "You want a yogurt?"

"Don't we have any *pastéis de Belém*?" he asked, sounding wistful.

"I'm afraid not. I think we ate the last of them from the *confeitaria* about ten minutes after we got to the airport."

"Dagnabbit," he said with a playful grin. "Then I suppose yogurt will have to do."

Over breakfast, they talked about Marc's plans for the day. He told her he intended to finish packing up his apartment; he said he didn't think that would take more than two more hours.

"I'll bring a load of stuff to the apartment and, if I have enough time before I leave for work, start packing some of our non-essential items here."

"Sounds like a plan. But remember: no lifting anything heavy with that arm."

He gave a resigned nod. "I know. Nothing over five pounds for six more weeks."

"Good. Meantime, I'll be in meetings and sessions all day. Plus, I'm on call tonight. Unless I get called in, I'll probably get home about the same time you do."

"We can always meet at the diner for coffee and French toast at midnight, like we used to."

"Ugh. All those calories right before bed?"

"So, we can come back here and work 'em all off." A seductive smile hitched the corners of Marc's mouth upward a second before he broke into a full-on grin.

Marie shook her head. "You were right: All you guys ever think about is food and sex." She got up from the table and gave him a kiss. "I gotta get going, sweetie. Thanks again for the coffee" – she held the bag aloft – "and for making my lunch. I love you."

Marc was finished at his apartment by eleven. Before heading to Seymour, he stopped at the building manager's office to say he would vacate the apartment at the end of August.

"I'm sorry to hear that," the manager told him. "You've always been one of my favorite tenants. You've been with us for years, you're quiet, you always pay your rent on time. We've never had an issue with you. Out of curiosity, why are you leaving?"

"I got married a few weeks back and we're moving out

of town."

"I'll sure be sorry to see you go." Then he tilted his head a bit and looked at Marc strangely.

Here it comes...

"Wait a second. Aren't you the guy who stopped the shooting incident on that airplane a few weeks ago? The hero of flight something or other?"

His patience seeping away, Marc glanced away. "Flight Seven Twenty. Yeah. That was me."

"I thought so. Hey, good for you, man! Good for you."

When the other man reached out and gave him a congratulatory thump on the shoulder, Marc flinched and sucked in a breath through his teeth.

"Ooh! Sorry – that where you got shot?"

"Yeah." He winced. "It's still a little tender."

"Geez, I'm sorry 'bout that," he fretted. "Are you okay? I didn't mea—"

Marc put up a placating hand. "It's fine. Don't worry about it."

Marc got home in plenty of time to shower, change and pack up something for supper later that evening. He decided to head in to work early; he expected a ton of production orders in his work queue that he'd have to catch up on.

When he opened the door to the station just after five, he suddenly wished he'd thought to put on the sling he'd recently abandoned wearing.

Almost the entire staff milled about in anticipation of his return. Those near the lobby applauded as Marc came through the door, and crowded around him in welcome. As they did, some of them inadvertently jostled his arm, making him wince.

Absent from the welcoming mob was Gary, who was in the midst of a commercial break.

All Marc wanted to do was slink away and seek refuge in the quiet of the production studio. But his colleagues all wanted to welcome him back and congratulate him for his heroic actions.

Marc had to remind himself none of them had seen him in three weeks, and they were eager not only to acknowledge his actions on the plane, but to congratulate him on his recent marriage – which by now they all knew about, thanks to the efforts of the national media. So while inwardly he was cringing, Marc put forth a positive appearance and accepted the outpouring of accolades from his peers.

Once he was able to escape their admiring clutches, he retreated to the relative safety of the jock-prep area. But there he found, on the walls, various news articles from every newspaper – local, regional and national – that had featured his story amid its pages. As he sat at his desk, Marc glanced around, profoundly disconcerted by images of his smiling face staring back wherever he looked.

Dropping his head into his hands, he let out a soft groan, shoved his show-prep materials aside and went to the broadcast studio for a bit before starting his production work.

"Hey!" Gary greeted him. "Welcome back, buddy."

"Hi." Some of the anxiety that had invaded his psyche earlier dissipated. He even managed a tentative smile. "It's good to be back."

Gary came around from behind the control board to give his brother-in-law a hug, careful to avoid his right shoulder and arm. He didn't mention a word about his friend's being a hero, didn't offer laudatory remarks, didn't make him feel uncomfortable. "It's great to see you back. Did'ja have a good time?"

Marie must have tipped him off. Marc could scarcely feel himself nod. "Yeah. Real nice time." Now he smiled – a genuine, relaxed smile. "We're already thinking about going back again someday.

"And thanks for taking care of Oscar. I hope he wasn't any trouble."

"Nah," Gary replied. "Perfect houseguest. Oh, and your car's fine. All I did was disconnect the battery – and I had it good to go before you guys even left her street."

"I know. Thanks," Marc replied. "Marie fessed up once we got to the airport."

"Man, I wish I coulda seen your face," he said, grinning. "There was no way you were gonna be back here on time – you must have been going nuts."

Giving Gary a grim headshake, Marc tried his darnedest to suppress a smile. "You damn Sheldons… you're just evil. It wasn't bad enough it took us practically forever to get to that stupid airport. Then that sister of yours goes and veers into long-term parking and I'm freaking out, trying to get her to turn around and head back the other way, to the short-term parking area. But Oblivious Girl just kept right on driving."

Gary did his best to force back a burst of laughter, both at Marc's telling of the story and his hilarious characterization of Marie. His laughter provided a fitting backdrop for Marc's next words.

"She finally pulled into a parking space and let me in on her little scheme. I swear, if she'd let it go on much longer, my head might well have exploded entir—"

"Stop! Stop!" Gary implored, waving him off from saying anything further, and at the same time trying to regain his composure. Donning his headphones, he cracked the mic and turned up the volume. "Sixteen minutes 'til seven, Z97-3. That's Phil Collins, *Take Me Home*. I'm Gary Sheldon hanging out with you for another few minutes. Then, speaking of home, Marc Lindsay's home from gallivanting across Europe the past few weeks. He's over his jet lag, he's bright eyed and bushy tailed and he'll be in at seven to tell you all about his adventures" – a sudden glare from Marc made him retract his statement – "or not. Stick around. Your Z97-3 weather's up next."

Pressing a button to activate the first of three thirty-second commercials, Gary tugged off his headphones.

"Sorry 'bout that."

Marc shrugged it off. "Aah. No biggie."

"So what did you say when she told you? I could totally envision your head about to fly off!"

"I'm glad you think it was funny. I was practically in heart failure by the time she clued me in."

Gary scribbled in the time the three spots played on his program log, then checked off each of the commercials. "And you had no idea?"

"None at all."

"C'mon. Not even about the wedding?"

He shook his head. "Totally blindsided. Not that I mind. Marrying that sister of yours was – no lie – the best thing I've ever done."

"Hold that thought." Gary pulled his headphones back on and held up a finger. "Fourteen minutes 'til seven, six forty-six if you're left handed, Z97-3. I'm Gary Sheldon, hanging out with you for another little while. Here's your forecast for the overnight…"

By the time Marc got home, his arm was throbbing. He hadn't expected doing a radio show would take that much of a physical toll and he wished he'd thought to take a pain pill before he left the apartment.

Marie wasn't home yet; she'd probably been called in to see a patient. He hoped she was at Danbury Hospital and not up in Waterbury. Locking the deadbolt on the front door, he greeted Oscar and went into the bathroom to retrieve his pain meds.

Oscar leapt onto the sink as Marc opened the medicine cabinet. "Prrrp?" he asked, rubbing against Marc's elbow.

"Hey, buddy." Marc scratched the little cat behind the ear. "How was your night? Aww, you like that, huh? Yeah…"

Oscar responded by standing on his rear legs, stretching up against Marc's chest, and head butting his arm. He began to purr, then batted at Marc's hand, as if asking to be petted.

Marc smiled and complied. "Yeah, we missed you, too."

Abruptly, the cat took his front paws from against Marc and settled all four feet on the sink. Marc flinched. Last time Oscar made a sudden move around him, not quite a year ago, he'd sunk his teeth into Marc's hand, ultimately sending him to the emergency room. And if there was one place Marc Lindemeyr was certain he didn't want to end up again any time soon, it was a hospital.

"Oh no you don't," he chided, backing a few inches away.

Oscar cocked his head, did a funny little dance on his back feet along the smooth porcelain edge of the sink, his front paws dangling a fraction of an inch above its surface. An instant later he sprang into the air like a furry guided missile and executed a graceful four-paw landing on Marc's left shoulder. "Mrrow."

Startled, Marc tried to hold as still as possible, to avoid ending up with eighteen claws dug into his shoulder. But Oscar seemed to have excellent balance and kept his claws retracted.

Marc turned his head to address the cat. "Okay with you if I take a pain pill?"

Oscar rubbed against his ear and purred.

"I'll take that as a yes." He reached into the medicine chest for the cobalt-hued bottle. He popped off the plastic lid and shook out a pill. He'd been judicious about taking his pain meds thus far, not wanting a second addiction to become an issue. Besides, he wasn't sure he'd be able to refill a prescription that originated in a foreign country. He peered inside. Eight pills left.

As Marc recapped the bottle, Oscar perched on his shoulder, eyeing him carefully. He barely shifted when Marc reached for the water glass and held it under the faucet to fill it.

Raising his arm to drink with a cat balanced on his

shoulder would pose a challenge, Marc realized. He hoped the cat wouldn't freak out and tear away half of the skin from his good shoulder.

Deciding not to take any chances, Marc set the glass of water on the sink, then walked into the bedroom. He leaned over the bed. "Down, please," he requested.

"Mrrrr," Oscar replied in mild throaty protest; still, he did as he was asked.

"Thank you." Marc petted Oscar's soft black head before disappearing into the bathroom.

About twenty minutes after he took the pill, the throbbing in his arm began to subside. Ten minutes after that, Marc was asleep.

When Marie arrived home at 2:45, she undressed in the dark and slid under the covers beside her sleeping husband, draping one arm around him. He barely stirred. But when she felt something soft move on the bed between them, she let out a startled gasp.

Unfazed by her expression of alarm, Oscar got up and stretched, rearranged his nap and settled back to sleep, purring.

"Oscar, you scared the hell out of me," she murmured, stroking the little cat's silken fur. She wondered at his sudden fondness for sleeping in bed with them, but fell asleep before she could give it too much thought.

When they awakened, Oscar was still asleep, rolled up in a little ball, his chin resting atop his back paws.

"Looks like something's come between us. And that didn't take long," Marc observed, giving Marie a smile that made her insides go all to goo. He reached over to stroke her cheek, then leaned in to kiss her.

"He's never done this before. I wonder why he started now."

"I don't know, but he was awfully attentive – even affectionate – when I got home last night. He must have missed us while we were away."

"I guess so."

"He jumped up on the sink, demanding attention. Then he leapt onto my shoulder, purring like crazy." Seeing Marie's expression register concern, he added, "Not that shoulder. And he just sat there, purring. It was the strangest thing. I came back in here and asked him to get down – I needed to take a pain pill."

"What did he do?"

"He got down. I guess I must have asked him nicely enough. I thought it was a little strange that he fell asleep next to me, but I didn't expect him to still be here this morning. I figured he'd have gone back to— hey, where *does* he normally sleep?"

Marie shrugged. "Beats me. Not on the bed, that's for sure."

"Do you want me to get him down? Is he not supposed to be up here?"

"He's fine. If he were a hundred-pound German shepherd, that'd be a different story, but he's an eight-pound cat."

As if realizing they were talking about him, Oscar raised his head. He gave a mighty yawn, got up and stretched, then rubbed his head against Marc's face.

"Pfff," Marc said, after getting a faceful of cat fur. He wiped a hand down his face to clear away the loose fur, then shook his head. "That was rude," he told the cat, who circled back for another pass. This time, Marc was ready for him and leaned backward, out of the way.

Well accustomed to Oscar's face-rubbing antics, Marie laughed. "You don't know rude 'til you've had him rub his butt against your face."

The rest of the week passed uneventfully. Marc settled back into his regular routine at work; eventually, folks stopped mentioning his heroism. Marie, meanwhile, resumed her schedule as chief of psychiatry at the Foxbridge

Institute in Newtown, seeing patients and overseeing daily operations.

She was on call until midnight a few nights a week, and had to be available to drive either to Danbury Hospital or Waterbury Hospital if a psychiatric emergency cropped up. When she didn't get called in, she arrived home around the same time as Marc.

When she wasn't on call, Marie was home before six, where she enjoyed sliding her tired feet into slippers. Because Marc took his supper to work every night, she only ever cooked meals to be reheated, which she found depressing. She'd cook just so there would be something in the fridge for Marc. Because she hated eating alone, Marie looked forward to the upcoming move; she envisioned sharing semi-regular meals with Val and Tim. She and Marc had grown quite fond of them – and she hoped the feeling was mutual.

Chapter 21

Marc and Marie spent much of the weekend schlepping cartons to the new apartment. By the time Sunday night rolled around and they accepted Val and Tim's invitation to join them downstairs for supper, all the boxes were gone from Marc's old apartment and the only thing left was furniture. They kept his bedroom furniture for the guest room. Because he didn't see the point of having two kitchen and living-room sets, Marc called Father Callahan, to see if he could use them for one of the interim-housing facilities he'd set up. The new accommodations would house men ready to leave the shelter but not prepared to face independent living.

By the time they showered and fell into bed late Sunday night, they were both achy but felt a real sense of accomplishment.

"Now we get to start moving stuff out of here," Marie said, adding acerbically, "and won't that be fun?"

"Don't remind me," Marc said with an audible groan as he settled into the softness of their bed. "Whose idea was this, anyway?"

"I think it was yours," she responded sleepily, cuddling close. "At least now we don't have to lug boxes down two flights of stairs," she pointed out, trying to sound optimistic.

"Thank God for small favors." Yawning, Marc turned out the light, then gave her a quick kiss. "We can worry about that next weekend."

By the time Marie murmured, "Good night," Marc was already asleep.

(10 a.m., Monday, August 2)
"C'mon in."
Without making eye contact, Marc stood and followed his therapist into her inner office.

Moving toward her seat, Dr. Merino turned on her towering heels and indicated his usual chair with a wave of her hand. As they sat, the psychiatrist folded her hands in her lap.

"Now, then," she sat back in her chair and crossed one leg over the other. "Shall we discuss how you're handling your unintended-hero syndrome?"

Marc swallowed hard. It felt like someone had thrown a porcupine at him. "There's a name for it?"

The therapist's glossy hair swished against the back of her chair as she shook her head. "Not officially, but there probably ought to be."

His head tilted in silent question.

"Any time I saw you being interviewed on the news, you looked so... beleaguered. Set upon. And uncomfortable. Like you dreaded the publicity and just wanted to slink away, unnoticed."

"That pretty much sums it up," Marc said. "They kept after me about how heroic I was and how I saved hundreds of people's lives, and that I was a national hero. The president even dubbed me the Hero of Flight Seven Twenty – and then all the media wonks picked up on it.

"And honestly, doc? Like I said on the phone, I didn't do anything particularly heroic. All I did was try to stop some jerk who put my wife in danger. Hell, I didn't even get the gun away from the guy – so I basically suck at this whole being-a-hero stuff." He sank his head into his hands and groaned. "I wish everyone would just stop making such a big fuss."

When he looked up again, Dr. Merino was nodding.

"That makes sense?"

She gestured with the hand holding her blue pen. "Of course it does, Marc."

Her slightly rolled "r" reminded him of how Avó Madalena spoke his name; the mere sound of it soothed his nerves. He met her gaze. "Good. Because right now I really need something to make sense in my life. I feel like I've been walking around with this great big neon arrow over my head for weeks with a sign that says, 'Hey! Look at this guy!'" Craning his neck, he looked upward. "I swear I can hear the damn thing humming up there."

She smiled. "At least you're trying to maintain a sense of humor about it. I know we talked about this on the phone, but why don't you go over what happened for me, from the beginning."

Marc felt as if he would rather lie down in the middle of North Main Street at rush hour. He couldn't bear to speak about it again. She couldn't be serious. "Really?" He sounded about as weary as he felt. "The whole thing?"

She gave a slight nod. "Please."

It was the last thing he wanted to do, but Marc trusted Dr. Merino; he had for years. In the past six years, she'd seen him through coming to terms with some of the roughest experiences in his life: Patrick's suicide in high school, alcoholism – even an AIDS scare. And he realized what she was asking of him now was, at its core, for his own well being. With a resigned sigh, he related the story for his therapist, from the hijacker's taking a flight attendant captive through his being whisked away by ambulance to the hospital when the plane landed in Lisbon.

The therapist listened, nodding from time to time. She let him recount his story, without interruption, prompting or questions.

When he finished, Marc slouched in his chair, feeling more exhausted by his just-completed verbal ordeal than he imagined he might have felt if he'd just swum the English Channel.

"Good job," Dr. Merino commended him. She uncrossed her legs and re-crossed them in the other direction. "The way I heard what you said just now, you acted – without thought for any possible ramifications or concern for your own safety – to come to your wife's aid... which, in the process, yielded the unintended consequence of sudden heroism. It's not something you sought out or wanted; it just happened. Is that pretty accurate?"

Marc nodded.

"Perhaps you even wish you could go back and undo it? – because the constant recognition and the attention in the wake of the shooting is so unwelcome. Does that sound about right?"

Another nod – and an expression of relief at being understood. "Yes! And all I want is to resume my normal, ordinary, insignificant life."

The therapist's eyebrow arched. "Insignificant?"

Marc shot a hand through his hair. "Gaah," he muttered. "You know what I mean."

Her slow, measured nod reassured him. "I do. And I understand that desire on your part."

"So I'm not being selfish? Or demanding? Or even unreasonable?"

A headshake swished her hair around her shoulders. "Not at all. You're perfectly normal. Okay, so maybe 'normal' is overstating it a bit. You're quirky," Dr. Merino teased, walking back her 'perfectly normal' assessment. "But otherwise absolutely normal."

"What should I do?"

"You mean when someone has the nerve to mention your heroics before all the hubbub dies down?" A slight smile curled about her mouth.

He cringed a little. "Yeah."

"What would you like to do?"

"Well, screaming 'Shut up!' at the top of my lungs probably would not be helpful."

"Granted." She shifted in her seat, then crossed her

legs in the other direction. "Although I imagine that might feel pretty satisfying."

Marc grinned. "I bet it would."

"Would you like to give it a try?" she suggested with a hand gesture in his direction.

"Right now?"

"Why not?" She tilted her head. "How's it feel to be a genuine hero?" she baited.

Marc hesitated.

She watched him expectantly.

He watched her.

"Aren't you going to say it?" she prompted.

"Uhh... you mean, now?"

"Come on. That was your cue. Don't wimp out on me," she goaded. "How's it feel to be a real-life, genuine, honest-to-goodness hero? Huh? How's it feel? How's it feel? Huh?"

Marc's fists clenched at his sides as she badgered him. His pulse quickened. His breathing grew rapid and shallow. "Shut up!" he blurted at last.

Dr. Merino smiled – a big, teeth-showing smile. "There!" she exclaimed. "I knew you could do it! Doesn't that feel better?"

Marc let out a lung-clearing sigh. "Yeah," he admitted. "It does." He took a deep breath, let it out slowly, then drew in and exhaled another.

"You look like it felt good."

"It really did. But, as satisfying as that felt just now, it's not a practical response for everyday interactions," he acknowledged. "Especially in otherwise-polite conversation."

"Agreed," she said with a nod. "But I wanted to give you that sense of satisfaction in a safe space where there would be no repercussions. And, that said, what do you suppose might be a more appropriate response?"

He wiped both hands down his face. Shook his head. "I have no idea. Maybe..." – he threw both hands in the air – "Oh, I don't know. Try to change the subject?"

"That's one option. Anything else you can think of?"

"Leap out the nearest window?"

She pursed her lips. "Marc!"

"Kidding!" He rolled his eyes. "Geez... lighten up."

Dr. Merino shook her head.

His knee jiggled.

She watched him.

He scratched the side of his nose with one finger. Shrugged. "Uhh..." His brain scrambled for words his mouth wouldn't speak. Finally he shrugged again. "I got nothin'," he admitted.

"Maybe your change-the-subject idea could work," the therapist acknowledged after a brief silence that somehow felt to Marc like twenty minutes of dead air.

He looked at her like he thought she was more in need of therapy than he was.

"Hear me out. Why not enlist a few trusted friends or colleagues to intercede on your behalf, to help defuse the situation?" She raised a hand to hush him from any protest. "So, say, if someone mentions it at work, you could have Gary step in with, 'Oh, I'm sure Marc's had his fill of discussing this.' Perhaps Marie could be one of those advocates, too. She can take folks aside privately and say, 'Gee, ya know, Marc really feels kind of uncomfortable talking about this. Can we please let it drop?' Folks might not even realize it bothers you. If someone close to you initiates efforts to quash it, that validates it even more."

Marc gave a contemplative nod. "That all makes a lot of sense. Thanks, doc. I'll give it a try."

"Just remember," she cautioned as he started to get to his feet, "folks who are making a big deal about this aren't setting out to make you feel uncomfortable. That's probably not even on their radar; they simply need something they can feel good about."

His brow furrowed. He sat down again, feeling confused. "How's that again?"

"To a lot of folks, being able to commend someone for doing something positive is often as close as they can get to that 'feel-good' emotion. So while it may be difficult for you to contend with the swirling emotions you're feeling right now, keep in mind it's something that gives others a sense of comfort, something to feel good about – even feel proud of vicariously. Everyone needs to feel good about something, even if it's someone else's accomplishment. That's why we feel such a sense of connectedness and pride when our country takes the gold in the Olympics, or our favorite team wins the World Series."

That evening, Marc approached his brother-in-law a little before they swapped places at the mic. "I kinda need your help with something."

Gary looked up from signing the log page for the six-o'clock hour. "Sure. What's up?"

Unaccustomed to asking for help, Marc took a deep breath. "I need you to run interference for me."

"How so?"

Using the discussion techniques he'd practiced with Dr. Merino during their session, he tried to convey how uncomfortable he felt with his sudden – and unwelcome – celebrity status, and asked for his brother-in-law's help to divert people's attention.

Gary gave a thoughtful nod. "Sounds like that's getting to be a real drag. Of course I'll help you. Whatever you need."

Two weeks later, Marc's nightmares hadn't abated. As Dr. Merino predicted, he was waking up in the middle of the night, enveloped by dread at seeing the gun being held on his wife, then hearing and feeling the gunshot over and over. In his worst nightmares, the gunman would shoot Marie. On those occasions, he'd watch the crimson stain seep across his wife's pretty blue dress, as all signs of life drained from her eyes.

(2:37 a.m., Monday, August 16)

As he watched the love of his life dying beside him, Marc's horrified screams ripped through the cabin of the airplane – and then through the quiet of their bedroom.

Oscar awakened and, with a sudden hiss, leapt across Marc's midsection, bolted off the bed and tore out of the room.

Jolted from her sleep, Marie sat up in bed. Now accustomed to his nightmares, she wrapped her arms around her traumatized husband, who clung to her, shaking like a birch tree in a windstorm and fighting back tears.

Still, her embrace couldn't calm him. "It's okay, Marc. Everything's fine," she reassured him. "It was just a bad dream."

But she knew the dreams would not resolve on their own.

In the morning, Marie suggested Marc contact his therapist to help him work through his terrifying dreams and find some way to seek resolution or closure on them.

He called Dr. Merino just after seven. She answered on the second ring. To Marc's dismay, she was completely booked and didn't even have time for a brief phone consultation that day.

"I know this is wearing on you, Marc. I can hear it in your voice. Can you come in first thing tomorrow?" she asked. "Would eight thirty work for you – or is that too early?"

Still getting used to daytime traffic patterns and travel times along his interim commute, Marc arrived at work just as the monthly one-thirty staff meeting started. During the impossibly long gathering, he found his already rattled nerves rubbed raw and stretched to their breaking point.

After an exhausting discussion about possible station promotions for the fall ratings period, during which nearly everyone shifted and squirmed in their seats, Pete stood.

Catching Pete's eye, Gary shook his head. He'd been tipped off that morning as to what was about to happen and had strongly advised against it: Pete intended to present Marc with a certificate of appreciation, a proclamation from the mayor of Middlebury and an engraved plaque from the Consul General of the Portuguese consulate in Waterbury, to honor him for his midair bravery.

On the heels of Marc's request for help in quashing such incidents, Gary suggested a simple certificate of appreciation might be more appropriate, and recommended Pete present it in private, minus any accompanying fanfare. But Pete insisted it be presented during the meeting; he wanted the whole team there and he wanted Marc to know how much the staff appreciated his efforts.

Now the rest of the staff looked at the program director, waiting for him to speak.

"That pretty much wraps things up for this month. But before we adjourn," he said, "I'd like to take a moment to recognize one of our own."

Marc glanced at Gary, who was eyeing Pete and shaking his head.

"Last month, as you all know, Marc Lindsay and Marie Sheldon eloped."

A few folks around the table offered halfhearted applause.

"And as you no doubt also know, as they were headed off on their honeymoon, an on-board incident on their flight to Portugal went horribly awry. Luckily, Marc was able to take control of the situation. And, while he was wounded in the effort, he saved a planeload of people from a pretty unpleasant fate. That said, I think it's fitting we take a moment now to acknowledge his herois—"

"Jesus, Pete! Would you get off it already?" Marc exploded, leaping to his feet. His chair skidded backward on its casters and slammed into the wall with a thud. The fury in his eyes boiled over into his voice. "I'm not some kind of fucking hero, alright? I'm not! And I'm sick to death of hearing that bravery shit. So just stop it!" Agitated beyond English, he slammed his fist against the table and lapsed into an angry tirade in Portuguese. When he finished hurling foreign expletives, Marc stalked out of the conference room, slamming the door as he went.

Raised eyebrows and startled looks accompanied the uncomfortable silence that filled the room in his absence.

Looking stricken, Pete sank into his chair and glanced at his afternoon-drive announcer.

Gary was shaking his head more visibly now, his expression somber. "Damn it, Peter, didn't I specifically tell you not to do that?" he intoned in a murmur. "I warned you it would end badly."

"I honestly didn't think he'd react like that," Pete replied just as quietly, looking shocked. He stared at his hands before him on the tabletop.

Giving an irritated sigh, Gary stood. "Well, if you'll excuse me," he said a little more sharply than he intended, "I'm gonna go find him and try to calm him down."

Pete nodded his approval — which he knew Gary neither sought nor required.

Gary found his fuming brother-in-law outside, at the far edge of the parking lot, muttering to himself. The scorching August sun beat relentlessly against the gravel surface and the humidity felt stifling; the midday heat shimmered off the hoods of the dozen-plus cars in the lot, making it seem even hotter.

At first, he kept his distance from his normally placid best friend, not wanting to intrude on Marc's obvious need for solitude to process his fury.

Mired in his swirling rage, Marc bent down and scooped up a handful of gravel. Standing again, he rattled the pieces like dice in his hand. Then, one by one, he picked out individual chunks of rock and hurled them at the oak and maple trees just beyond the parking lot. Whenever a stone missed its mark, he uttered an expletive.

Standing in the receding shadow of the building, Gary watched Marc. After a few minutes, he ventured out across the parking lot. When he was about twenty feet away, he took a misstep and his sneaker crunched audibly against the gravel.

Marc turned toward Gary. The hand with the gravel in it balled up into a fist and his eyes grew even more stormy.

Before his brother-in-law could hurl invective at him, Gary, who had stopped walking, put up both hands, palms forward. "I come in peace."

The greeting cracked Marc's wrathful veneer; his half smile seemed to be a reflex action. He unclenched his fist and let the rest of the gravel tumble harmlessly back to the ground at his feet.

"Want some company?"

"Not really," he mumbled, "but, well, since it's you…" His words trailed away to silence.

Gary advanced slowly. "I didn't get to warn you," he told Marc, reaching out one open hand, palm upward, in an apologetic gesture when he was about ten feet away. "You know I would have."

It was as if he hadn't spoken.

"I tried to tell Pete not to do that during the meeting," Gary continued, "but you know how he is about listening to other people sometimes."

Marc nodded. Some of his earlier intensity returned to his voice. "He shouldn't have done it at all," he grumbled. "Meeting or no meeting."

"He meant well," Gary offered. Now he was just a few feet away. He felt like he was trying to creep up on a feral cat whom he expected to bolt at any second.

Smirking, Marc bent down and picked up more gravel. Standing again, he rattled the jagged rocks in his open palm. "Yeah, well, he shouldn't have done it," he repeated. He began to fire small chunks of gravel sidelong into the woods, as if attempting to skip flat stones across a lake.

When he spoke again, his voice sounded hesitant. "Are

they mad at me? For ruining their little – whatever it was?"

That's a strange thing for him to be worried about. Gary shook his head. "I don't think so. I think it's more that they're worried about you. You gotta admit, that eruption was kind of out of character for you. We're all used to you normally being so easygoing. They probably weren't expecting such – well, such an intense reaction."

Marc turned away and stared at the ground. But before he did, Gary noticed the flush of embarrassment rising in his cheeks.

"I can't go back in there," Marc muttered, shaking his head. His voice wavered. "I can't face them. Not after... not after that outburst."

"It might not be as hard as you think."

"Who're you trying to kid?" he sputtered.

"Just c'mon back," he went on, as if Marc hadn't spoken. "It won't be that bad. You'll see."

Marc shook his head, his back still turned. Without a word, he fired a rock into the woods. And a second. Then he threw two more. All four rocks struck trees with little *thwip* sounds.

"You gonna keep assaulting those trees all afternoon?" Gary kept his tone gentle, as though he were addressing a small child.

Marc's back stiffened. His shoulders squared. He let out an audible sigh. "You're not gonna leave me alone, are you?"

"'Fraid not."

"And you're gonna pester me 'til I go back inside, huh?" His voice sounded strained.

"That's the plan."

Marc's shoulders sagged in resignation. When he turned to look at his brother-in-law, Gary pretended not to notice how damp and frightened the other man's eyes looked.

"C'mere," Gary whispered. He put an arm around Marc's shoulder and drew him in to a comforting embrace.

Marc tensed slightly but did not pull away. He let Gary hug him. His defenses crumbled and, as Gary wrapped his other arm around him, Marc let out a hiccupping gasp.

"It's just so fucking hard," he wailed, succumbing to his overwhelming anger and frustration. "I just can't do it anymore..."

"Of course it's hard," Gary agreed, holding his friend close. "I know we don't understand what you've been through. But, Marc, no one expects you to go it alone. We just want you to know how much we love you, and we want to be supportive of you, whatever you're dealing with."

Marc took a shuddering breath.

"Like Pete always says, we're sort of a family here. And like a family, we truly care about one another. So even when one of us, say, blows up and swears a blue streak during a staff meeting and then cruelly assaults defenseless trees" – he grinned as Marc let out an unexpected chuckle through his tears – "our response is always going to be one of compassion and support. Everybody in that building over there loves you, Marc, and they're concerned about you. And I can guarantee not one of them is thinking ill of you. Not one. You're the only one beating yourself up over this."

Marc didn't respond.

"And I know Pete feels terrible about embarrassing you in there. Despite what it might feel like, that was never his intent. You must know that... right?"

Now Marc nodded.

"So how about you stop assailing those poor trees – because they've never done anything to you – and come on back inside? Think you can do that now?"

Gary waited for Marc's nod before he released the embrace.

Not looking at his brother-in-law, Marc sniffled. Turning away, he swiped at his eyes. Then he dug a handkerchief out of his pocket and blew his nose.

"Why don't you take a minute to pull yourself together," Gary advised, one arm still draped around Marc's shoulder. "I'll go on ahead and get the troops to back off. Meanwhile, you can duck into my office and hang out there for a bit. Okay?"

Marc nodded. Now he looked up at his friend with a tentative smile. "Thanks, Gar'."

Gary shrugged. "That's what family's for." He gave Marc's shoulder a squeeze and offered him a benevolent smile. "I'll see you inside."

He strode back toward the station. When he entered the building, Brenda, the receptionist, met him just inside the door. She looked at him with question in her eyes. She hadn't been in the conference room for the meeting, but she'd heard Marc's outburst and saw him go tearing out of the building – and Gary racing out after him.

"He'll be in in a minute. I think it'd be best if you" – Gary motioned down the hall – "were maybe in the sales office when he got back."

Brenda nodded her understanding. She smiled. "You're a good friend, Gary." Returning to her desk to retrieve a stack of phone messages for various staff members, she hurried down the hall to the sales department.

Gary made his way around the office to ask the rest of the staff to please curtail any mention of heroism regarding Marc. Everyone agreed not to bring it up again.

When Marc returned a few minutes later, he glanced around the lobby. Finding no one there, and the building curiously quiet, he darted down the hall to the music department. The door to Gary's office was open, but the room was empty. Marc slipped inside and shut the door behind him.

He looked at his watch. It was nearly three. Gary was in the on-air studio. Marc slumped into one of the chairs opposite Gary's desk and, with a deep sigh, let his head droop into his hands.

Fifteen minutes later, Marc decided he couldn't put off facing Pete any longer. He got to his feet and poked his head out the door; the corridor was still deserted. He made his way down the hall and knocked at the program director's open door.

"Yeah," Pete responded to the knock, still focused on the report he was reading. When he looked up, he seemed startled to see Marc standing there.

"Can I come in?" His voice wavered.

With a welcoming smile, Pete motioned him in. "Of course. Have a seat."

Marc shut the door and sat.

Neither man said anything for a while.

At last, Marc met his boss' gaze. "I owe you an apology."

Pete shook his head. "No. You don't. I'm the one who should be apologizing to you, Marc. I never should have put you on the spot during a staff meeting. It was dead wrong and I'm sorry."

Marc half shrugged. "Maybe so, but I was out of line, storming out of there like that. While I can't exactly promise it'll never happen again," he added with a reticent grin, "going forward, I'll do my best to keep my emotions in check at work."

"Fair enough," Pete said. "More than that I can't ask."

Smiling, Marc took the hand his boss extended. "Thanks."

The next morning, Marc arrived a few minutes early for his eight-thirty appointment and settled into a chair in the waiting room. His knee jiggled almost uncontrollably.

"Good morning, Marc," Dr. Merino greeted him when she opened the door. "C'mon in."

"Hi," he mumbled as he slunk into the office and took his usual seat.

She opened her notebook. "What's going on?" When he didn't respond, she tried a different approach. "You sounded really upset yesterday. Do you want to talk about what happened?"

Marc looked away, ashamed. He couldn't remember why he'd called. His blowup yesterday completely eclipsed everything else. Slumping forward, he sank his head into his hands. "I had a meltdown at work."

"Is that why you called me?"

He shook his head. "No, that was a whole other mess."

The therapist gave a reflective nod. "Okay. Let's start there," she suggested. "Why don't you tell me what happened at work."

Marc told her about Pete's intent to honor him, and how he stormed out of the conference room. "That was so unlike me." He told her how Gary had found him, used gentle humor to divert him from his out-of-control thinking and eventually got him to come back inside – where he offered him a safe space to work through his runaway emotions, away from the rest of the staff.

"He sounds like a good friend," she observed.

Marc nodded. "He really is. I don't know what I would have done if he hadn't been there to reach out to me and talk me down." He gave a short, barking laugh. "I'd probably still be out there throwing rocks at trees."

Dr. Merino let him marinate in awkward silence for a minute or so. "What else is going on?"

Marc shifted in his seat. Part of him wanted to talk about it, but wasn't sure how it would be received; but another part of him didn't want to acknowledge the truth in what he was about to say. "You were right."

"About what?"

He averted his eyes. "The nightmares."

Dr. Merino nodded. She jotted in her notepad. "I see."

"I'm not having flashbacks," he said, "but the nightmares are" – he shook his head – "I just don't know what to do about them. They're really taking a toll. I think that's at the heart of why I blew up at my boss yesterday, because I was so – rattled about those stupid nightmares."

"Why don't you tell me about them," she offered, gesturing toward him with one hand.

"I know I said last time we talked I wasn't having nightmares, but that's 'cause I didn't want you to think I was so... so weak I couldn't handle a few bad dreams," he confessed in a low voice.

"There's no shame in that, Marc," she assured him. "And you certainly wouldn't be the first guy to admit that."

She motioned toward the couch. "Do you want to lie down? Sometimes it can be easier to talk about difficult subjects when you're not sitting face to face."

Marc shrugged. "It couldn't hurt." He went to the couch, lay down and stared at the ceiling. "What do you want to know?"

"Tell me about the nightmares," she invited. "Are they always the same or do there seem to be different ones sometimes?"

"They always start when the guy with the gun points it at Marie. But sometimes, instead of fighting with me for control of the gun, he shoots her..." His speech was starting to slow.

Dr. Merino knew he was beginning to see the action unfold as he spoke.

"I hear the gun go off. It's loud. And there's blood seeping through her dress. It spreads out across it, and she looks up at me as she's dying... like she's begging me to do something. The dress kind of matches her eyes, but the blood spreads across it and" – Marc's voice snagged in his throat – "and it's ruined. I can see her life draining away. It scares the hell out of me, because I know there's nothing I can do to save her." He took a tremulous breath to calm himself. "That's when I wake up screaming."

Dr. Merino reached forward and handed Marc a tissue.

"Thank you," he said in a voice that was barely there.

He wiped at his eyes.

"How often do you have this particular dream?"

"At least once a night – usually more often than that. Two, maybe three times a night."

"Have you talked to Marie about these dreams?"

Sniffling, Marc sat up. He shook his head. "She's having her own nightmares. When one of us wakes up screaming, the other one's there to offer comfort. So far, we haven't had them at the same time, so one of us can always offer reassurance. But yeah, Marie knows I'm having them, too."

"Is this something you could talk about in couples therapy? Your combined approach to facing a common adversary?" Dr. Merino proposed. "Are you still doing the couples therapy?"

"Yeah... not as often, though. We're going once a month."

"Okay. Good. I think you should bring it up at your next session. Perhaps being able to face your fears together can unite you against the common enemy and help you both move past your nightmares."

"That makes sense."

"In the meantime, I'd like you and Marie to sit down and talk about them together. And not when one of you has just woken up from one. Often, talking things out – apart from the emotional overwhelm – is a good way to help put them to rest. You may also find, now that you've described your nightmare and we've talked through it here, in a therapeutic setting, you might not have it as often. There's something else I'd like you to try, too."

"What's that?"

"I want you to try rewriting the ending."

Marc did a double take. "I'm sorry, what now?"

"Rewrite the ending. There's a technique that often helps people dispel recurrent nightmares. It's called imagery rehearsal treatment, or IRT. The premise behind IRT is if you can successfully change the bad stuff that happens during the nightmare, it loses its power."

He sat forward. "How do you mean?"

"Maybe, for example, his gun shoots hot fudge instead of bullets. Or a little flag pops out of the barrel that says 'Bang.' Or, instead of the gunman getting an opportunity to shoot Marie, what if she whacks him over the head with her purse and knocks the gun out of his hand? Then, suppose she takes a length of rope from her bag, hogties him and leaves him squirming in the aisle, helpless?"

Marc let out a chuckle. "That could work."

Dr. Merino nodded. "It really could. Several recent studies have shown remarkable results implementing IRT. Basically, you change the ending while you're awake so you no longer perceive it as a threat. And then, still awake, you rehearse the new ending of the dream in your mind, until it becomes almost second nature to you. So when you have the nightmare again, your subconscious goes, 'Hey, I know what to do with this,' and it substitutes the new ending for the scary one."

Noticing the time, Marc got to his feet, aware their session time had dwindled. "That makes a lot of sense. Thanks, doc."

Dr. Merino stood and accompanied him to the exit. "I think you'll find once the nightmares subside, you'll also feel less anxious about the whole heroism-recognition situation. For now, while you're still actively dealing with the nightmares, I'd like you to come back weekly – at least until your classes start. Does Monday at ten still work for you?"

He nodded. "That works. Thanks."

"You're doing fine," she reassured him, laying a hand on his shoulder. "Just remember to start rewriting the ends of those nightmares – and talk with Marie about them. Okay? We'll revisit this again next week."

Chapter 22

(7:27 a.m., Friday, August 20)
Little by little, Marc and Marie began moving household items over to the new place. Finally, it was moving day. Marie had a nine a.m. session, so Marc oversaw the move.

He met the crew at their apartment, where they loaded all the cartons and the furniture into the truck, then drove to his apartment. There they loaded up the furniture they were keeping, followed by the pieces to be donated to the interim-housing facility.

They dropped off the donated furniture at the address Father Callahan had given him, then transported the rest to the new apartment in Seymour.

At that point, Marc wisely stayed out of the way and let the professionals do their thing. He brought Oscar to the front balcony and opened the door of his carrier. The cat emerged and sniffed around the enclosed area, to assess his new environment. When he was satisfied it met his approval, he returned to his open carrier, curled up inside and went to sleep.

All the cartons had been clearly labeled with the name of the room into which they were to go – and each room was identified so as to avoid confusion.

At eleven thirty, based on the workmen's topping preferences, Marc ordered several pizzas to be delivered; he set them on the counter, along with sodas and bottled water he'd stowed in the fridge the week before, and summoned the movers to the kitchen.

The crew chief instructed two of his men to continue working while the others ate quickly, and then switch, taking turns so the work of unloading the truck wouldn't stop.

"No," Marc refuted him quietly. "I want them all to stop and have lunch. It's hot out there, and those guys need a real lunch break."

"But you're paying us by the hour," the crew chief explained. "By law, we would have to bill you for that time, even if nobody was working."

"I understand," Marc said with a nod. "I still want them all to take a half-hour lunch break." He also insisted the guys take frequent water – and bathroom – breaks as needed.

After the boss reversed his initial directive and told his workers all to take thirty for lunch, at the customer's insistence, one of the guys sought Marc out right away.

"Thanks, mister," the young man said, breathing hard as he mopped his sweaty brow with a wrinkled red paisley bandana. "That sure is nice of you. I wish more customers were like you."

After lunch, as the crew returned to work, each of them thanked Marc for providing lunch and drinks.

He assured them it was his pleasure.

During the afternoon, he noticed all the crew members took particular care while carrying in and setting up the furniture. Once they finished unloading all the cartons, they ensured each one was in its proper room before gathering their moving blankets, hand carts and dollies, to bring them out to the truck. Finally, they did a quick check of the apartment to pick up empty water bottles, soda cans, napkins and discarded pizza crusts, leaving the apartment in pristine condition.

As they were about to leave, Marc personally thanked each member of the crew, addressing each man by name, and tipped them all handsomely.

Before he left for work, he brought Oscar in from the porch and left him to roam inside the new apartment. He filled the cat's food and water bowls in the kitchen, then set up the litter box in the hallway and showed Oscar where it was.

When Marie got home from work, her old apartment was empty. All that was left to do was chase after a few cat-hair tumbleweeds and crumpled wads of discarded packing tape. Once that was done, she locked the place up and drove home to Seymour.

Marc had made up the bed, unpacked a carton of bath towels, hung the shower curtain and set an assortment of bath salts and scented candles on the counter. He'd even taped a note to the bathroom mirror: "Have a nice bath. I'll be home before 1."

When Marc arrived home at 12:25, Marie was in bed, reading. As he entered the bedroom, she laid aside her book and got up to greet him, wearing a sheer green peignoir.

"Hi," she purred, sliding up against him as she stretched on tiptoe to kiss his mouth.

Marc slid his good arm around her and pulled her close. "Hi. Mmm, you smell great." He kissed her upturned mouth softly, sliding his hand down her back, where it came to rest along the shapely, tantalizing curve of her bottom.

"I'm so glad you're home." Pressing her breasts against him, she kissed him with a sense of urgency. She tugged his shirttails free of his jeans, unhooked his belt and undid his fly. She rubbed her pelvis against his crotch, smiling in quiet delight as she felt him stiffen at her teasing ministrations. "I've been wanting you all night. Come to bed."

An enticing smile crossed his face. His left eyebrow arched upward. "Time to christen this apartment?"

"You catch on quick." Her breath was hot against the side of his throat.

"Can I at least brush my teeth first?"

Marie had figured he would ask that. She gave a knowing smile. "Okay, but don't keep me waiting too long," she cautioned. Then she bit her lower lip and fixed him with a smoldering gaze. "I don't like being kept waiting."

Marc retreated into the bathroom and came back far too quickly to have brushed his teeth. "What is this?"

Marie, who had shed her negligee, met him partway to the bed. She watched Marc looking at her, assessing her physically. She knew her breasts were fuller and more voluptuous than he'd likely ever seen them.

Biting her lower lip again, she shifted from one foot to the other and asked innocently, "What's it look like?"

"It looks like one of those pee-on-a-stick pregnancy tests."

"Well" – she twisted her hands together in front of her tummy and shook her head – "no. Not exactly."

"What do you mean, 'not exactly'? That's clearly what it is."

"Kind of." Marie hesitated. "It's a *positive* pee-on-a-stick pregnancy test."

She watched as his face registered recognition. His jaw fell slack. He swallowed hard and his eyes seemed to bulge. "You're... pregnant?"

Her eyes twinkled with excitement. A tiny smile spread across her face until it encompassed her rosy cheeks. She gave an excited nod. "Mm-hmm."

Before Marie could ask if he was excited about her news, Marc closed the distance between them. An instant later, he swept her into his arms, wincing slightly at the leftover twinge in his bicep.

Marie squealed with glee as he spun her around and then set her back on her feet. His mouth covered hers in an exuberant kiss. His hands framed her face, then plunged into the thick softness of her auburn curls, drawing her close. Moments later, his hands slid downward to cup her breasts. She arched her back and let out a whimper as he tweaked her nipples to bring them to attention.

Lowering his head to her creamy breasts, Marc flicked the tip of his tongue across first one erect pink nipple, then the other, sending little shock waves through his shuddering wife.

Marie moaned aloud and pressed her breast fervently into his mouth, and her pelvis to his. She wrapped her arms around his neck and pulled his mouth more firmly against her breast.

"Quit fooling around and take me already," she breathed hotly, her head dropping backward.

Marc scooped her up and carried her to the bed. Laying her down gently, he stepped back and stripped off his clothes.

Coming back, he lay atop her; he nudged her knees apart and entered her as passion coursed like fire through his veins. He scarcely noticed the spasm in his bicep as he took control and thrust powerfully into Marie, making her squeal.

Marc rolled off his wife and lay, breathless, at her side. "Not that I have a single complaint about these past six weeks, but I almost forgot how much I enjoy being on top," he panted when he'd recovered sufficient breath to speak.

Marie let out a deep sigh of gratification. "I second that," she managed wearily. She cuddled close and rested her head against his chest.

Marc wrapped an arm around her and held her close.

Within minutes, both were asleep.

(10:15 a.m., Saturday, August 21)

"You haven't begun figuring out seating arrangements yet, have you?" Marc asked Marie as he entered the living room. As he joined her on the couch, Oscar leapt up beside his new best pal and settled into his lap, purring.

Marie looked up from reading a medical journal. "Not yet. I was going to start working on that this afternoon. Why?"

Petting the cat with one hand, Marc hedged. "I hate to do this to you...but can we add two more people to the guest list? I'd like to seat them with my parents."

Marie looked at him in confusion. "Sure, but where'd we get two more? Who are they?"

"Friends of my mom," he replied glibly. "In Portugal."

"Weren't they on the list to begin with?"

"Originally, yeah. Then my mom said we should take them off because she figured they'd never make the trip, because they're older. Then she hesitated to ask us if we could still invite them because, in the wake of... July," he said as he'd begun referring to the shooting, "she figured they might come, if only to make the effort to pay their respects, so to speak." He paused. "Can we work that out?"

"I don't see why not."

"Just... just don't mention anything to my mom – she already feels bad enough about the last-minute ask."

Marie looked surprised. "Of course not. I'll add two more to the meal count for the hall."

"Thanks, hon. And while we're on the subject of guests, we did invite Val and Tim, right?"

"Of course."

"What about Steve and Paola Merino?" He looked uncomfortable about making that query.

"We invited them. I talked with Paola the other day. They've accepted provisionally."

"What's that mean?"

"She wanted to be sure you didn't have any issue with her being there."

"If I did, we wouldn't have invited them."

"I told her that. She's just trying to keep boundaries in place, that's all. Especially now, since you've started seeing her again. If it makes you at all awkward to have her there, she said she's fine with declining the invitation."

"A year ago it would have been awkward. I'm fine with it now. She's your friend and, yeah, she happens to be a service provider. If I were friends with the plumber or the florist or the HVAC guy, I doubt we would be having this discussion."

"We might if you were friends with my gynecologist."

Marc considered this. "Okay. I'll give you that. That would be weird."

"But you're okay with Steve and Paola being there?"

"Yes. And when I posed the question, I even identified her as 'Paola' and not 'Dr. Merino.' See? I can acknowledge and respect boundaries as well as the next guy." He flashed a playful smile.

"I did notice that. I thought that showed remarkable growth on your part."

"Thank you." Getting to his feet, Marc planted a kiss on his wife's forehead, then gently placed Oscar onto her lap. "Here, this is for you. I gotta make a call. Then I'll head out to the grocery store."

Back in the bedroom, Marc shut the door; he picked up the phone and dialed the number on the card he pulled from his wallet.

As the connection went through and the ringtone buzzed in his ear, his insides clenched. He suddenly recalled his teasing words to Marie in the airport, about starting their marriage with deceit and obfuscation.

When the line clicked and he heard, "*Olá*," Marc nearly hung up.

***

(11:40 a.m. Monday, August 23)

Right after his session with Dr. Merino, Marc drove to Yale to register for fall classes. As a prerequisite to an architecture course he hoped to take come spring, he took 20th Century History. And as he hadn't suffered quite enough torture last semester with trig, he signed up for Calculus of Functions of One Variable I. Rounding out his fall courses, he registered for a first-year seminar, Reading Recent North American Short Fiction, and Drawing Architecture, one of the architecture classes actually open to first-year students.

While he was in town, Marc checked out the practice pool on the third floor of the Payne Whitney Gym. It was less than a half-mile walk from the architecture school, so he could resume the daily swimming regimen he'd had to abandon months earlier.

When he was ready to leave, it was too late to meet Marie for lunch, but he really wanted to see her. He stopped at the diner for two decafs to go – extra light with one sugar, on the off chance she could get away for a short break.

Elisa buzzed into Marie's office. "Doctor Lindemeyr, Mister Midnight Coffee is here."

Marc smiled at the nickname Marie's assistant bestowed on him when they started dating.

"He says he's a few hours early. I hope that's okay."

Marc could hear Marie's playful grin in her tone through the intercom. "Has he got coffee?"

"He's got two cups of something," she replied. She sniffed the air. "Sure smells like coffee."

"Send him in. If it's not, I'll schedule him for six sessions of electroconvulsive therapy. That oughta teach 'im."

Elisa raised an eyebrow. "Hmm, only six; guess she likes you." She motioned to the closed door. "You heard the boss lady. Go ahead in. And I hope for your sake that really is coffee."

Marc laughed at her easy teasing. "You two need serious help."

Marie swung the door open and greeted her husband. "To what do I owe this pleasure?" she asked, shutting the door behind him.

He handed her one of the to-go cups and leaned in to kiss her. "I missed you. That's all."

Her grin broadened. "I'm glad to see you," she replied. "And I'm glad you brought coffee."

"It's decaf. I hope that won't warrant any electroshock therapy."

She patted his cheek and kissed him. "It gets you extra

points for thoughtfulness."

"I didn't say anything about its being decaf because I didn't want to raise suspicions."

"Good thinking. I'm not planning on saying anything 'til I begin to show." Motioning him to the couch, she glanced at her watch. "I've got forty minutes 'til my next session. What's up?"

"I got the classes I wanted. And I checked out the on-campus pool; it's open to all students, and it's within easy walking distance."

"That's terrific!"

"Now you don't have to worry about me going all to flab," he said, patting his still-firm abs.

"I was thinking more about its being excellent therapy to rebuild that poor muscle," Marie replied, caressing his right bicep. She snuggled close. "I'm so glad you came to see me. It's been such a long day already. And I'm on call tonight. I swear, all I want to do is sleep!"

"Can you nap while you're on call and just keep an ear out for your pager?"

"I'd love to, but that's a dangerous habit to get into. What if I were to fall so deeply asleep I didn't hear it go off?"

"You, my dear, are a remarkable woman – and a dedicated professional." He kissed the end of her nose. "Tell you what" – he scooched to the end of the couch and coaxed her toward him, resting her head in his lap – "you nap for awhile. I'll wake you up in half an hour."

"What if you fall asleep, too?" she fretted.

"Shh," he replied, smoothing his wife's hair. "I won't. Just rest."

Within minutes, Marc felt Marie's breathing slow and deepen; she was out. He set an alarm on his watch for ten minutes to three and continued stroking her hair while she slept.

Chapter 23

(9:56 a.m. Saturday, September 11, 1993)
"Nervous?"

"Why should I be? This makes the most sense of anything I've ever done in my life."

Gary kissed his sister's cheek. "I'm glad to hear that." He clasped her hand. "I love you, sis. And Marc is one lucky guy; I hope he realizes that."

Tears formed at the corners of her eyes. She was always weepy these days. "Thanks, Gary – for being so supportive. I always could count on you." Marie shifted her bouquet of white roses and purple irises to her left hand and dabbed at her eyes with the iris-embroidered handkerchief in her right hand.

"Well, I seem to recall you being there for me... through *many* a rough patch."

The siblings watched Joey escort their mother to her seat; then Clive escorted Marc's mother to hers. The grey-tuxedoed groomsmen returned to the back of the church to roll out the aisle runner, just as they had practiced during the rehearsal the previous evening.

Gary squeezed Marie's hand. "If you guys are even half as happy together as Micki and I have been, you're in for a great next fifty or sixty years."

Not wanting to smear her lipstick, Marie rested her head against his shoulder. He was tall and sturdy; he kind of reminded her of Grandpa. And she told him so. "Only, much, much younger."

Gary's surprised laugh was full and rich and hearty. It carried through the church over the sound of the subdued organ music. Much like Grandpa's laugh would have.

Aunt Viv and several of Marc's even-more-ancient great aunts turned with pursed lips to cast disapproving glares toward the vestibule.

"Oh, that's just great," Marie remarked. "Get me in trouble with his family on my wedding day!"

"It is not your wedding day and you know it," Gary countered. "That was months ago."

"Yeah, but now I'll never have a moment's peace at family gatherings."

"*You're* the doctor; just explain I'm the unstable brother nobody mentions and I'm going straight back to the facility afterward. I'll be sure to be unduly awed by shiny things."

She snickered. "You're too much. But it might just work. If I can pull that off, I owe you one."

"You can pay me back in nieces and nephews. And I want plenty of 'em."

Impish secrecy flickered across Marie's face. "I wasn't going to say anything yet..."

Gary's eyes darted toward his sister's satin-swathed middle. A conspiratorial twinkle lighted his eyes. "Something new?"

Marie gave a tiny, excited nod; a squeal bubbled up and escaped before she could squelch it. She clamped a hand to her mouth; her face glowed with exhilaration at the finally shared secret.

Moments later, when she'd barely had time to compose herself, the ushers returned to the vestibule. Marie's attendants exited the bridal prep room with their bouquets and were now waiting to process in for the start of the Mass. Erin hopped excitedly from foot to foot, then spun in a circle just to feel the swooshy material of her full-skirted chiffon dress twirling around her legs.

Michaela tapped Erin on the shoulder. "Settle down, sweetie." She handed her bouquet to her stepdaughter so she could make a last-minute adjustment to Marie's veil.

Once everyone was in place, the organist began the opening strains of *Jesu, Joy of Man's Desiring*, to signal the attendants' procession up the aisle. Emily and Clive went first, followed by Joey, escorting Erin. Finally, Michaela, Marie's matron of honor, made her way up the aisle.

When Michaela arrived at the front of the church, near where Marc waited alongside Father Callahan, the organist slid seamlessly into *Trumpet Voluntary*.

Marie processed down the aisle on her brother's arm, as they'd rehearsed. Once they reached the sanctuary, Gary would take his place beside Marc, as best man.

Catching sight of her mother, two-year-old Amanda chirped, "Mama!" She stood on the pew beside her grandfather, in a pretty green satin-and-tulle dress.

Micki turned around and put a finger to her lips to quiet the toddler.

Before Michael could react, the little girl scrambled down and galloped toward her mother. Then she noticed her godfather standing nearby. "Unca Mahc!" she gasped.

Michaela tried to catch her daughter as she darted past, but the child was too fast.

Amanda looked up at him with an adoring gaze and exclaimed, "You wook so pwetty!"

Several pews of guests chuckled at the toddler's proclamation.

Marc smiled as he gamely swept the child into his arms. "Thank you. So do you."

Ignoring his white-rose boutonniere with its dark-blue ribbon, her little fingers went directly to the small gold insignia affixed to the lapel of his grey tuxedo, the one that identified him as a Grand Cross member of the Order of Prince Henry. He gave his goddaughter a little kiss before handing her back over to her mother.

Amanda did not want to be corralled. She squirmed and fussed in her mother's arms and demanded to be let down. Finally, in frustration, the child yelled, "Shit!" at the top of her lungs.

A collective gasp escaped the guests. Terrible stillness filled the sanctuary – except for the organist, who was still playing the processional as if nothing out of the ordinary were unfolding.

Gary winced. "Oh dear God," he whispered, covering his face with one hand.

Mortified, Michaela marched over to her father, the struggling tot still in her arms. "Dad, hang on to her – and *please* try to keep her quiet."

Marc cringed and turned away, ostensibly to confer discreetly with Father Callahan. The two men stood at the sanctuary, red faced – Marc with embarrassment and Father Callahan from trying to repress his mirth.

Marie, meanwhile, stopped walking and gripped her brother's arm.

Gary gave a hesitant glance at his sister, afraid to see the expression on her face.

An unearthly sound escaped her throat. A strangled, horrible sound.

Panic swept through Gary. Chagrin at his daughter's having spoiled her aunt's wedding overwhelmed him.

Now Marie bent at the waist, convulsing, as the horrible, gasping sounds surged through her.

At last, Gary realized, the noises emerging from Marie weren't anguished, guttural cries of ruination, but uncontrollable laughter. He tried to subdue his sister, but her infectious laughter left him stifling chortles as they approached the sanctuary – much to Micki's consternation.

By the time Marie and Marc stood together at the foot of the sanctuary, the entire wedding party was aflush – either from embarrassment or the effort of trying to squelch their laughter. Or, as in Marc's case, both.

Father Callahan ascended to the altar to greet the assembled guests.

"Good mornin' to ye," he boomed, rosy cheeked and mirthful. "We gather here this lovely morning, in the Name of the Father and of the Son and of the Holy Ghost, not only to celebrate the holy sacrifice of the Mass, but to recognize and convalidate the union of this fine couple... and to acknowledge that even when it seems things have gone most wildly out of control, God is still in His heaven, He's here present among us, and He remains with us every step o' the way along our paths through life. And in case there was any doubt, He sometimes throws us a curveball just to remind us He has quite a hearty sense o' humor."

A murmur swept through the church at his words.

"I'm given to understand we can thank our groom for teachin' that darling little monkey to cuss like that," he added. "Marcus assures me he extends his deepest apologies to anyone who may have been scandalized – especially the parents of said little monkey."

Realizing there was nothing they could do about it now, Gary and Micki exchanged a look of resigned awkwardness.

"But what's behind us is behind us," Father Callahan continued. "And now I invite ye lovely people to join me in prayer..."

It wasn't until partway through the Mass, when she and Marc faced one another, about to restate their vows, that Marie happened to glance out into the pews, to scan the rows of guests. She noticed four unfamiliar dark-suited men in the fourth pew. Then she recognized the dignified couple seated in the third pew, just behind Marc's parents. Her breath caught in her throat.

She leaned slightly toward Marc. "How did they get here?" she breathed, her slightly parted, smiling lips not even moving. She knew he would know precisely who she meant.

"Shh," he replied, his mouth equally still. "I'll tell you later."

Just before the end of the Mass, Father Callahan introduced the newly married couple. "I present to ye, for the first time in public since being united in holy matrimony in the Catholic Church, Mr. and Mrs. Marc Lindemeyr. And don't they make a right handsome couple?"

At his words, the guests burst into enthusiastic applause.

After the final blessing and the dismissal, the newlyweds, trailed by their attendants, exited to a spirited rendition of Mouret's *Rondeau*.

After they greeted nearly all their guests in the receiving line, Marie noted the surprise guests hadn't yet emerged. As she was about to wonder aloud to Marc what had become of them, she saw Isabella and Paolo surrounded by their quartet of dark-suited guards. On her husband's arm, Isabella looked radiant in a bright-blue dress with simple diamond-stud earrings. And Paolo looked every inch the dignified head of state in his classic cut dark-grey suit.

"It's so wonderful to see you again!" Marie squealed, giving the first lady an exuberant hug. Tears appeared at the corners of her eyes. "What a lovely surprise!"

"We couldn't have missed this," Isabella told Marie, her dark eyes shining. "And you look so beautiful! Congratulations!"

The first lady continued along the line to greet Marc. "Congratulations, dear!" She gave him an enthusiastic hug. "What a lovely couple – and such a beautiful ceremony!"

His smile radiated the warmth of his affection for her. "Thank you, Isabella. I'm so thrilled you and Paolo were able to make it."

"We're delighted to be here – and the timing worked out beautifully. He's due to visit the consulate tomorrow and then he'll be addressing the United Nations on Monday."

"That worked out great! I'm so glad," Marc said. "Let me introduce you to the others."

"That would be wonderful. But" – Isabella laid a cautionary hand on his arm – "please just introduce us as Paolo and Isabella. No titles. We're here simply as friends."

Marc nodded with a courteous smile. "Understood."

The introductions went smoothly, with no one being any the wiser. But as he presented the first couple to his parents, Fernanda Lindemeyr's eyes widened in immediate recognition.

"*Senhor Presidente*," she stammered, clasping the hand he extended to her. Her gaze left the president's only long enough to flicker to her son's face and back. "*Isso é uma grande honra. Obrigado por ter vindo.*" This is a great honor. Thank you for coming.

"It is our pleasure to be here," he assured her graciously, in flawless English. "Your son and his wife are a lovely couple, and we wanted to be here with them to celebrate this special and holy occasion. Thank you for permitting us to share the day with you."

Chapter 24

As the semester progressed, Marc's enthusiasm for his classes thrived. He commandeered the third bedroom as his study space – and kept the door shut when he wasn't there, so Oscar couldn't get in and trash any of his projects. Mostly Marc worked in there on weekends, as he did the bulk of his homework and studying in the New Haven Public Library before going to work.

And now that he was back to swimming nearly every day, his energy level and his stress level had swapped places. This enabled him to cut back to seeing Dr. Merino monthly and, before long, every three months. His nightmares had also subsided and he was sleeping through the night again.

(2:30 p.m., Saturday, October 23)
A knock at the back door startled Marie, who nearly dropped the apple she was peeling. Setting the half-peeled fruit on the cutting board, she wiped her hands on her apron and went to answer the door.

"Hi, Tim," she greeted the landlord. "What's goin' on?"

"Can Marc come out and play?"

Marie smiled at the question. "Not right now. He's studying for his calculus midterm."

Tim made a face. "Ugh. Math. Well, better him than me. But when he needs a break, tell him to come on down. Sebastian dearly wants to go for a walk and he doesn't seem to have any use for me these days. He much prefers his walkabout buddy."

Marie grinned. "I'll be sure to tell him. He'll get a kick out of that."

"What're you up to?"

"Peeling some apples for pie. Maybe you and Val can come up later for dessert and coffee?"

Tim's eyes widened in delight. "Ooh! Sounds good to me. I'm sure Val wouldn't turn down an offer of your apple pie, either. We'll bring the ice cream."

"Only if it's vanilla," Marc called from the other room.

Marie shook her head. "I swear, that boy's got the hearing of a bat!"

"Hey, don't you have studying to do?" Tim called back.

Marc, wearing sweats and thick socks, padded into the kitchen. "Well I was studying," he remarked, "until I was interrupted by all this talk of pie and ice cream."

"That's your fault for getting so easily distracted," Tim replied.

"Actually, I could kind of use a break," Marc admitted. "Only so much calculus I can take at any one time."

"Great. You wanna come with me to take Sebastian for a walk?" Tim asked. "We'll probably only go to the end of the block and back – not too long – so you can get a little break from studying and then get back to it."

When Marc returned, the pie was on the counter, in a state of partial completion. The fridge stood open and Marie was gone.

Marc shut the refrigerator door. "Hon?" he called out to the empty room.

No answer.

He looked for her in the living room, then the bedroom. He found her standing by the toilet, arms folded across her middle, looking pale and queasy. "Honey? Are you okay?"

Marie took a deep breath and let it out. It was as if she hadn't heard him.

"Marie?"

She continued to stare at the toilet, as though mystified by it.

Marc reached out and touched her on the shoulder. "Are you alright?"

Giving a start, she stared at her husband, then nodded woodenly. "Can you finish making the pie? I" – she hesitated – "I can't…"

"What's the matter?"

When she turned to look at him, it was like she was seeing him for the first time. "You know those roundish things we keep in the refrigerator?"

Where's this coming from? Marc squinted in perplexity. "What?" He shook his head, confused.

"Those" – she drew her hands close together, indicating a small object – "those little white things… in the refrigerator."

"White things in the…? You mean eg—"

"Shh!" Looking as though she was about to vomit any second, Marie reached out a hand to cover Marc's mouth before he could finish the word. "Don't say it," she warned, shaking her head. She took several deep breaths, in an obvious attempt to stave off a rush of nausea, then edged closer to the toilet.

She looked at his worried face, her expression grim. "I need you to never say that word," she implored. "I can't see them. I can't hear about them. And I – for sure – can't smell them."

Marc gave a slow, deliberate nod, placating her. "Okay. What brought this on?"

She patted her slightly pregnant tummy.

"Ahh. Food aversions. Emily couldn't stand the smell, taste or texture of beef or onions for months. Then, suddenly, she couldn't wolf down enough of 'em. And then coconut was *odio cibum*."

"Was what?"

"Unwelcome food."

"Oh." Marie wrinkled her nose. "I hate it when you

speak Latin. It makes me feel so stupid."

"Sorry." He kissed her on the forehead. "Why don't you go lie down. I'll finish that pie and then get back to studying."

"Thank you." Marie slid her arms around his midsection. "How did I ever get so lucky?"

He shrugged. "That may remain one of the world's great unanswered questions."

Chapter 25

(Friday, December 24 – Christmas Eve)
That year Marc and Marie agreed they'd spend Christmas Eve with her family, and Christmas Day with his. Holding to a family tradition that started while Grandpa was alive, Gary hosted Christmas Eve at the cottage in Milford. That made it convenient for Sam and Martha Johnson, who lived four houses up and who'd been Edward and Josephine Sheldon's dearest friends, to join in the festivities.

Customarily, they celebrated with the standard Italian seven-fishes meal. In years past, Gary, and Marie handled the cooking, working from Grandma Jo's well-worn cookbooks. Now, though, Gary and Micki assumed the kitchen duties.

This year, there'd be eleven of them: Gary, Micki and the girls; Micki's dad; Gary's mother and brother; Sam and Martha; and Marc and Marie. It would be snug quarters, but as Edward was fond of saying, "We've always been a close family." They'd had fourteen for Thanksgiving the year before, so eleven seemed almost spacious.

This was Marc's first Christmas Eve with the Sheldons, and he couldn't help comparing it with his own family's ethnic traditions.

Over dinner, he casually revealed that not only was Marie four and a half months pregnant, but they'd just learned a few days earlier they were expecting twins.

A great commotion erupted around the table.

Erin squealed and hugged Uncle Marc.

Diane patted her daughter's arm. "That's wonderful! You're going to be a fantastic mom!"

Gary gave his sister a knowing wink. He hadn't even told Michaela, who let out a gasp and nearly dropped the platter of scallops.

Joey did some quick math. "Wait a minute. Weren't you guys just married in September?"

Marc and Marie exchanged a hand squeeze beneath the table.

"No," Marc replied, aware of Erin's keen attention. "We've been married since July. But the marriage was convalidated in September."

"Call it what you want," Joey teased, waving his fork with a ring of fried calamari on it. "All I remember is a church wedding only three months ago."

"If it makes you feel better to be scandalized, little brother," Marie piped up, "then go right ahead."

Across the table, Sam and Martha beamed as proudly as if Marc and Marie were their own grandchildren.

After dinner, when they had a quiet moment together, Sam and Martha sat down with the expectant parents.

"This is such wonderful news," Martha said, clasping their hands. "We're both so happy for you. You two are going to be fabulous parents."

Sam looked at Marc curiously.

"What's the matter?" Marie asked.

Sam nodded. "I recognize that ring," he said with a smile, indicating Marc's wedding band.

"And I recognize those rings," Martha added, lifting Marie's hand.

"Grandpa left them to Gary and me," Marie explained, snuggling close to her husband, "and when Marc and I got engaged last Christmas, Gary gave him Grandpa's ring."

"It's nice to see them on the hands of young people in love again," Sam commented. "May you enjoy many happy years wearing them together."

When it came time to open presents, everyone exclaimed with delight over the gifts Marc and Marie brought back.

For Martha, they'd gotten a brightly colored woven tablecloth and some handmade pottery serving pieces. And they couldn't have chosen anything better than the pair of sheepskin slippers for Sam.

Diane, the other architect in the family, declared her leather attaché case "perfect!"

The bottle of Port and a leather business-card case were the ideal gift for Michael.

Erin's dark-brown eyes widened in delight as she clutched her new leather-bound journal. "I love it!" she exclaimed, hugging her aunt and uncle. "Ohh, I just know I'm gonna do so much great writing in this book! Thank you!"

For Joey, they bought a pair of fine leather driving gloves.

"Ooh!" Micki exclaimed, holding up her new red-leather miniskirt. "You guys! This is so—"

"Hot," Gary finished.

"Well, if we'd known you'd enjoy *her* gift so much, we wouldn't have gotten you this," Marc teased, handing over a small package.

"For when you actually have to dress like a grownup," Marie added.

Inside was a pair of blue miniature ceramic-tile cufflinks and a matching tie clip.

And finally, for Amanda, a life-size stuffed Portuguese water dog. She squealed with delight and hugged the nearly two-foot-tall plush black and white toy.

"What are you going to name her?" her mom asked.

Clutching her new toy close to herself, Amanda looked up at her mother, her eyes big and round. "I name her Unca Mahc!"

While Christmas Eve festivities at the cottage often

carried on until nearly midnight, Marc and Marie left just after ten. It was a half hour drive home and by the time they got back, they were both eager to fall into bed.

"Want to go to midnight Mass?" Marc asked as he helped her out of the car.

Marie stared at her husband in exhausted disbelief. "Tell me you're joking."

He hugged her. "Yes, I'm joking. The only place you're going is right to bed."

They were almost asleep when Marie sat up with a gasp. "Oh no!" she lamented.

Instantly alert, Marc snapped on the bedside lamp. "What's the matter?"

"I just remembered – I was supposed to make the *bolo rei* this year. Remember? I got the fava bean last year." Tears immediately sprang to her eyes. "I totally forgot 'til just now!"

Marc gently wiped away his overly emotional wife's tears. He drew her close and stroked her hair. "Hush, *querida*. We told my mom weeks ago we wouldn't be there tonight. I'm sure she made one. C'mon, go back to sleep."

In the morning, Marc and Marie walked to church with Tim and Val for eight-thirty Mass. On their way back, Val invited the other couple back to their apartment for a light breakfast and to exchange gifts.

After breakfast, while Tim cleared the table and refilled everyone's coffee, Marc ran upstairs to retrieve the presents for their friends, and Val pulled Marc and Marie's gifts from beneath the Christmas tree.

Val drew in her breath when she opened her gift, a pair of silver earrings and a silk scarf in a bold floral print.

Tim laughed aloud as he opened the cube-shaped box that bore his name; he knew the ice-cream maker had to have been Marc's idea. "Let me guess – the recipe book was Marie's idea."

The Unintended Hero

"Of course," she admitted. "Someone had to be practical."

Marie's gift from their friends was a back-porch container garden, complete with wheeled pots, soil mix and a set of basic gardening tools – plus two packets of zucchini seeds.

"So you can have all the fried zucchini flowers you want," Val chirped, hugging her friend.

Marc roared with laughter as he opened the same ice-cream maker he'd gotten for Tim.

"Now you can make your own vanilla ice cream," Tim said with a chuckle.

"Hey, can you blame me if I don't think butter pecan exactly goes well with apple pie?"

"I can't help it if you're not open to new experiences," Tim sniped back.

Marie and Val shook their heads and laughed.

Sebastian nosed his way over and plopped himself into Marc's lap.

Marc rubbed the pooch's belly. "Hey, buddy. How ya doin'? You wanna go for a little walk?"

The puppy jumped up and licked Marc's face.

"Not 'til he's opened his present," Marie said, pulling forth one final package.

"Oh, you shouldn't have," Val told her, accepting the gift.

It was a tin of homemade dog cookies.

"The round ones are peanut butter and the rectangular ones are bacon," Marie explained.

"Where'd you find time to bake dog cookies?" Tim marveled.

"Forget that," Marc said, acting affronted. "How come you never bake *me* cookies?"

Marie grinned and patted his cheek. "I'll bake you dog cookies, sweetheart."

"Thanks," he grumbled. "C'mon, Sebastian, let's go find your leash."

Before leaving for his parents' house, Marc and Marie

exchanged gifts. They had agreed to keep Christmas low key, and to give each other one small but meaningful gift apiece: for her, a blue-topaz pendant; and for Marc, an electronic keyboard. Marie looked a bit miffed when she noticed the gift with her name on it that remained under their little tabletop tree.

"That's not from me," Marc replied when she called him on it.

"Then where'd it come from?"

"It showed up in the mail earlier this week."

Eyeing him suspiciously, Marie accepted the package. It felt squashy, like a scarf. She peeled away the wrapping to find a tissue-wrapped parcel. An envelope taped to it had her name on it.

The envelope contained a hand-written note.

> *Dearest Marie,*
> *I was so thrilled when Marc shared with me the news of your pregnancy. What a wonderful and exciting time this must be for you both!*
> *This gown, hand stitched by my grandmother, is the one I wore at my baptism. I had always intended to pass it down to my own children, but God's plans for me did not include babies.*
> *I hope you and Marc have plenty of occasions to put it to use.*
> *With all my love and affection,*
> *Isabella*

Tears flooded Marie's eyes. As soon as she wiped them, more took their place. She handed Marc the note and, with trembling hands, opened the tissue. Inside lay a white satin garment, with tiny pearls sewn into the hand smocking. With an audible breath, she lifted the satin gown from its tissue bed. She ran her hand lovingly over the smooth material, marveling at the intricate details of the hand-smocked front.

Marc's eyes misted as he read the note. "That's beautiful," he said, handing it back.

Her eyes still streaming with tears, Marie looked up at him. "I have to call her."

"Absolutely." Marc pulled out his wallet and took out the card with the first couple's private number. "Tell them I said '*Feliz Natal.*'"

Later that night, Marc and Marie settled onto the couch to enjoy some quiet time together before turning in.

"Did you have a nice Christmas?"

Marie smiled. "I did. I still can't get over that gift from Isabella! That was so sweet!"

"It really was," Marc agreed.

"It was so great getting to spend time with family. The kids are all getting so big! Erin and Mandy are growing like weeds! And Felicity looked darling in that little Christmas-tree dress with all the ornaments on it."

He smirked. "I thought she looked ridiculous."

"Marc! How can you say that?" she exclaimed. "It was adorable!"

"Call it what you want. I thought it was silly," he scoffed. "I hope you're not planning to dress our kids in stupid getups like that. You're not, are you?"

"When did you get to be such an old poop?"

"I just think it's unnecessary to dress kids like stage props – simply because parents think it's 'cute.' It's one thing if you want to wear a Santa hat, an ugly sweater or a dopey bit of fake mistletoe on a spring over your head."

"Or a pair of elf ears?" she interjected, recalling the way he'd showed up at her doorstep the previous Christmas Eve.

"Yes," he replied. "My point exactly. That was my choice. But kids don't get a say about whether they're made to look absurd. They're not accessories, for crying out loud! They're people."

Then, made uneasy by Marie's continued scrutiny, he gave kind of a half-smile and admitted, "Alright, it did look kind of cute." He shook a playful finger at her. "Don't go getting any ideas for next year. I will not have you dressing our kids like a candy cane and a yule log."

"Fine," she teased, ruffling his hair. "I still think you're being an old poop."

"I've been thinking," he said a minute later, kissing the side of his wife's throat as she relaxed in his arms. "What if I were to take a year off from school t—"

"What?" She stared at him. "But you're just getting started. Why would you do that?"

"So I can care for the kids. You can go back to seeing patients after your maternity leave, and the babies get to stay home instead of having to go to daycare, or get shuffled back and forth between sets of grandparents all the time."

Marie looked doubtful. "Do you think you'll be able to handle both of them?"

"No less well than you could. No one ever asks moms that. It's just assumed they'll be fine juggling kids. Of course, I won't be doing any breastfeeding, so you'll have to be pumping regularly. But how's that sound to you?"

She gave a slow nod. "Sounds like it could work. Let's talk about it again as it gets closer."

"You don't like the idea, do you?"

"It's not that. It's just... I hate for you to put your dreams on hold."

"I wouldn't be putting my dreams on hold," he countered. "Yale's just one of my dreams. I have plenty of dreams – fatherhood among them. I'll just be temporarily trading one for the other. And it's worth it. Think about it, *querida*. Your patients depend on your being there. If you were to take even a few months off, they'd have to find other therapists. And I totally get how scary it is to consider starting over once you've established a level of trust with someone."

Marie considered this. She nodded in reluctant agreement.

"Anyway, how many dads get to be home with their kids full time?"

"That's a good point. Would you still keep working at the station?"

"I'd like to, yeah. At least for a while."

"Okay. I should be home well before you have to leave. But what about when I'm on call?"

Marc frowned, drumming his fingers against his wife's pregnant tummy. "I didn't consider that. I guess that won't work very well then, will it?"

Marie was silent for a time. "Maybe it can." She interlaced her fingers with his and kissed his cheek. "I could tell them I can't be on call anymore. They can find someone else to do it. There's no reason you should have to be the only one making sacrifices for the family."

"Can you do that?"

She raked a hand through her hair. "I don't see why not. I never signed on to do permanent on-call duty the rest of my life. My primary responsibility is to my family. If they can't accommodate that, it's their problem, not mine. I'll let them know next week, so they have plenty of time to find a replacement. When were you thinking of implementing this full-time dad arrangement?"

Marc glanced around. "I don't see any babies around here just yet," he replied with a teasing grin, "so I'm figuring after exams. That'll be May, and you'll still be on maternity leave, so the timing should work out well. We'll have some overlap before you go back, which'll give us both a chance to ease into parenthood."

"The more I think about it, the better I like the idea," she admitted, settling back into Marc's embrace. She patted his arm. "I think it'll be nice, having you with them full time. I'm glad you brought it up."

Chapter 26

For the spring semester, since he still qualified as a freshman, Marc took another first-year seminar, Jazz and Architecture. He also registered for Mapping the Dialects of American English, Intensive Elementary Italian and Engineering Improv: An Introduction to Engineering Analysis.

The months sped by. Midterms came and went and his late-semester engineering project and final papers for his seminar and English class loomed. Marc spent nearly all his free time studying or working on term projects. He apologized for being absent so much. But Marie, who had entered her nesting phase, assured him she didn't feel abandoned, and insisted he focus on his schoolwork.

Before his study schedule grew too hectic, they shopped for cribs, dressers, a pair of rocking chairs and a changing table, plus car seats, a breast pump and dozens of bottles.

Toward the end of March, with help from Tim and Val, they set up the nursery.

(7:39 p.m. Wednesday, April 13, 1994)

Marc jotted requests while taking calls for Seventies at Seven. He pressed the flashing button for the next caller. "Hi, Z97-3."

"Honey, it's me. Val's bringing me to the hospital. My water broke."

"Already?" he squeaked. "Isn't it kinda soon?"

"It's a few weeks early, but that's not uncommon with twins."

"Will you be okay 'til I get there? I'll leave here as soon as I can."

Marie took a deep, calming breath. "I'll be fine, sweetheart. It's only been a few minutes. No need to rush. The contractions are still about ten minutes apart. You've got plenty of time."

As soon as Marc hung up with Marie, he got Rob Tyler on the phone. The fill-in guy had long since been advised Marc might have to duck out on short notice.

"Hang tight, bud. I'll be there in twenty," Rob told him.

No sooner had he hung up with Rob than Marc realized he couldn't remember which hospital she said she was going to.

When Rob arrived just past eight, Marc was a wreck. Val might have taken Marie to one of at least seven hospitals.

"Calm down," Rob said. He and Cindy had four kids and were no strangers to the which-hospital-are-you-at issue. "Marie's a doctor, right? Doesn't she have a mobile phone?"

Marc nodded. "Yeah. Yeah, I guess she does."

Rob patted the younger man on the shoulder. "Okay. Take a deep breath and give her a call. You know the number, right?"

Just then the auxiliary line in the studio rang. It was Marie.

"Hi, honey," she said, panting through a contraction. "Val bet me you wouldn't remember which hospital we're going to…"

By eight fifteen, Marc was on his way to St. Mary's Hospital in Waterbury.

By the time Marc arrived, Marie had already been assigned to a labor-and-delivery suite. She'd been given an epidural and had fetal heart monitors strapped to her belly.

"Are you okay?" Marc asked, rushing to her side.

"I'm fine. Everything's going well. When it's time to deliver, they'll wheel me down to the OR – that's standard procedure with twins," she reassured him, reaching for his hands. "If they need to do a C-section for one or both of them, I'm already there."

Marc nodded his understanding. "Okay. What do you need me to do?"

"Just coach me through it, feed me ice chips and remind me to breathe. Oh, and this is key: Stay well out of striking distance once the next contraction hits. They say I've got a hell of a reach."

(7:11 a.m., Thursday, April 14, 1994)

Marc swept the damp hair off his wife's forehead and gazed at the newborns resting in their mother's arms. "They're beautiful." He kissed her flushed cheek. "Absolutely perfect."

Marie managed an exhausted smile as she kissed their tiny heads. "I'm glad you think so. I'm never sleeping with you again."

He grinned. "Oh, you say that now…"

She shook her head. "Mark my words, buddy boy. Separate bedrooms. Now and forever."

Just before eight thirty, Marc reluctantly left his wife and babies to go to school. He could scarcely keep his mind on his classes; he had a hard enough time staying conscious.

After startling himself awake twice in the first ten minutes of Italian class, his teacher called him out. *"A tarda notte, signor Lindemeyr?"* Late night?

"Scusate, Signora Conforti," he replied. *"Mia moglie ha avuto due gemelli questa mattina."* Sorry, my wife had twins this morning.

Mrs. Conforti's eyes widened and she nodded. *"Congratulazioni!"*

Calls of *"Auguri!"* – Best wishes! – came from fellow students around the room.

Marc glanced around at his classmates and raised a

hand in acknowledgment. "*Grazie.*"

"*Abituarsi a non dormire,*" the teacher added with a smile. Get used to not sleeping.

He nodded. "Yeah."

She shook a finger at him. "*In italiano, per favore.*"

"*Sì.*"

"*Hai più lezioni dopo questo?*" Do you have more classes after this?

He shook his head. "*Non oggi.*" Not today.

She made a shooing motion. "*Andare a casa. Riposati.*" Go home. Get some rest.

Weary but grateful, Marc gathered his books and got up to leave. "*Grazie, Signora. Ciao.*"

Marie managed little cat naps between the onslaught of visitors. The first one, just after ten, was her mother, eager to snuggle her new grandbabies.

"Look at all that dark hair," Diane gushed. "You two make beautiful babies!"

When Gary and Micki arrived, a posted sign indicated no children under five, except siblings, could enter. They took turns visiting Marie and the babies while the other stayed in the waiting room with Amanda.

When Marc's parents arrived, Marc had just returned to the hospital, after a nap, a shower and a call to the station to say he'd be out again that night – and probably the next. By then, Marie was asleep, so the babies had been returned to their cribs in the nursery.

Marc greeted his parents with a weary hug. "Hi, Mom, Dad. Or should I call you *Avó* and *Bestefar*?" That was Norwegian for Grandpa. "Have you seen the twins yet?"

Fernanda Lindemeyr shook her head. "We just got here and saw Marie was asleep. The poor dear looks exhausted!"

"I know. She was in labor almost twelve hours."

"For a first pregnancy, that's short. I was in labor with you for twenty-six hours."

"Twenty-six?" Marc looked horrified. "How did you

stand it?"

"It was a breeze for me," Willem Lindemeyr joked. "Back then, they didn't allow fathers in the delivery room. So I slept through most of it."

His wife shot him an irritable look. "You could sleep through an earthquake." She turned back to Marc. "It wasn't contractions and pushing the whole time, but it was no picnic, either."

"I hope I was at least worth it."

"You are now." She patted his cheek. "So, where are these grandchildren of mine?"

That evening, Val and Tim came to visit. They knocked at the slightly open door. "Where are these babies we've heard so much about?" Val asked, peeking her head into the room.

"C'mon in," Marie welcomed them. "They're just about to have their supper."

"Oh, they're darling!" Val enthused, gazing at the babies in their parents' arms.

"I dunno," Tim mused. "They look kind of scrawny to me."

Marc and Marie laughed.

Val did not. "Must you?" she asked. "Really?"

"Someone had to say it," Tim replied. "Do they have names yet, or are we just going to call them Thing One and Thing Two?"

"Sorry to disappoint you, Tim, but we've named them," Marie told him.

"I bet they're not terrific names. Tim and Val are nice names," Tim suggested. "At least, Tim is. Come to think of it, maybe not Val, after all. But Tim's a great name."

Marc laughed wearily at his friend's comment.

"Don't encourage him, Marc," Val warned.

"This is Edward Lucas," Marie told them, gazing down at the little boy in her arms.

"And this," Marc said, turning the baby girl to face them, "is Isabella Fernanda."

***

The next afternoon, the Lindemeyrs brought their twins home to their new apartment.

"Welcome home, babies," Marc cooed as they came through the door with the infants in their carriers. He and Marie set the carriers on the kitchen table and hugged each other.

"Ready to do this parenting thing?" Marc asked as they drew back from one another.

"Whether I am or not, it's gonna happen," Marie replied. "Let's do this."

A sudden stab of panic ran through Marc and he stared at his wife. "Holy crap, Marie! What are we doing? We can't raise kids. We don't have the first clue how to do this."

"It's okay," she said, laying a hand on his arm. "We feed them when they're hungry, change them when they're wet and put them down for naps when they're tired."

He still didn't look comforted. "You forgot bathe them when they start to stink."

"Before then, I would hope," Marie said with a weary smile as she reached up to caress his cheek. "And be as good to each other as we can in the process. It'll be fine, Marc. Now, c'mon, let's get them into their cribs and go get the rest of the stuff from the car."

"No." He laid a hand on her arm. "Let's get them into their cribs and I'll go get the rest of the stuff from the car. You go get some sleep."

Chapter 27

Weeks raced by as Marie and Marc adjusted to parenthood and life as a family of four. Marie seemed to spend much of her time breastfeeding the babies. When Marc wasn't at work, in class or studying, he changed, held and rocked them. Often, he held or rocked them while studying overnight.

During a visit when the twins were a week old, Marc's mother had asked if she could sew their baptismal gowns.

"That's a really generous offer," Marc told her, rocking his fussing son, "and we'd love to have you make one for Edward, but we've already been given a gown for Isabella."

Mrs. Lindemeyr looked perplexed. "Who gives you a gown for one baby and not the other?"

"Someone who didn't know we were having twins," he replied delicately, shifting the baby to his other arm.

"Well, who wouldn't know that?"

The name rolled off his tongue. "Isabella Raposa da Costa."

Fernanda's eyes bulged when she recognized the name. Speech eluded her.

Marc stroked his son's soft dark hair. "She sent Marie the baptismal gown her grandmother made for her." Doing his best not to disturb his son's sleep, Marc retrieved the gifted garment.

Fernanda inspected it carefully. "This is beautiful, Marc. The smocking is so intricate! And the pearls... oh, it's lovely!"

"Think you can make one to match?"

Her lips forming a slim line, she shook her head. "I'll do my best, but I don't think it'll even come close."

Marc kissed his mom on the cheek. "I'm sure it'll be gorgeous. Now here, do you want to hold your grandson?"

(Sunday, May 15)

The twins' baptism took place during the ten-thirty Mass at St. Augustine's. Marc and Marie asked Gary and Micki to be Edward's godparents, and Emily and Tim to be Isabella's. The infants looked darling in their hand-smocked satin gowns, and both slept through the entire ceremony.

Following the Mass, they had a celebratory lunch at Conforti's, a local Italian eatery in Seymour.

While Marc and Marie were settling the babies, one of the waitresses came by to put pitchers of ice water on the tables.

"*Signor Lindemeyr*," a familiar voice hailed him. "*Questi sono i tuoi nuovi bambini?*"

Without thinking, he replied, "*Sì. Sono stati appena battezzati questa mattina.*"

Now he turned to see his Italian instructor in a white tuxedo shirt and black apron. "*Signora Conforti. Che sorpresa vederti qui!*"

Her laughter filled the room. "We're not in class now, Marc; you don't have to speak Italian to me. And yes, it is rather a surprise. It's my husband's restaurant. I help out on weekends."

"I never put two and two together with the name. We love it here."

"I'm glad to hear that."

Marc motioned Marie over. "Sweetheart, this is my Italian teacher, *Signora* Conforti. *Signora*, my wife, Marie."

The two women shook hands. "Pleasure to meet you, Marie. Your babies are beautiful. And Marc's spoken highly of you – in perfect Italian. Please, call me Angela. And be sure to let me know if there's anything I can get you."

"Now that you mention it, an A on my final exam would be great."

She laughed and shook a finger at him. "Don't push it."

The following day, just after his Italian final, Marc sat down with his academic adviser.

Dr. Erich Phillips looked both startled and annoyed at his advisee's news. "Why would you do that?"

"I'm taking time off to be a stay-at-home dad so my wife can resume seeing patients. She's a therapist and continuity of care is important."

The other man leaned back in his chair, folding his arms across his chest. "What happened to your wanting to study architecture? Last semester you were quite intent upon that."

"I still am, Dr. Phillips. But for now, my priorities have shifted. It's not a decision I've come to lightly. I've given this a lot of thought. What it comes down to is this: Yale has been around for two centuries; it'll still be here when I'm ready to come back. But babies are only little for a while."

"I hope you know what you're doing."

"I do," Marc replied with a confident nod. "I've learned that for a building to last, you need a firm foundation, constructed of sturdy materials and erected on solid ground. It's a basic premise of architecture, and that's what I'm doing here. I'm laying a firm foundation. Only this one is for my family. Right now, my twins need their dad. And I won't skimp on building that foundation."

Dr. Phillips nodded and gave Marc the closest he would ever get to a smile. "Your reasoning is sound." He stood and shook his advisee's hand. "I wish you all the best, Marc – and I'll look forward to seeing you back here next fall."

As he exited his adviser's office, Marc heard Edward's voice in his head: *Sometimes, Marc, it's the little things that define a true hero.*